*P*raise for Melanie Dickerson

"*The Piper's Pursuit* is a lovely tale of adventure, romance, and redemption. Kat and Steffan's righteous quest will have you rooting them on until the very satisfying end!"

—LORIE LANGDON, AUTHOR OF *OLIVIA TWIST* AND
THE *DOON* SERIES

"Christian fiction fans will relish Dickerson's eloquent story."

—SCHOOL LIBRARY JOURNAL ON *THE ORPHAN'S WISH*

"*The Goose Girl*, a little retold fairy tale, sparkles in Dickerson's hands, with endearing characters and a charming setting that will appeal to teens and adults alike."

—RT BOOK REVIEWS, 4 1/2 STARS, TOP PICK! ON *THE NOBLE SERVANT*

"Dickerson is a masterful storyteller with a carefully crafted plot, richly drawn characters, and a detailed setting. The reader is easily pulled into the story. Does everything end happily ever after? Read it and see! Recommended for young adults and adults who are young at heart."

—CHRISTIAN LIBRARY JOURNAL ON *THE NOBLE SERVANT*

"[*The Silent Songbird*] will have you jumping out of your seat with anticipation at times. Moderate to fast-paced, you will not want this book to end. Recommended for all, especially lovers of historical romance."

—RT BOOK REVIEWS, 4 STARS

"A terrific YA crossover medieval romance from the author of *The Golden Braid*."

—LIBRARY JOURNAL ON *THE SILENT SONGBIRD*

"When it comes to happily-ever-afters, Melanie Dickerson is the un-disputed queen of fairy-tale romance, and all I can say is—long live the queen! From start to finish *The Beautiful Pretender* is yet another brilliant gem in her crown, spinning a medieval love story that will steal you away—heart, soul, and sleep!"

—JULIE LESSMAN, AWARD-WINNING AUTHOR OF THE
DAUGHTERS OF BOSTON, WINDS OF CHANGE, AND
HEART OF SAN FRANCISCO SERIES

"I couldn't stop reading! Melanie has done what so many other his-torical novelists have tried and failed: she's created a heroine that is at once both smart and self-assured without seeming modern. A woman so fixed in her time and place that she is able to speak to ours as well."

—SIRI MITCHELL, AUTHOR OF *FLIRTATION WALK* AND
CHATEAU OF ECHOES, ON *THE BEAUTIFUL PRETENDER*

"Dickerson breathes life into the age-old story of Rapunzel, blending it seamlessly with the other YA novels she has written in this time and place . . . The character development is solid, and she captures religious medieval life splendidly."

—*BOOKLIST* ON *THE GOLDEN BRAID*

"Readers who love getting lost in a fairy-tale romance will cheer for Rapunzel's courage as she rises above her overwhelming past. The sur-prising way Dickerson weaves threads of this enchanting companion novel with those of her other Hagenheim stories is simply delightful. Her fans will love it."

—JILL WILLIAMSON, CHRISTY AWARD–WINNING AUTHOR
OF THE BLOOD OF KINGS TRILOGY AND THE KINSMAN
CHRONICLES, ON *THE GOLDEN BRAID*

"Readers will find themselves supporting the romance between the sweet yet determined Odette and the insecure but hardworking Jorgen from the beginning. Dickerson spins a retelling of Robin Hood with emotionally compelling characters, offering hope that love may indeed conquer all as they unite in a shared desire to serve both the Lord and those in need."

—RT Book Reviews, 4¹/₂ stars, on *The Huntress of Thornbeck Forest*

"Melanie Dickerson does it again! Full of danger, intrigue, and romance, this beautifully crafted story will transport you to another place and time."

—Sarah E. Ladd, author of *The Curiosity Keeper* and the Whispers on the Moors series, on *The Huntress of Thornbeck Forest*

THE
PIPER'S
$\mathcal{P}$URSUIT

ALSO BY MELANIE DICKERSON

YOUNG ADULT FAIRY TALE ROMANCE SERIES

The Healer's Apprentice

The Merchant's Daughter

The Fairest Beauty

The Captive Maiden

The Princess Spy

The Golden Braid

The Silent Songbird

The Orphan's Wish

The Warrior Maiden

A MEDIEVAL FAIRY TALE SERIES

The Huntress of Thornbeck Forest

The Beautiful Pretender

The Noble Servant

REGENCY SPIES OF LONDON SERIES

A Spy's Devotion

A Viscount's Proposal

A Dangerous Engagement

THE
PIPER'S
PURSUIT

MELANIE
DICKERSON

THOMAS NELSON
Since 1798

The Piper's Pursuit

© 2019 Melanie Dickerson

Published in Nashville, Tennessee, by Thomas Nelson. Thomas Nelson is a registered trademark of HarperCollins Christian Publishing, Inc.

Thomas Nelson titles may be purchased in bulk for educational, business, fund-raising, or sales promotional use. For information, please email SpecialMarkets@ThomasNelson.com.

Publisher's Note: This novel is a work of fiction. Names, characters, places, and incidents are either products of the author's imagination or used fictitiously. All characters are fictional, and any similarity to people living or dead is purely coincidental.

ISBN 978-0-7852-2805-9 (e-book)
ISBN 978-0-7852-2832-5 (audio download)

Library of Congress Cataloging-in-Publication Data

Names: Dickerson, Melanie, author.
Title: The piper's pursuit / Melanie Dickerson.
Description: Nashville, Tennessee : Thomas Nelson, [2019] | Audience: Ages 13+. | Audience: Grades 10-12. | Summary: In 1424 Hamlin, Katerina reluctantly allies with the handsome but brash Steffan to protect herself and her city from formidable dangers--missing children, hordes of rats, a marauding beast, and her devious stepfather, the town's mayor.
Identifiers: LCCN 2019030162 (print) | LCCN 2019030163 (ebook) | ISBN 9780785228141 (hardback) | ISBN 9780785228059 (e-book) | ISBN 9780785228325 (audio download)
Subjects: CYAC: Missing children--Fiction. | Family life--Fiction. | Christian life--Fiction. | Middle Ages--Fiction.
Classification: LCC PZ7.D5575 Pi 2019 (print) | LCC PZ7.D5575 (ebook) | DDC [Fic]--dc23
LC record available at https://lccn.loc.gov/2019030162
LC ebook record available at https://lccn.loc.gov/2019030163

Printed in the United States of America

19 20 21 22 23 LSC 5 4 3 2 1

One

Did Katerina dare to stay out hunting past dark? The sun was going down, casting long shadows as she skirted the forest on her right and an empty meadow on the left. At least the town gate was visible ahead.

She checked her crossbow, making sure the arrow was strung and ready. Her unruly brown hair was starting to come free from the leather tie taming it at the nape of her neck.

She picked up her pace as she passed a particularly dark section of the forest. She could easily imagine the giant wolf, or whatever the beast was that had killed so many, coming out of those dense trees and leaping at her. Would she have time to aim her crossbow before she fired? She would only get one shot.

She laid a hand on the long dagger she kept in the sheath on her belt. If she missed, she might have time to stab the animal before it attacked.

Were her ears playing tricks on her? Or was that a rustling sound coming from the trees?

She stopped and raised the crossbow. Her heart thumped hard against her chest, so hard she could barely breathe. If she died, what would happen to Mother?

It was probably just a rabbit. She kept the crossbow aimed at the dark trees while moving her feet slowly in the direction of town.

Something was shifting the shadows. The bushes were shaking. Leaves gave way.

Wait until you're certain you have the best shot possible. She willed her hands not to shake, holding the crossbow up to her eye to make sure she could aim quickly.

A figure stepped out.

A child stood staring blankly at her. Katerina lowered her crossbow to her side.

The breath rushed out of Katerina's chest. A child! How could a small child be alone outside the walls of town? Everyone knew the beast was killing men, women, and children out here.

When she was able to draw in enough breath to speak, Katerina approached the child. "What are you doing out here, little one?"

The girl was filthy. Her face was nearly black with soot or dirt, Katerina couldn't tell which. Her hair was as tangled as a field mouse's nest. The child's wide blue eyes stared unwaveringly at Katerina's face.

"Mama. I want Mama." But her expression didn't change and she didn't move.

She must be one of the missing children that had been presumed killed and eaten by the Beast of Hamlin. Tears gathered behind Katerina's eyes. *Thank You, God, for letting me find her.* Katerina wanted to pick up the child and run for town. But that might frighten her.

Blinking back her tears, Kat asked, "What's your name?"

"Bridda."

"How long have you been lost, Bridda?"

The child's expression didn't change and she didn't answer.

"Are there any other children with you?"

Bridda shook her head.

Katerina hung her crossbow over her shoulder and across her back, then walked toward Bridda until she was close enough to reach for her hand. She squatted in front of her. "Are you all right?"

The little girl lifted her hand slowly. It was as dirty as the rest of her. Katerina took it between hers and squeezed gently. The poor child just stared into her eyes.

"How old are you, *Schätzchen*?" Katerina used the term of endearment her own mother used for her. Kat's heart twisted at the tired, almost hopeless look in the little girl's eyes.

"Six."

"Are you from Hamlin?"

No response.

"What is your father's name?"

Her expression held a tinge of confusion. Then her eyes lit up. It was as if a memory came to her, and she said, "Johannes."

A surge of breath rushed into Kat's chest. "Come. I'll take you to Hamlin and we'll see if we can find your father and mother." Katerina stood, still holding on to the girl's hand, and started walking, anxious to get the little girl safely out of the forest.

The little girl gazed up at her and tugged ever so slightly on her hand.

Katerina bent down. "What is it, Bridda?"

"Don't let him get me." Her voice was a whisper.

Katerina shivered, her gaze flicking back toward the trees. "Don't worry. I won't let the beast get you."

Katerina hurried toward Hamlin's town gate with the little girl's hand held firmly in hers. A minute later, Katerina noticed the poor child was walking slower and slower.

Katerina squatted. "May I carry you?"

The child looked her in the eye and nodded. Katerina put her arms around her and lifted her up, holding her snugly.

As they entered the town gate, Katerina spied a guard she knew, her friend Hans.

Hans saw her as well, and his mouth fell open. He started toward her.

"Hans, this is Bridda. I found her outside the wall. Do you know of a man named Johannes who's missing a six-year-old daughter?"

Hans stared at the girl from beneath thick brown hair that fell across his forehead. He breathed, "It's a miracle. How . . ."

"Do you know her?"

"I know her father. Wait here. I'll go find him."

Hans started to leave, but Katerina put her hand on his arm to stop him. "Before you go . . . how long has she been missing?"

"About five months."

Hans turned and started running.

Katerina stared at the tiny face next to hers. "Where have you been for five months?"

Bridda just stared back at her.

As they waited for Hans to return, Bridda's pale blue eyes started to look livelier, shedding the lost, stunned expression as she tentatively turned her head to look around her. Her gaze seemed to fix on certain points. Was she recognizing buildings or maybe people? She also seemed to be watching the rats running through the streets. The plague of rats had descended on the town about the same time the beast had started its killing rampage. Katerina wondered, not for the first time, if the two things were related, though she couldn't imagine how.

So many questions were running through Katerina's head. How had this little girl avoided being killed by the beast while she was in the woods? And even stranger, how had she survived on her own for five months?

———•✦•———

Hungry, dusty, and tired, Steffan was thankful when he came to a small village. He'd been wandering toward home since he'd left his brother Wolfgang and Wolfgang's new wife in Poland. A bed, no matter how lumpy, and a warm meal would be a welcome change after sleeping on the hard ground and eating mostly what he could kill or forage.

He spotted the village inn and went inside, even though he had no money for either food or a room.

The innkeeper was friendly, so while the man stroked his graying beard, Steffan said, "I am very good at playing the pipe. I could play for your patrons in exchange for a meal."

The innkeeper nodded. "You play for one hour, then my wife will serve you the finest stew in the Holy Roman Empire, then you play a bit more. Yes?"

Steffan had already extracted his pipe from his bag. He placed it against his lips and began to play.

Everyone in the room turned to face him, most of them smiling. By their looks, music was a rarity here.

When he had played about an hour, the innkeeper's wife brought him a tankard of ale, a bowl of mutton stew, and a slab of bread. He sat to eat, and the innkeeper joined him.

"You're not from nearby, are you?"

"I'm from Hagenheim originally, but I haven't been there in over a year."

"You may not have heard, then." The innkeeper leaned forward, fixing his eyes on Steffan's.

"Heard?"

"Of the plague of rats that has been tormenting the town of Hamlin."

Hamlin was a town under his father's authority, in the region of Hagenheim.

"I have heard tales of this plague of rats. I thought they might have only been the fanciful stories people invent to distract children."

"Indeed, they are not just fanciful stories. The plague of rats is real. I have seen it with my own eyes." The grizzled innkeeper lowered his voice. "But there is something else plaguing Hamlin, something more terrible than rats."

"What do you mean?" Steffan shoveled another bite of stew into his mouth. Truly, the innkeeper was not exaggerating overmuch when he'd said it was the best in the Holy Roman Empire.

"People are being taken, gone—more than sixty people, last I heard."

Steffan rested his wooden spoon on the side of his bowl and stared back at the man. Was he daft? An outrageous liar? Surely sixty people could not have simply gone missing from Hamlin.

"What do you think is happening to them?"

"They say a beast is dragging them off and eating them."

"A beast? What sort of beast?"

"No one knows exactly. Some think it could be a wolf, or a large dog gone wild."

"It would take a very large and vicious dog to kill a man, and wolves rarely kill people, especially in town. Is there proof?"

"Would the bodies of several half-eaten villagers be proof enough for you? A woman was found with her arm torn off, the rest of her body partially eaten, and her throat . . . The poor woman's head was nearly separated from her body."

Steffan winced at the gruesome images his mind conjured up, familiar images of his time fighting in Poland. He had to blink hard to rid them from his thoughts and remember where he was.

"Has anyone actually seen the beast or been attacked and lived to tell of it?"

"*Ja*, there have been two or three. One man was attacked on his way through his field outside Hamlin town. He said it looked like a giant wolf. The beast bit him on the ankle, but the man beat it with his walking stick until the animal let go. But the wound took on a putridness and the man died a few weeks later."

If only the poor man had had some of the healing salve Steffan's sister-in-law had given him.

"I have been traveling for a while and have not heard about this. All I've heard about are the rats."

"The mayor of Hamlin is my sister's brother-in-law's cousin," the innkeeper went on, his gaze shifting to the door as two men walked in and seated themselves, "and he does not want the news to be spread abroad."

"Why is that? Does he not want the creature captured or killed?" Steffan resumed his eating, taking a bite of stew then of bread.

"The mayor's lord is the Duke of Hagenheim, and the mayor is afraid of being held accountable for allowing the beast to kill so many people. He's offering a reward to anyone who will either kill or capture it, but no one has been able to find it. Or they are too afraid to go looking."

"A reward, you say?" Steffan leaned in, remembering the one silver guilder in the pouch on his belt—all the money he had.

"The mayor says he'll give one thousand silver guilders and his daughter's hand in marriage to the man who can kill the beast that's wreaking havoc and frightening the townspeople."

When the innkeeper said the words "a thousand silver guilders," Steffan's heart jumped into his throat. The money was a very enticing reward, though he was hardly anxious to marry a mayor's daughter he'd never seen before. Hamlin suddenly seemed a very interesting place.

"Has this creature come into town?"

"People believe so, because several children have been taken from inside the town walls. But often it's attacked those outside the town walls, people who farm small plots of land or have gone to visit families in the countryside."

Steffan listened to everything the innkeeper had to say about the Beast of Hamlin, but when he started to talk about other things, Steffan's mind wandered back to the reward.

He must kill this beast.

It was just the sort of noble feat that could bring him glory, get his name into a popular ballad sung by the troubadours and Minnesingers or his likeness onto a church mural or stained glass window. The story would be told everywhere, including Hagenheim. Then he wouldn't be ashamed to go home again and face his father.

For a year he'd been on a quest for adventure, treasure to discover, or any task that might earn him money—except what he had done in Poland, which was to fight and kill someone else's enemy. His most recent quest had been to save two pigs that had fallen into an old well, which he had accomplished after many hours of effort. His reward had been a hot meal and a bed to sleep in.

It seemed good deeds and money seldom went hand-in-hand. The last real coin he'd earned had been from playing his pipe in a harvest festival at least a month ago.

His family was very musical, as his father played the lute and most of his siblings sang and played various instruments. Steffan found his pipe useful for entertaining himself and his fellow soldiers. Now that he was traveling alone, it helped distract him when his thoughts wandered to unwanted places.

But if he could succeed in slaying this man-eating beast, his father would surely hear of it. Perhaps that would make up for all the bad things he had done. And perhaps then Steffan wouldn't feel as if he were the least of all his brothers—the one bad apple in the Gerstenberg family tree.

———

Katerina watched the townspeople hurrying home before dusk turned to night. No one seemed to notice her or the child in her arms who was covered in dust and grime.

Hans came running down the street toward them with a man by his side. The man's face was pinched and tense, almost as if he were in pain. His gaze landed on Bridda. He cried out and ran faster, pulling ahead of Hans.

He was crying when he reached them, his face twisted, as he reached out his hands toward her.

The child hesitated, but only for a moment. Her little hands extended, her eyes brightened, and she said, "Papa."

Bridda's father plucked her from Katerina's arms, clutching her tenderly to his chest. Sobs erupted from his throat, but he quickly pressed his lips together and held her out so he could look at her.

"Oh, my little *Schätzchen*. It is a miracle."

Tears welled up in Katerina's eyes at the joyful reunion. Her chest ached as she whispered, "Thank You, God."

The father was still gazing hungrily into his daughter's face. "Are you well? Are you hungry? Are you hurt?"

Bridda patted his cheeks with her little grimy fingers. He grabbed them and kissed them.

"Mama."

"She is home. I shall take you to her. Shall I?"

Bridda nodded, still keeping her eyes pinned on her father's face, as if he might disappear if she looked away.

He kissed her cheek. Then, over Bridda's head, his teary eyes met Katerina's. "I thank you, Fräulein. How did you find her?"

"I was outside the wall, just now. She simply walked out of the forest."

"I thank God, thank God. But where has she been?"

"I don't know. Hans"—Katerina motioned at the tall guard— "will you walk with Johannes and Bridda back to their home?" While Johannes was talking to his daughter, she leaned closer to Hans. "Come back and tell me where they live. And tell him I shall come to them tomorrow, to ask questions."

"Yes, Fräulein Katerina."

Katerina watched them leave and took a deep breath. It truly was a miracle that the girl was found alive, but Katerina wondered again at the mystery of where she had been and how she had avoided being killed by the beast.

As she stood waiting for Hans to return, she noticed an unfamiliar man on horseback riding at a slow walk through the town gate. There was something about his face—relaxed and yet sharp-eyed—that caught her eye. He might also be considered quite good-looking, sitting tall in the saddle of his large warhorse, but when his gaze met hers, his expression changed and his lips curled upward. She would have sworn he was thinking, *You find me handsome, don't you?*

How she detested arrogant men.

She gave him her sternest look and turned away from him. Now that she thought about it, he wasn't so handsome after all. She preferred short dark hair and brown eyes, and his hair was long and blond, his eyes also a light color, probably blue or green. She couldn't tell from this distance. Not that she cared. She only hoped he was astute enough to understand she was not interested.

But the clopping of his horse's hooves on the cobblestone street behind her grew louder. Still, she refused to turn around and look at him. She had no time to waste on this stranger. Her mind was on Bridda and solving the mystery of where she'd been for the last five months. Tomorrow she would question both the parents and Bridda, if the parents would allow it.

"If you please, Fräulein," a male voice said behind her.

Katerina turned to see the arrogant stranger sitting atop his horse, looking down on her.

She glared at him.

"I am in search of the *Bürgermeister* of Hamlin."

Katerina looked him over. Why did he want to speak to the mayor? This stranger did not wear the clothing of a nobleman. He could possibly be a knight, though he wore none of the trappings—no mail shirt or colors or quilted gambeson. But perhaps that could be attributed to the fact that the summer air this day had been so hot.

"This is Hamlin town, is it not?"

"It is." She studied him a moment longer. He did not have a vicious look, but one could never be too careful.

"I said, could you tell me where I might find the Bürgermeister?" He spoke each word deliberately. His brows drew together and now he was frowning.

Good. She had annoyed him. "He's probably at his home, as it is nearly suppertime."

"And do you know the location of his house?"

"I should. I am going there myself."

Just then she saw Hans walking toward her, though he was still many steps away.

The stranger sat a little taller in the saddle. "I am Steffan of Hagenheim. And I would be much obliged if you would allow me to accompany you there."

Did he think he was entitled to her deference just because he was from Hagenheim, the seat of power for this region? At least his tone was respectful, though there was an edge to it, as if he were still annoyed but trying to hide it.

"Very well."

Hans reached her then and leaned close to her ear. In a low

voice, he told her where to find little Bridda's house. She thanked him, and he went back to his post at the gate.

Katerina started walking toward her home, then glanced over her shoulder at Steffan of Hagenheim. The glance was the only invitation he would get, so he'd better take it.

$\mathcal{T}$ wo

$\mathcal{S}$teffan gazed down at the wavy-haired beauty. Her attitude was as unruly as her hair, and there was a spark in her blue eyes. He was intrigued, as he couldn't remember a young woman treating him with so much contrariness—other than his sisters.

He followed her down the street after she turned her crossbow-laden back to him. Was she a hunter? A young woman carrying a crossbow might have struck him more strangely had he not recently spent time with his brother and sister-in-law, both of whom were lauded and famous for fighting in the recent liberation of Poland from the Teutonic Knights.

This rather tall girl, with her wild hair and even wilder expression, looked as if she could take on a few knights herself—and win.

He wished he'd asked her name. She walked with a sway that was both confident and feminine. Most women who held their heads that high were aristocratic, wore embroidered silk clothing, and were fine-boned and dainty. This girl looked quite sturdy and wore the clothing of a poor laborer's daughter.

Surely she had not been out hunting, not with the Beast of Hamlin on the loose.

Steffan had been to Hamlin when he was a young boy, so the

streets seemed vaguely familiar. The town, in fact, was closely connected to his family, and reminded him so much of Hagenheim that it caused a pang to shoot through his middle.

He wasn't that far away now—only two or three days' ride. After he killed the Beast of Hamlin, he'd go back, even though he'd have to see his parents' disappointment in him, and that thought stirred up the old angry feeling that made him want to do something stupid like defy his father's wishes and join with the Teutonic Knights. But he had to face his father's disapproval sooner or later, and he knew he deserved it, even if it did still make him angry.

His thoughts were suddenly redirected by a sight he'd never seen before—a herd of rats moving down the street, streaming into an alleyway up ahead. They roiled as they crawled and tumbled over each other, making faint screeching sounds, mingling with the collective clicking of their tiny claws on the cobblestones.

A man walking into the path of the rats suddenly cried out and started to back away. The rats reached him before he could escape, engulfing his feet as he cried out again, lifting one foot then the other. Steffan held his breath, too far away to help the man as he tried to walk on top of the rats. When he lifted one foot, a rat hung by its teeth from his ankle.

The man flailed his arms, running as best he could. He was nearly out of the teeming rats when he fell to his knees amidst the furry bodies. He jumped up and ran some more, until he finally disappeared down an open street.

On the vermin came.

A woman ahead of them was carrying a large cloth bundle in front of her, across her arms, obstructing her view.

"Watch out!" the girl with the crossbow yelled, hurrying

toward the woman, but it was too late. The rodents surrounded the woman's feet. She lifted a foot, teetering, then fell to her knees among them and screamed.

Steffan slid from his saddle and ran toward her, but the young woman with the crossbow raced ahead of him and began kicking a path through the rats.

Steffan used his booted feet to sweep the rodents out of the way. The girl reached the woman first and grabbed her under her arms, yanking her to her feet. Steffan picked up the woman's bundle. He shook off a rat that had sunk its teeth into it, then kicked at the rats that were still swarming around them, clearing a circle of safety around the two women.

Finally, the herd of rats moved on down the street.

"Thank you, Fräulein Katerina." The woman let out a loud breath, then laughed shakily. "And you." She took her bundle from him. "Thank you."

So the girl's name was Katerina.

"You are welcome, Frau," Steffan said.

"Frau Walpurg, this is Steffan of Hagenheim."

"I thank you, Herr Steffan." Frau Walpurg bowed, then smiled at him.

It amused him to hear someone call him "Herr" when the proper way to address him was "Lord Steffan," but he didn't correct her.

"We shall walk with you as far as my house," Katerina said.

Her house? Was she a servant of the Bürgermeister? Steffan would have to speak to him about letting his servant girl go hunting alone with the beast stalking about.

"Are you not one of our town's guards, a big strapping man like you?" Frau Walpurg asked.

"I am not."

"I'm sure the Bürgermeister would be grateful to have your services."

"Steffan of Hagenheim is only passing through," Katerina said.

"That is probably true, Fräulein Katerina, though one never can be certain of the future."

She frowned and leaned away when he spoke her name.

Frau Walpurg turned to Katerina. "Please tell Herr Hennek to find someone to get rid of these rats." The woman's eyes filled with tears.

"Of course. I will." Katerina laid a comforting hand on the woman's arm.

"Fare well, Katerina," Frau Walpurg said, moving away from them, "and thank you again, Herr Steffan of Hagenheim."

"You are most welcome." He gave her a gallant bow.

"The Bürgermeister will think of a way to rid us of these rats, and the beast too. God will reveal it to him. Hennek is a good Bürgermeister."

Steffan noticed Katerina cringing at the woman's words, then she gave the woman a weak half smile. "Can you make it the rest of the way home?"

"Yes, yes." With one last "fare well," the woman hurried away down the street.

Katerina strode toward a large, four-story, half-timber house, colorfully decorated with fantastical painted-on animals and flowers. A young man was coming around the side of the house.

"Please take this man's horse to the stable." Katerina inclined her head toward Steffan and his horse.

"Of course." The young servant reached for the reins and Steffan handed them over.

Steffan waited for her to go first, then followed her to the giant wooden front door with the head of a lion two feet wide carved into it at eye level. She opened the door and went ahead of him, her shoulders tilted back, her head high, unlike any servant girl he'd ever seen.

A well-dressed woman came gliding down the stairs as they stood in the entryway of the large house. Katerina slipped off her crossbow and addressed her.

"Mother, this man wishes to speak to my stepfather."

So Katerina was the mayor's stepdaughter.

The woman said softly, "Change your clothing quickly, darling."

Katerina hurried up the steps without even a backward glance.

Steffan stared as she made her way up to the top of the staircase and disappeared from view. Was she also the daughter whose hand in marriage the mayor was giving as part of the reward?

"May I ask your name?" The lovely woman whom Katerina had called Mother wore a gentle, refined expression. Katerina had obviously acquired her lovely eyes and mouth from her mother, who did not look much older than Katerina.

"I am Steffan of Hagenheim." He might as well tell her the truth. "My father is Duke Wilhelm of Hagenheim."

The woman's eyes widened in surprise. She bowed her head to him. "Lord Steffan, you are most welcome here. I am Ayla Grymmelin, and my husband is Hennek Grymmelin."

"I am honored, Frau Grymmelin." Steffan bowed.

"The servant will take your saddlebag."

He'd forgotten he'd slung it over his shoulder. It contained nearly all he owned, and his sword and scabbard were strapped to it.

A servant who had been lurking in the shadows came forward, and Steffan handed it to him.

"Won't you please stay for supper?" Frau Grymmelin's voice was soft and pleasing. "We would be honored to have you as our guest for as long as you would like to stay."

Her voice was mild but her eyes studied him, and in them he saw a glimmer of something—fear, hope, desperation, or maybe all three.

She turned and led him through a doorway to a dining hall dominated by a large table and ornately carved chairs.

Heavy footsteps sounded on the stairs behind them, too heavy to be Katerina's. Frau Grymmelin took a step back, toward the wall. A moment later, a large man almost as tall as Steffan entered the room.

"Husband, this is Lord Steffan of Hagenheim." Something about her expression made a memory spring to Steffan's mind. Years ago he and his brother Wolfgang had been walking through the *Marktplatz* when they saw a man beating a dog. They had rescued the pup, taking her and keeping her as a pet, but he'd never forgotten the way the dog had cowered before the man.

The mayor of Hamlin had thick black hair interspersed with white and equally thick black eyebrows. A few wrinkles around his eyes hardly took away from his otherwise smooth face and even smoother smile, which broke out on his face when his wife introduced him.

"It is an honor to meet you. You are the duke's son, yes?" He raised his brows as he stared hard at Steffan's face.

"I am."

"An honor indeed! And I am the duke's humble servant, Hennek Grymmelin, Bürgermeister of this fine town. Please, sit at my right hand and enjoy the best I have to offer. Ayla, have the food brought in."

Steffan and the mayor sat while Frau Grymmelin hurried away.

"Shall I play my pipe for you while we wait?"

Steffan must have looked surprised, because the mayor said, "You did not think the Mayor of Hamlin would play such a humble instrument?"

"No, it's just that . . . I also play the pipe." Steffan extracted his own small pipe from inside his outer garment.

"Oh-ho! You wish to best me, no doubt."

"No, no, please play something. I rarely get to listen. I'm usually the one playing."

"Very well, then." The mayor placed the flute to his lips and started playing a popular tune, a well-known song Steffan was often asked to play.

The mayor was proficient, but Steffan noticed he skipped a note here and there. He had barely reached the end of one verse and chorus when he stopped.

"That is enough of that. I should be asking you all the news of Hagenheim. It has been more than two years since Duke Wilhelm paid us a visit." Herr Hennek held eye contact with Steffan. "But Lord Hamlin was here nine months ago, just before all our trouble started."

"I am surprised he did not come at once to help hunt down the beast." Such a thing was just what his oldest brother, Valten, loved.

"He may not have heard about the beast yet." Herr Hennek glanced away.

"That seems like something the duke should know about."

"We do not like to ask for help with problems we can solve ourselves. I would not worry the duke with things that do not affect him."

Steffan opened his mouth to say that such problems were very important to the duke, since they had to do with the safety of his people. But just then Frau Ayla entered the room, the servants behind her carrying large platters with bowls and spoons, and began setting four places.

Hennek sat at the head of the table while Frau Ayla sat across from Steffan and smiled. The servants placed pottery bowls in front of each of them, with an extra one beside Frau Ayla. They served the bread and spooned frumenty into the bowls.

"Do we need to wait for Katerina or will she not be joining us?" Bürgermeister Hennek cast a hard stare at Frau Ayla.

"She is readying herself and should be here any moment." The lovely woman smiled, but her eyes darted past Hennek's head, down to the table, then down at her lap. Still smiling, she glanced up at Steffan. "What brings you to Hamlin, Lord Steffan?"

"Can you not guess, my dear?" Hennek's voice boomed, filling the room. "Do you truly need to ask?"

Just then Katerina caught Steffan's eye as she reached the bottom of the stairs. She approached the room slowly as her stepfather went on.

"Are you so daft as not to guess his intentions? He has heard of our daughter's beauty and has come to win her by killing the beast!"

Katerina entered the room, her jaw set, her chin rigid as stone. She sent a narrow-eyed glance at Mayor Hennek, paused, then sat down across from Steffan. She kept her head high as one of the servants placed a bowl in front her.

He didn't have to wonder what she thought of him or what she thought of the Bürgermeister offering her as a reward. Her jaw was still hard and her lips pursed.

Something stirred inside his chest. This beautiful young woman might already be predisposed to hate him, and he might not be the most worthy son of his father, and he didn't intend to marry her even if he did win her. But he had an inexplicable desire to change her mind.

Katerina's fury at her boorish stepfather was like a fire in her head. How dare he speak to Mother in his usual arrogant way in front of this equally arrogant man? And why had her stepfather invited him to sup with them? Probably Mother, feeling sorry for him, invited him before she had time to think. He did look a bit hungry, but he was strong. He could kill and eat the small game that ran wild all over the forests of this region. If he wasn't afraid to hunt the beast, he should be able to get his own food.

And why should she care? She had more important concerns—namely, what was happening to the town's children. She was beginning to wonder if the rats were carrying them off. They seemed to be getting bigger and bolder and more numerous by the day.

She would kill the beast herself. And she would not be "given" *by* anyone or *to* anyone. Especially not to this man.

"You were late, Katerina. Were you killing rats again? You know that frightens people."

"And the rats do not frighten people?" Katerina said the words in a low voice and immediately wished she'd kept silent. Heat crept up her neck to her cheeks as her mind went on alert.

"Lateness is a very bad trait. If you had a husband—"

Katerina's mother's frumenty bowl slipped off the edge of the table and crashed to the floor, breaking and spilling at her feet.

It was just like her mother to cause a distraction when Hennek was saying something especially malevolent. Katerina laughed, a quick bark. She glanced at her stepfather, knowing he'd be furious at her mother for breaking the bowl. Indeed, Hennek wore a pinched, hard look on his face.

A servant rushed into the room and began cleaning up the mess while another servant girl quickly brought in a full bowl and placed it in front of her mother.

Mother would rather endure Hennek's sullen, cold treatment of her for the next several days—which would be the punishment for knocking her frumenty onto the floor—than allow Katerina to be humiliated by her stepfather's words in front of this stranger from Hagenheim.

She also did it to stop Katerina from saying what she would have said next, which likely would have turned into one of their heated arguments. Katerina did not often argue with Hennek, but when she did, it always grew ugly, with him accusing and insinuating nasty things—that she was coldhearted and would never marry, that she was greedy, and that she only pretended to love her mother but was actually too selfish to care about anyone but herself. She'd long noticed his practice of accusing others of what he himself was guilty of.

Katerina would somehow find a way to save herself and her mother from Hennek. And she would not have to marry some man in order to do it. First she would kill the beast and make sure no other children were harmed. Then she would force Hennek to give her the reward money. And then she would somehow convince her mother to leave Hennek, who was more evil and insidious than any beast, and they would begin anew in a new town.

Her thoughts darted to the little girl Bridda. She almost trembled with the impulse to run over to her home and ask her questions. But that would not be wise. Better to let her soak up her parents' love for one night, to feel safe again. Then she'd be more apt to answer Katerina's questions.

She just had to wait.

Hennek's pinched look was slowly changing into a snide little smile, then a toothy grin as he turned toward Steffan.

"I wish you success, Lord Steffan, in hunting the beast."

Lord Steffan? Wasn't that taking things a bit far in addressing a simple mercenary like this man?

"I honed my hunting skills in the Harz Mountains just outside of Hagenheim. And I fought in the Polish-Teutonic battles a year ago."

"A soldier! Very good!" Hennek boomed.

Her stepfather never liked anyone else showing him up, and since he had never fought in a battle, he became quite loud to draw the attention back to himself—one of his many grating traits.

Steffan stared down at his frumenty. Was that regret in his expression?

"Kill many Poles, did you?" Hennek's smile was obscenely broad.

Steffan cleared his throat, not quite meeting Hennek's eyes. "I was fighting with the Teutonic Knights, but I've since parted company with them."

"Parted company? Fighting was not to your liking, then?"

"No, it wasn't." Steffan seemed to let out a breath he was holding. He reached for his goblet and drank a gulp.

"Couldn't stomach killing men, eh? But killing wolves is more to your liking?"

Steffan gazed down at his bowl. "You could say that."

Well, perhaps the stranger from Hagenheim did have a bit of humility inside him.

Then he looked up at Hennek, the sad, humble look completely gone, if it had ever been there. He gave Hennek a wry smile. "My father taught me and my brothers and sisters to do good, never evil, with whatever skills or resources we have."

"Oh yes, the Duke of Hagenheim would certainly teach his sons to do right. That is exactly how I live my life as well. I support the orphanage in town with my own money, and I do not use the town's coffers for any of the orphans' expenses. That has always been my way. I please God in all that I do. God is our ultimate Sovereign, and He requires we do good. When I was . . ."

Hennek began one of his hypocritical stories about some good deed he had done, but Katerina was no longer listening. Was Steffan the son of Duke Wilhelm of Hagenheim? That must be why Hennek allowed him to come to dinner and called him Lord Steffan. Her cheeks heated. That might explain why he was so arrogant. And she had not exactly treated him with deference.

He must think her ridiculous, a mayor's daughter giving him disdainful looks, judging him when he was the powerful Duke of Hagenheim's son. But then, why should she care if he was a duke's son? He was a man just like anyone else. God was no respecter of persons, so why should she be? And if God hated haughty eyes and prideful looks, Katerina could hate them too.

". . . and then the duke appointed me mayor of Hamlin." Hennek sat back and crossed his arms over his broad chest. "Now, tell us about your oldest brother, Lord Hamlin. We are due a visit from him soon. Has he been helping his father keep the rabble in their place?" He laughed as though it were a very amusing jest.

"I am not certain what my brother Valten has been doing. I've been away, as I mentioned." Steffan turned his eyes on Katerina and gave her a look that at first seemed humble. But then his lips stretched into a small smile, and he winked, a movement so quick . . .

Humble, ha! He was no more humble than Hennek was. Probably the two men were quite similar, bullying their way through life, squashing ordinary people under their feet to get ahead. Oh yes, she'd heard of this younger son of Duke Wilhelm's. The rumors were that he was a drinker and carouser and that he had left his father's soldiers and gone instead to the enemy side, the Teutonic Knights, to satisfy his own ambition. These dukes and earls and their sons were all the same. They seduced women and laughed at their pain when they abandoned them. No doubt Steffan had done the same everywhere he went. She had heard Duke Wilhelm was a good and God-fearing man, though many people thought Hennek was as well. A reputation for righteousness meant very little in Katerina's mind after living with a man who proclaimed, very loudly, his own.

But perhaps what she'd heard about the Duke of Hagenheim had been true and this Steffan had not been pleased to live under his rule. Perhaps that was why he hadn't been home in so long.

"Katerina, you would like it if Lord Steffan killed the beast, would you not?" Hennek met her eye before he started laughing again, that fake laugh that went on and on, one of his many ways of controlling those around him, forcing them to wait until his loud laughter stopped before they could speak and be heard.

No one spoke. Everyone's eyes were on her, even Mother's.

No doubt she worried what Katerina might say in front of Lord Steffan, the son of the lord of this land.

"I would be very glad if Lord Steffan was able to kill the beast," Katerina said. "Then the people of Hamlin would no longer have to be afraid."

Hennek chuckled. "She is a smart girl after all. My daughter would like being married to a duke's son, would she not?"

She gave Hennek, then Steffan, her coldest look. "I am a free woman in the eyes of the Church, and I will not marry against my will. And it most certainly is *not* my will to marry."

Three

Steffan couldn't say he was surprised at the cold look the Bürgermeister's daughter sent his way, but he was a bit surprised at her giving the same look to her stepfather. No one even moved for several seconds after her softly spoken but biting words.

She was not impressed that he was Duke Wilhelm's son, then. He admired that. After all, he had done nothing to merit his status. And Katerina was just the sort of woman to only respect and admire people who had earned her respect and admiration.

Another sensation went through his chest. He suddenly wanted to earn her respect.

Her chestnut-brown hair lay uncovered and unfettered over her shoulders, her eyes sparking as she stared back at him. Her dress was colorful and fine, transforming her from the peasant girl she had appeared to be on the street into a wealthy burgher's daughter. But he barely saw the dress because he couldn't tear his gaze away from her deep blue eyes.

He would never try to force anyone to marry him. However, if she ended up *wanting* to marry him . . .

He closed his eyes, shutting out her lovely face, and mentally shook himself. The girl was beautiful, but he was not ready to marry.

He focused on the food in his bowl. The frumenty contained

juicy chunks of pork and was delicious. And he didn't even like frumenty. As soon as he'd inhaled the last spoonful, the servants entered and whisked away his bowl, replacing it with a plate. A servant laid a slice of bread in the middle of the plate, then ladled meat and gravy on the bread. More dishes—stewed fruit and cooked vegetables swimming in sauces, all steaming hot—were brought in on large platters and set in the middle of the table.

"Take some of everything," Hennek boomed. "A young man like you needs his strength! Eat up! There's plenty of food in the kitchen!"

The food looked delicious, but Steffan got a niggling sensation in his gut over how Hennek had treated his wife and daughter. Hennek seemed jolly and cordial enough, and his words, which had angered Katerina so much, seemed more careless than spiteful. But it was the looks on the two women's faces and their reactions to Hennek that made Steffan uneasy. Hennek had unnecessarily mentioned Katerina marrying, more than once, which obviously infuriated her.

He'd never really thought about it before, but it would be humiliating to have someone offer you in marriage, especially when you did not know the person to whom you were being offered. It made him want to protect this girl.

The mayor had such a friendly smile. Perhaps he meant no harm. Though Steffan had never heard or seen his father embarrass his sisters or push a man on them. He couldn't even imagine it.

In the past year, after what had happened with Wolfgang and the Teutonic Knights, Steffan had realized how wise his father was. Everything he'd said about the Teutonic Knights, which Steffan had thought reflected his father's unjust prejudice, had actually been true. And his father was kind. His orders, telling Steffan what to do and what not to do, had only been a father trying to save his son from pain. His brothers and sisters had seemed to know that all along. Why had it taken Steffan so long to realize that his father and mother were good? That they had only had his best interest at heart all along?

But hadn't he changed? He'd saved his brother's life, after all. He still bore the scar above his eye from that tilt.

Hennek ladled stewed fruit onto Steffan's plate. "Try this," Hennek said, "and tell me if the cooks at Hagenheim Castle have anything this good."

Steffan tasted the fruit. "It's good." But he refused to say it was better than Hagenheim's cooks' fruit. Could he be feeling a new-found loyalty to home?

Hennek began talking again, his blustery voice filling the room.

"My daughter here thinks she can kill the beast herself. What say you, Steffan? Do you think you can out-track her?"

"I do not know." Truthfully, he had never done much tracking. His father had a master tracker who led their hunting parties. He'd done his own tracking in the last year, whenever he'd tried to fell a deer—with little success. But he wasn't about to tell them that.

"Is Katerina a good tracker?" Steffan addressed the question to Hennek but kept his gaze on Katerina. Her lips thinned and she glared at him, her blue eyes darkening.

"I guess you will find out." Katerina completely ignored her stepfather and went back to eating her food.

"My daughter likes to feign this fractious attitude." Hennek laughed, a forced, aggressive sound. "She goes out every day with her crossbow and tells the servants she's going to kill the beast, but she hasn't killed it yet. Perhaps she feels pity for it and doesn't truly want to kill it. Women are such gentle creatures. Not fierce like men."

"I am fierce enough to slay a beast that kills children." Katerina's voice was quiet but seemed to shiver with a hard edge. "And you will find that I am not too gentle to put a bolt through the skull of any animal that bares its teeth at me, including ones that walk on two feet."

With this she slowly and deliberately turned her head to stare straight at Hennek. But it was the look on Hennek's face as he returned her stare that sent a jolt of heat up Steffan's neck and across his shoulders. Would he have to defend the girl?

Hennek licked his lips and looked away from her. Then he laughed.

"Have you ever heard such talk from one of your sisters, Lord Steffan? I imagine your sisters are much more submissive."

"Less than you might think." Steffan glanced back at Katerina. "They've been known to fight back when someone threatens them and would no doubt approve of her hunting—"

Hennek cut him off by shouting at the servants to bring out the rest of the food. Then he said, "No one has been able to kill this beast. Soon there may be so many people hunting it that you'll be likelier to shoot each other."

Hennek's laugh this time was even less genuine than before, sounding brittle and fake. Steffan glanced at both Katerina's and her mother's expressions. The girl's face was red, tight-lipped, and her jaw hard as stone, while her mother's was white, her bottom lip trembling, her eyes blinking rapidly.

"How many people have tried to kill the beast so far?" Steffan asked, trying to keep Hennek from further upsetting the women.

"Oh, there have been some, but they were not fierce hunters, only peasants from the area, and one or two of them were killed by the beast." Hennek eyed Steffan as he took another bite of food. "But you, Lord Steffan, should be in Hagenheim helping your father, trying to curry your brother's favor so you can inherit a grand estate somewhere."

Heat leapt to Steffan's cheeks.

"Oh, I know you are wanting to make your own way in the world. I understand that, of course! Look at me. I earned my success. I did not wait for my father to leave me an inheritance. He was the illegitimate son of the Duke of Braunschweig, and he distinguished himself in the Duke of Hagenheim's guard. He was a captain when your grandfather was still alive. And he made sure his son was educated in some of the best households in the Holy Roman Empire. Now I'm the Bürgermeister of Hamlin, and you will also do well for yourself. A man who goes out seeking adventure, however, must be ready for it when it comes." The shrewd look he aimed at Steffan did not match his smile.

The only sound for a moment was of Hennek's knife scraping his plate. He shoved a huge bite of pheasant and gravy-soaked bread into his big mouth as the brown sauce dripped from his lip.

"Dear," he said, addressing his wife, "why don't you tell Steffan about Hamlin's history, how much more prosperous we have been since I took over."

Frau Grymmelin sat up straighter and cleared her throat before looking up and smiling as she began to tell how much money had been taken in taxes, the industries that were flourishing, and how many new homes and warehouses had been built since her husband had been appointed mayor. But her eyes never quite met his.

"I never boast myself, but the town has done very well." Hennek actually stuck out his chest.

Katerina's lip curled as she stared down at her plate. "Please excuse me. I must go to my room now."

"We haven't finished our meal. The cooks are working on a special dessert. You are too thin. You'll waste away if you keep refusing to eat the special dishes they make for us. Besides, don't you want to hear how Lord Steffan plans to kill the beast? He may reveal his secrets if you stay and listen. I might even ply him with strong drink. Eh? Lord Steffan, what is your weakness?" He raised his brows high, then laughed.

He was guffawing so loudly no one could have heard anyone's reply, even if they'd made one. The longer his raucous laughter went on, the more set Katerina's jawline became.

Finally, when the annoying sound dissipated, she said quietly, "I have eaten sufficiently and would like to go to my chamber. Enjoy yourselves." She stood without receiving his permission and slipped away.

"She is quite a beauty, would you not agree, Lord Steffan?" Hennek winked.

"She is a lovely young lady, Herr Hennek."

And true to his word, after the sweetmeats arrived, Hennek plied him with strong drink. Steffan refused it, however, remembering his promise to himself. He had not let himself get drunk since he and Wolfgang had been at Malbork Castle, since he'd left Poland.

He couldn't quite decide what, but something about Mayor Hennek was not right. He seemed jolly and eager to please one minute, insulting the next, and then laughing as though he was in jest. But the reactions of his wife and stepdaughter to his bluster stuck in Steffan's mind. If anyone would know the intentions of this man, it would be his family members who lived with him.

Even so, when Hennek urged him to stay the night in his home, Steffan had no better options, so he accepted. Besides, he wanted to kill the beast, get the reward money, and stay long enough to make certain that the beautiful and spirited Katerina was safe, because, in spite of her confident defiance, she was too much at the mercy of this man Hennek for Steffan's liking.

Four

"I see you are an early riser."

Katerina startled and spun around at the voice behind her. *Ack.* It was that Steffan fellow. Why wouldn't he leave?

Katerina didn't reply to his statement, but he didn't seem to mind. He followed her down the stairs.

"Your mother is quite lovely. I might almost have mistaken her for your sister."

"She was young when I was born. What of it?" Was he interested in her mother? Katerina went toward the kitchen and he kept following her.

"I have already broken my fast and thought I would ask you where the best place was to hunt the beast."

"You should ask my stepfather."

"He didn't seem as knowledgeable about the animal's habits as someone who had experience hunting it. Someone like you."

Katerina entered the kitchen. Hilde and Grette smiled and greeted her, then started gathering her usual breakfast into a cloth.

"Oh, may I have one of those?" Steffan leaned over her shoulder.

"Of course, Lord Steffan." The cooks smiled and hurried to wrap up an identical bundle of bread, cheese, and cold pork, and they gave it to Lord Steffan at the same time they gave Katerina hers. Grette and Hilde were glancing from Katerina to Steffan and back again.

"Thank you." Katerina bolted from the room as Steffan thanked each of them. Why was he fawning over the servants? No doubt he wanted something from them, or he just enjoyed the way they were smiling and blushing at his attention. But she wasn't waiting to see any more. She had to get rid of him before he followed her to little Bridda's home.

Out on the street, she took up a brisk pace. Almost immediately, heavy footfalls sounded behind her. She clenched her teeth, preparing herself to tell him to get away from her.

A woman and two children were walking down the other side of the street. The woman was holding a small child on her hip while a slightly older child held her hand.

"Mama, look at this!" The older child let go of her hand and darted ahead.

"Caspar, no!" The woman fairly screamed.

The child stopped, his face turning pale. He turned and went back to his mother.

"Hold my hand, you naughty—" She stopped and her face began to crumple.

"Don't cry, Mama. I'm sorry. I'll hold your hand now." The little boy grasped his mother's hand.

"I just don't want the beast to get you. You know that."

They walked on past.

"The people here are very frightened, aren't they?" Steffan appeared at her side. He had already opened his bundle and was taking a bite of bread and cheese.

"I thought you already broke your fast."

"I did." He chewed and swallowed. "I got hungry again."

His smile was so friendly it made her angry. She shouldn't have said anything to him. She opened her own bundle and took a bite, keeping her head turned away from the talkative duke's son.

"So, have you actually seen this Beast of Hamlin?"

Katerina considered ignoring him, but finally she shook her head.

"I heard a rumor that a few people have seen it and lived to tell of it."

"Two people. A man was attacked but beat it off with a stick."

"May I talk to him?"

"He's dead. Died of a putrid fever from his wounds."

"And the other person?"

"A woman who beat it off with a broken tree limb." Katerina spoke around the food in her mouth. Let him think her uncouth and unmannerly. She certainly had no wish to impress him.

"And where were these two people attacked?"

"You will have to excuse me, *Lord* Steffan." Katerina glanced at him as she neared the front door of Bridda's home. "I have business here. Fare well."

She turned her back on him, stuffed the remainder of her breakfast in her shoulder bag, and knocked on the wooden door that was fancifully painted and carved with a unicorn and a lion facing each other, vines and leaves surrounding them.

A woman answered the door looking distracted. "Yes?"

"I am Katerina, the mayor's daughter." She cringed inwardly at the words that so disgusted her, but the people actually looked up to her stepfather as sort of a savior of the town, more because that was how he portrayed himself than because of anything he had done. And she would use the fact that the mayor was her stepfather if it helped her discover the truth about the disappearances of Hamlin's children. "May I come in?"

"Oh." The woman covered her mouth, her eyes filling with tears. She quickly stepped back and opened the door wide. "I am so grateful to you for finding my little girl."

As Katerina stepped inside, she felt something brush against her back. She looked over her shoulder and there was Steffan, hovering right behind her.

"What are you doing?" she whispered up at him. "Get out."

He shook his head, a slight movement, then whispered back, "Let me stay. I can help."

Katerina barely had time to whisper, "No!" when Bridda's mother lifted her red eyes to Katerina's and grabbed her hand. "Thank you, Fräulein Katerina. I cannot tell you how grateful we are."

Bridda's mother's sincere emotion drove away Kat's fury at Steffan. But if he betrayed her or Bridda's family in any way, she would make him rue it.

"I only found her wandering out of the woods. Has she told you what happened and where she had been staying?"

The woman sniffed and shook her head as she led them through the corridor.

Kat turned to glare at Steffan, and her nose nearly touched his chest, so close was he following her. But he only shuffled his feet as if anxious to catch up with Bridda's mother.

They both followed the mother into a room with a trestle table, two benches, and some large wooden chairs against the wall filled with pillows and blankets. In one of those chairs sat Johannes holding Bridda in his lap.

All the black dust had been cleaned from her face and hair.

She wore clean clothes and was eating a small apple while resting her head and shoulder against her father's chest.

When she saw Katerina walk in, Bridda's eyes grew slightly wider as they fixed on Kat, following her, never even blinking.

"Fräulein Katerina!" Johannes's eyes were misty as he sat up, still holding Bridda close to his chest. "Please come and sit down." He indicated the chair beside him.

"And I am Steffan." The duke's son still hovered just behind her.

She could explain who he was to make it less awkward, but she had not invited him, nor did she even want him here.

"I am a friend of Fräulein Katerina and her father, Herr Hennek."

"Steffan?" Johannes studied his face. "We heard the son of the Duke of Hagenheim was in Hamlin. Are you he?"

"I am."

"It is an honor, my lord." Johannes nodded and indicated a chair. "Please sit and be comfortable. My house is yours."

Katerina forced herself not to glare at Steffan. Could she trust him not to tell Hennek anything of their conversation? If anyone should be disinterested and unable to be bribed by Hennek, wouldn't it be the son of the powerful and wealthy Duke of Hagenheim? But what if the rumors were true and Steffan hated his father? What if his character was so corrupt that he could be persuaded to join with Hennek in some way?

Trustworthy or not, she'd deal with him later.

Katerina smiled at Bridda. "Good morning, *Schätzchen*. Do you remember me?"

Bridda shrank a little closer to her father's chest.

She addressed Johannes. "May I ask your daughter a few questions?"

"Of course, but she has hardly spoken."

"I only want to ask you what you remember about where you have been."

The girl only stared back at her with large blue eyes. Her expression didn't change, and her lips stayed closed.

"How did you get lost from your mama?"

Still she didn't speak.

Johannes squeezed his daughter's arm. "It is well, Bridda. You may tell her what happened. She is Katerina, the mayor's daughter."

The little girl's gaze moved from Katerina to the man behind her and her eyes locked on to him. Still, she neither moved nor made a sound.

Katerina turned slightly and spoke to Steffan. "Lord Steffan, I think she might be more likely to talk to me if you were not here. Your presence seems to disturb her."

"I do not think she is disturbed by me." Steffan's gaze flitted from her to little Bridda, to Johannes, and back to her. "But if you think it best, I shall wait outside." He stood and bowed.

"Please, take some food and drink, my lord," Johannes said. "My wife makes very good cherry pasties and nut bread."

Bridda's mother stood in the doorway and urged Steffan to go with her.

Good. He was gone.

"Bridda, did someone take you away from your home?"

Still she didn't speak.

"She was playing," Johannes said softly. "In the alley beside the Rathous. She was with Verena, our neighbor's daughter. They were waiting for my wife to finish her business in the Rathous— she was paying the land tax. Verena is twelve years old, so my wife thought she could watch over her and they would be safe for a few minutes, but when my wife came out of the Rathous, the children were gone."

Bridda's eyes seemed to get droopy while her father talked. Kat had hoped his words might awaken a memory, but Bridda seemed more likely to fall asleep than to reveal anything.

"The guards speculated that the beast must have attacked one of the children, the other tried to stop him, then the beast dragged them both away." Johannes shook his head and stared thoughtfully at the floor for a moment. "I just couldn't understand how two children could go missing at once, especially with no trace of blood or ripped clothing, and no one having seen the animal that took them. It was daylight and in the middle of town." He stared into Kat's eyes. "Does that make any sense to you?"

"No." Kat shook her head. "No, it doesn't." Indeed, it was very strange. Nothing about the missing children made sense. Now that she thought about it, she couldn't remember a single incident where a child's body had been found with teeth marks or any sign of an animal having attacked it. Only adults had been found obviously marred by an animal.

Perhaps the Beast of Hamlin was not responsible for the missing children at all.

Bridda's eyes had closed.

"Were there any injuries or marks on her body? Did she appear to have been harmed?"

"No."

Whispering now, Kat said, "Can you turn her hand over so that I can see her palm?"

Johannes gently turned the child's tiny hand over. Kat found herself staring at the pink palm. Several callouses and scrapes marred the otherwise childlike hand. Hardened callouses on what should have been perfectly smooth, plump skin.

"I had not noticed . . ." Johannes's brows drew together. "It looks as if she's been working with her hands. What could she have been doing?"

Katerina shook her head. "Johannes, I know you and your wife are overjoyed to have your precious daughter home, but how many people have you told of her return?"

"I haven't told anyone. My wife may have told a few people."

"I told a few of my friends," the mother answered from the doorway.

"I'd like to ask you not to talk to anyone else about Bridda being found, and ask your friends to keep it a secret for now, though I know news has a way of traveling quickly. I think it is possible that someone may be responsible for taking her—a person and not the beast."

"Do you think she's in danger? That someone will try to take her again?" Johannes's face was tense and hard.

Kat hesitated, then said, "I don't know, but it's hard to believe that a wild animal would take her but leave her unharmed."

"You must allow me to help you search for this wicked person."

"I don't think that would be wise. I need you to stay quiet for now, keep Bridda in the house, and ask anyone who knows of her being found not to speak of it. And if Bridda tells you anything about where she's been, anything that might be helpful, please let me know."

Johannes and his wife exchanged a look. Then he nodded. "We trust you, Fräulein Katerina. I am sure Herr Hennek will be able to discover what is happening."

Kat's stomach sank at the mention of Hennek, at the way these people seemed to think their mayor was a good and well-meaning person. But was it worth warning them? They probably would only become suspicious of her, not Hennek.

"Please give our best wishes to your mother and Mayor Hennek. And after what you have done for us, finding Bridda . . . we will do any task you bid us. You only need to send us word."

"Thank you." She looked at the precious little face, relaxed in sleep, safe in her father's arms.

Katerina knew how it felt to be alone in an unsafe place. Were there other children in the forest somewhere? Children who were away from their parents' loving arms, alone and afraid? If they were out there, Katerina would find them, no matter what she had to do.

She excused herself from Johannes, and Bridda's mother walked her to the front corridor. Kat said, "I'll let you know of any new information."

A man stepped out of the shadowy doorway. Katerina startled and turned.

"Thank you for the pasties." Steffan bowed to their hostess.

The man was like a louse, clinging to her. And how much could he eat? Three breakfasts in one morning?

Kat smiled at Bridda's mother and said, "Fare well," ignoring Steffan.

On the street she opened her mouth to tell him he was not welcome to follow her any longer, but he placed a hand on her shoulder.

"There is a man—"

"Get your hand off me." Kat jerked away from him.

Steffan quickly removed his hand. "I'm trying to tell you, there is a man following us. He trailed us from your stepfather's house."

Kat looked over her shoulder.

"Don't look!" Steffan's whisper was loud and urgent.

The large man—as wide as two regular men and a head taller—stood staring at them from beneath droopy eyelids, his bald head shining in the morning light. He glanced away when she met his eye.

"That's just Otto. Are you afraid of him? He is bigger than you." Her lips twitched.

"Afraid? Of course not." He blew out an audible breath between pursed lips. "He would be no match for me. I've been training for battle my whole life." But there was a look about his mouth and eyes that told her he wasn't convinced that he could defeat Otto, and he wasn't even trying very hard to convince her. He had the same expression as a jongleur she had seen performing once, trying to make everyone laugh.

"Don't worry." She made sure to infuse her tone with irony. "He follows me all the time."

"Why?"

Kat shrugged and kept walking. Truthfully, it infuriated her that Hennek sent his men to spy on her, and now Otto had seen her leaving Bridda's house. But it was too late to try to evade him now.

She had an unsettled feeling in her stomach. Kat had noticed the way Hennek looked whenever he learned of another child going missing or of someone being attacked by the beast—shrewd and unsurprised. She wondered what he knew, or if he somehow had something to do with the beast or the disappearances.

"What is going on here?" Steffan asked in a slightly louder tone. "If that child was missing, then where was she? You have to admit it's very suspi—"

"Would you be quiet?" She walked faster, then ducked into a bakery. Glancing around, she saw there was only one customer in the shop besides the woman behind the counter reaching for a loaf of bread.

Stepping into a corner, she spun on her heel to face him.

"You may be the son of a duke," she said in a quiet voice, "but I don't have to tell you anything. I am a free woman and I do not answer to you. You are not welcome here. Go back to Hagenheim and your comfortable home and leave me to protect the people. These are my people."

Her voice was shaking by the end of her outburst, and she was already regretting her harsh words. His expression was stunned, then guarded. His throat bobbed as he swallowed.

Did he expect her to ask for forgiveness? Well, she wouldn't. Mother might cower before a man, but she would not, not even if he was the son of a duke.

$\mathcal{F}$ive

$\mathcal{S}$teffan took a step back.

He couldn't remember anyone talking to him the way Katerina did—at least no one outside of his family. And his sisters only spoke to him this way when he'd been teasing them mercilessly and they were fed up. But he was not teasing Katerina. He just wanted to help.

"Some kind of treachery is afoot. I came here to kill the beast, but it appears something else is going on. I could help if you—"

"We don't need your help. *I* don't need your help."

"Do you hate everyone? Or is it only me? You know, I may be a duke's son but—"

"I don't have time to stand here talking to you."

Katerina slid past him, careful not to brush against his arm, and rushed out the doorway.

What was the matter with her? Her anger was unfounded and unfair. But nothing, not even that giant of a man who was following them, could keep him from going after her. He had to know what was going on for his own curiosity's sake, but it was more than that. His father needed to know what was happening in Hamlin, and if Steffan was able to discover what it was, perhaps his father would cease to see him as the son who never did anything right.

He burst out the door behind Katerina. He pursued her down the cobblestone street, but not before he noted the hulking man pushing himself off the shop front he was leaning against and coming after them.

She was walking fast. He stayed just behind her. Perhaps he could wait until she was less angry before trying to convince her to trust him.

He knew a lot about anger. He'd spent the last year realizing how foolish his own anger had been. Now, when that anger rose up, instead of drinking too much to make it go away, he asked himself where it was coming from. Oftentimes he realized he was blaming someone else for something that was mostly his own fault. The person he was most angry at was himself.

What was behind Katerina's anger? Steffan was fairly certain he hadn't done anything worse than be persistent.

A group of rats were chittering as they ran across the cobblestones. The people on the street gave the rodents a wide berth and a wary eye but continued on their way, obviously accustomed to seeing them.

After he killed the beast he'd have to figure out a way to get rid of those rats.

He matched his pace to Katerina's and watched the way her crossbow bounced ever so slightly against her back. She was dressed as she had been when he first saw her, with a peasant's rough linen skirt that came just above her ankles to allow for extra movement and thin hose encasing her legs. She was a most unusual girl. Her stepfather was the mayor of a large town, appointed and well-paid by Steffan's father, and yet she dressed defiantly and went out hunting against her stepfather's wishes.

Again, she reminded Steffan of himself. The difference was

that Katerina had a good reason for defying convention and her annoying stepfather. She wanted to find out what was happening to the children who were going missing, and she wanted to protect her people by killing the beast. He couldn't help but feel a swell of admiration for this girl. Even if she did seem to hate him.

They were heading out of town, toward one of the town gates. He glanced over his shoulder. The giant was still there, still following after them.

Katerina reached the gate. The guards standing there gave her a slight smile and a quiet greeting. She returned their greeting.

So she wasn't rude to everyone, or even all men.

She passed through the gate and began to walk faster. Steffan jogged to catch up to her.

"Good day, Fräulein," he said in his most jovial tone.

She tossed over her shoulder, "I need you to be quiet or go away. I'm going to hunt the beast."

"As am I."

"Where are your weapons?"

"I have my longbow here. See?" He tried to get her to look at where he was pointing to his bow and arrows slung over his shoulder, but she barely glanced at him. "And I have my short sword strapped to my belt. I don't like to go hunting without my weapons."

She frowned, acknowledging his weak jest whether she wanted to or not.

"Do we not *want* to attract the animal's attention? After all, it's hunting too, and if it hears us, it'll come in our direction." Not entirely a wise plan, but he couldn't resist trying to goad her into speaking.

She ignored him, heading toward the forest.

"Is this where you found the little girl?" He spoke softly enough that the man following them could not overhear.

She turned toward him and whispered, "No one is supposed to know about that."

"I cannot imagine you could keep something like that a secret for long."

She didn't reply as they continued walking. Soon they entered the brush, ferns, and beech trees of a thick forest at the foot of a large hill, and they started climbing the gradual incline.

"Otto is still following us. Shall I dispatch him for you?"

She made a contemptuous sound of breath rushing through her pursed lips. "I can't imagine you could."

"Do you doubt my abilities? I'll have you know I'm a warrior."

"Of the German Order of Teutonic Knights, I believe you said."

"No, not officially a Teutonic Knight, but I did some fighting for them." He'd rather not go into that.

"Didn't wish to take your vows and become a monk?" A wry smile twisted her pretty mouth. The Teutonic Knights were a religious order and therefore had to take a vow of celibacy.

"God has other plans for me."

Her smile widened. "Not surprising."

"What's not surprising?"

"It has been my experience that dishonorable men often blame their failings on God."

"You think I am dishonorable? Based on what?"

"You are a man. You're arrogant. And . . . I suppose that is enough."

Steffan knew he could be arrogant at times, but sometimes he pretended arrogance to deflect his shame at his own failings, or he pretended arrogance to elicit a laugh. But he hated that she thought him arrogant. "You misjudge me."

She only shrugged.

"Perhaps I can stay in Hamlin long enough to change your mind about me."

"Oh, please, don't stay on my account."

"And if I am the one to kill the beast . . . we'll be getting to know each other quite well, as man and wife."

He only said it to tease her, to make her laugh. Marriage was for people who wanted to settle down in one place and have children. And the thought of having a child filled him with dread. He didn't like children.

Katerina suddenly turned, her fist raised, forcing him to stop. He lost his balance and nearly fell into her.

"I will kill the man who tries to wed me. Is that understood?"

"Perfectly." He held up his hands, palms out. Her expression had changed so much, she didn't even look like the same person who had, half an hour earlier, spoken so compassionately to the little girl and her parents.

How could he ever get her to look at him with that softened expression?

But it hit him suddenly that that fierce, hard look was fear.

"Did someone hurt you? Is that why you'd rather murder a man than marry him?"

Her expression went slack. She spun around and started walking again. But just as quickly, she spun again to face him.

"How do you dare assume anything about me? All you need to know is that I will kill the man who lays a finger on me. Including you."

"Of course. I understand. You look quite capable of protecting yourself, and I would never touch you, or any woman, without their permission, I assure you."

"And you will never gain my permission."

"Understood. Forgive me for teasing you about marriage. Sometimes I try too hard to make people laugh. It is one of my many faults, and I beg you to forgive me." He placed his hand over his heart and looked her in the eye.

Was it his imagination or did her eyes soften? He'd never know, because she turned away and marched off through the brush, crushing ferns and twigs under her feet. He followed.

When she didn't speak, he asked, "So, do you forgive me?"

She blew out a long sigh as she walked. "Are you always so annoying? And talkative?"

"Not always." He couldn't help smiling. Already she was beginning to soften toward him. After all, he might not be as handsome as Wolfgang, but he could be quite charming when he wanted to be, as he had been told more than once. How could she resist him?

Perhaps he was arrogant after all.

———————

Katerina wished she could punch the big, annoying duke's son in the stomach and send him back where he came from. No doubt he was only entertaining himself, following her around, and he'd get tired of the game and find someone else who was more receptive.

She knew just the type of woman who would welcome his attention—those girls who laughed behind their hands when she walked by with her crossbow, pointing and giggling, protected darlings who never had to fend for themselves. Whenever a young man possessing handsome features was around, they blinked like there was something in their eyes, "accidentally" touched the man's arm, and laughed at his weak jests. No doubt Steffan was acquainted with many of those young women, had flirted with them, and . . . more than flirted.

Ignoring him, she pulled her crossbow off her shoulder and loaded it with a metal bolt, heavier and stouter than a longbow's wooden arrow.

"Has the beast been seen in this area?" Lord Steffan whispered.

"He attacked a man near here, the one who later died of a putrid fever."

"How did he describe the beast?"

"He said he looked like a wolf, or a giant dog; he was unsure. He was a shop owner who rarely ventured out of the town gates and had never actually seen a wolf before." He'd only been in the woods because he was meeting a woman who was not his wife. Stupid man's only weapon had been his walking stick.

As they walked, Steffan was finally quiet, and she hadn't heard Otto breaking any twigs or rustling any leaves in a while. Was he still behind them?

They were climbing the hill now, and the trees were becoming sparser, with fewer bushes and undergrowth. Very few people ventured this way anymore, not since all the reports of the Beast of Hamlin and so many people had gone missing. And yet, she saw evidence of people having recently climbed the hill on the very path they were taking, including fresh footprints, trampled leaves, and broken twigs.

Steffan stepped up beside her and bent over and picked up a bruised leaf. He looked at her and lifted a brow. "Who would be coming this way with the beast on the loose?"

Kat shrugged slightly and shook her head. She took a few

more steps, Steffan just behind her. The trail was becoming rockier as it went straight up, but a newer trail, less worn, was just visible, forking off to the left. Steffan seemed to notice it the same time she did, as he bent forward and peered in that direction. He looked at her and motioned with his head.

He was smarter than she thought. How annoying.

They took the left fork, where the trees were a little more dense, and found themselves winding between tree branches and bushes. Kat was in the lead, but when a branch blocked her way, Steffan held it up to let her pass under it.

She didn't say thank you. A tiny nudge of guilt pinched her chest. But why should she thank him? It was nothing heroic. And she didn't want him to think she wanted him here. He was an arrogant mercenary, and she didn't need his help.

They continued following the path as it wound around the side of the hill, coming to the far side, away from town. Then, instead of continuing up, the path started down.

Kat got a strange feeling, a prickling at the back of her neck, as if something were breathing just behind her. She turned, but only Steffan was there, slightly behind and to the side of her. Beyond him were dark, shadowy trees. The sky seemed to have become overcast, hiding the sun and making the forest even darker.

She continued forward. How had she never seen this path before? Or gone this way? It must be a very new path. A fallen tree lay up ahead. She vaguely remembered seeing it before, lying against a large boulder, half covered. But today there were other downed trees that looked to have been piled up around it, covering the boulder, if indeed her memory was correct.

The trees, though their trunks were sawed through, were still full of green leaves, as if freshly cut.

A growl erupted, loud and close. It came from the other side of the pile of trees.

Kat's whole body tensed. She already held her crossbow at the ready, so she stopped and waited. Steffan stepped up beside her. He had drawn his sword without her hearing it.

An animal with long skinny legs stepped out from behind the pile of trees. The unusually large creature bared its teeth and hunched low, crouching and readying itself.

Steffan stepped forward as she raised her crossbow. Thankfully, he stayed well to the side so that she had a clear shot.

Kat raised her crossbow, aimed, and just as she loosed the arrow, the animal leapt.

Six

Steffan waited as Katerina aimed her crossbow. *Shoot.* The enormous animal was preparing to leap at them. *Shoot.*

She shot, but at the same moment the animal sprang at them.

Steffan jumped in front of Katerina with his sword raised. The beast's eyes glowed as it sailed through the air. Steffan stabbed, but his sword tip struck the animal's shoulder instead of its heart, as its full weight crashed down on Steffan's head and shoulders, knocking him on his back.

Sharp teeth were so close they almost touched his nose. Steffan's left hand tightened around the wolf's throat, holding it off as it snarled and dripped saliva on Steffan's chin. He couldn't pull his sword back far enough to stab the animal. He slashed and beat at the animal's side, but the wolf heeded it not.

The wolf's lips were drawn back, and Steffan could see every sharp fang, every grinding tooth. The creature drew back until Steffan almost lost his grip on its neck. Should he let go and hope to have enough room to stab it? But then it lunged down at him. He locked his elbow, but the animal turned its head and sank its teeth into Steffan's forearm.

He had to let go of his sword to grip the wolf's head, but it did not loosen its bite.

If this was how his life would end, a victim of the Beast of Hamlin . . . Poor Mother and Father. He never got to tell them he was sorry.

Katerina's bolt missed the animal. A tight fist gripped her heart at the fatal mistake. Had Steffan really stepped in front of her? Now he was lying on the ground, grappling with the enormous beast.

She grabbed the extra crossbow bolt from her bag. Standing over the animal, she lifted the metal arrow and used it to stab the beast through the back, hopefully in its heart, while trying not to stab Steffan.

The animal's mouth was latched onto Steffan's arm. It didn't let go even when she stabbed it. She grabbed the bolt sticking out of its back and pulled it out. Before she could stab it again, the beast jumped off of Steffan and whirled on her, snarling and snapping its jaws. She held the bolt, pointing out. The animal jumped at her, twisting its body to avoid her weapon, and landed on its side on the ground. It was a bit slow getting back on its feet.

In that moment Kat stabbed the creature in the shoulder, just as Steffan's sword point came down on the back of its neck. The animal slumped to the ground and didn't move.

Blood was running down Steffan's arm. "Are you hurt?" he asked.

He was asking if *she* was hurt? She blinked, distracted by his blue eyes staring back at her.

Steffan lifted his uninjured arm and placed his hand on her shoulder.

His hand was so warm. Her heart pounded. He had stepped

between her and danger. He was wounded while protecting *her*. She had a sudden urge to throw her arms around him.

Strange, ridiculous thought. She would never, ever put her arms around Steffan. She hated him.

Except . . . she didn't seem to hate him anymore.

Her heart pounded against her breastbone, stealing her breath for a moment. She quickly turned away from him, shrugging the gentle hand from her shoulder.

She stared down at the wolf. With her foot she nudged the large animal and blinked away all of the confusing emotions that had been coursing through her. The animal didn't move.

Suddenly, Kat heard a growl, a snarl that raised the hair on her arms. She glanced at Steffan. His eyes met hers, but only for a moment.

Steffan sprang forward and grabbed his sword, which was still sticking up from the base of the animal's skull, pinning it to the ground. He pulled the weapon free and held it up in a defensive stance.

Kat snatched her crossbow off the ground and fitted the bloody arrow into the mechanism, loading it by bracing the bow on the ground with her foot as she pulled the arrow and string taut.

Kat saw the eyes before she saw the rest of the beast's body. It stalked toward them. Kat and Steffan backed away, putting the dead beast between them and this new animal. As it came closer, Kat gasped. It was just as big and gangly as the other one. Were her eyes playing tricks on her? How could it be that there were not one but two enormous beasts? Was that why so many people had gone missing?

Steffan was retreating slowly, just as Kat was, but he kept

his own body between her and the wolf, waving his sword at the creature and yelling, "Stay back! Back!"

The animal crouched, then did a crawl-step, easing carefully toward the dead wolf on the ground. It sniffed the ground next to the carcass, then made a high, whining sound. Then it turned and trotted away, looking back over its shoulder at Steffan and Kat.

They both stood staring after the animal.

"Do you think it will double back and come around from another direction?" Kat watched as Steffan lowered his sword, his shoulders relaxing.

"I don't think so, but we should go just in case."

Once again, Steffan had placed himself between her and danger.

"I probably should have shot at it while I had the chance," Katerina said. Why had she not? She must have been so shocked she wasn't thinking.

"I'm just glad we lived to tell the tale." Steffan looked at her, then down at his bleeding arm.

She forced a no-nonsense tone. "We need to see about that wound. Do you have any bandages?"

He shook his head. "It's not bad. I've seen much worse."

He probably had. He had two scars on his face, one below his eye and one above. Somehow they didn't seem to detract from his handsomeness. But outward beauty did not matter. Handsome men could be just as dastardly as the ugly ones.

But then she remembered the man who died from his wounds after being attacked by the wolf. Would Steffan's wound also become putrid?

"We must get you to a healer. Come."

She retrieved her other arrow—the one that she had shot at

the beast and missed. When she came back, Steffan was still staring down at the animal.

"There's something about it." He squatted beside the mangled animal. "It doesn't look like a normal wolf. Or a normal anything." He stretched out one of its legs. "It's so large, it must be the Beast of Hamlin. And yet the second one looked exactly like it."

Kat knelt on the other side of it. "It's a wolf. Look at its head. But you're right. It doesn't look normal. The legs are longer and the body is bigger than any other wolf I've seen, but it's also so skinny."

"As if it was starving. Maybe that's why it was so aggressive. But why would it be starving? There are plenty of hares and squirrels around these woods and fields."

"And rats." Hundreds and hundreds of rats. "But the rats all seem to be in town."

"You live in a strange place, Katerina Grymmelin."

"My name is not Grymmelin." Katerina's body tensed at hearing Hennek's surname applied to her.

"Oh, yes. Forgive me." He looked chagrined.

"My name is Katerina Ludken. And I thank you for . . . not letting the wolf . . . that is . . ." Why was it so difficult to say, "Thank you for saving my life"? All the breath had left her lungs. She just couldn't.

Finally she said, "Thank you for helping me kill the wolf." There. If he turned out to be a wolf himself, she wouldn't hate herself for thanking him, as he *had* helped her kill it.

Steffan turned all his attention on her and even leaned toward her, over the wolf's body. "You are welcome for me stepping in front of the wolf to protect you."

"And you are welcome for me keeping the wolf from gnawing

off your arm by stabbing it with my crossbow bolt." She glared, daring him to argue with her.

"You aren't going to acknowledge that I sacrificed myself to save you, are you?" He widened his eyes and let his mouth hang open.

She clenched her teeth. She couldn't discern if he was making a jest or in earnest, but either way, he was throwing it up at her, and it was obnoxious.

His lips curved only the tiniest bit, and his eyes were laughing. "You know, I could tell your stepfather that I killed the beast. Then he—"

"Then he what?"

"Well, he might tell me I can marry you."

If she'd ever wished she could shoot crossbow bolts from her eyes, it was now. "I will never marry you, and there isn't a priest in Hamlin who would force me."

"Never?" He laid his right hand, the uninjured one, against his heart. "You wound me."

Kat huffed. He was so irritating. "I didn't wound you, but you are wounded, so let us get back before you bleed out."

Her hands were starting to shake, a late reaction to the terror of the beast attacking them as they fought for their lives. But she had no intention of letting Steffan see her hands shaking or any other indication that she felt any effects from the attack, so she started down the path at a faster pace than when they'd walked up.

Now that Steffan was behind her and couldn't see her face, she let herself remember him jumping in front of her as the beast leapt at her. Her heart beat faster just thinking about it. Probably only because she was surprised the irritating man would do something so selfless. But that was not true, and she knew it. It was more because she'd longed for, even needed someone to protect her so many times in the past, but no one ever had. Instead, when men had tried to harm them, she'd been the only one to protect her mother and herself. And it sent such a strong feeling through her—she wasn't sure what to call it—to have someone protect her, even if it was Steffan.

She should not think of it anymore.

But her conscience nudged her that she had actually treated him ungraciously and had not thanked him as she should have for saving her.

Perhaps later, after his wound had been treated, she would. But how could she thank him without being overwhelmed by that strange feeling again? And he was so arrogant, he would probably get the wrong impression of her and would think she had romantic intentions toward him.

Her thoughts were warring inside her when Steffan said, "I thank you, Katerina, for stabbing that animal with your arrow."

This was her opportunity. She said quickly, "And thank you for stepping in front of him when he pounced."

She glanced over her shoulder. As she suspected, he was grinning on one side of his mouth, one brow lifting in a jocular expression.

She clamped her lips closed. She would not give him the satisfaction of admitting he had saved her life. She had saved herself too many times, and she'd long prided herself on never giving in to what men wanted. She wasn't about to start giving in to this one.

"Why will you not say it?"

"Because we helped each other. We both killed the beast. And if you don't be quiet, I may leave you here to bleed to death."

"It's not bleeding that much." His voice was cheerful, without the least bit of anger or resentment at her refusal to give him what he wanted. "Is your healer any good? I have a recipe for a wound remedy. It's said to heal wounds without fail, a curative against any putridness or fever. Perhaps your healer could make some of it."

"I have heard of this remedy. The maker of it was accused of witchcraft."

"Yes, but she was found innocent."

Steffan suddenly seemed thoughtful and fell silent. She glanced over her shoulder and saw he was staring at the ground, his brows drawn together.

She shouldn't ask him about it. A lack of curiosity was a safeguard against trouble. But she asked anyway. "This was your brother's mother-in-law who created this healing salve? She is still alive?"

He drew in a slow breath before answering. "She was alive when I left them nearly a year ago."

"Where did you leave them?"

"On the border of Poland and Germany, near Thornbeck. My brother was awarded a castle and lands by Duke Konrad of Poland. Wolfgang and his wife, Mulan, live there with Mulan's mother, who is a healer."

"I have heard of this Mulan. She was a warrior." *Like me.*

"Yes. She was a soldier and a captain of the duke's guard. You remind me of her."

Her heart lifted at the compliment.

"But she is rather more . . ."

"More what?" Again foolish curiosity got the better of her.

"Well, she was fierce in battle, but kinder and more sweetly mannered."

How dare he say that to me! But no doubt it was true. Kindness, at least toward men, was not something she had ever been able to afford. Her father had left them with nothing when he died, and her mother . . . Well, she had been young and foolish and had not protected either herself or Kat very well. Kat learned very early that protecting herself and her mother was more important than being kind. When had men been kind to her? Men could not be trusted. She had learned this lesson well.

Steffan touched her shoulder. She flinched and spun to face him.

He stared into her eyes. "A man hurt one of my sisters. After that she was different. Quieter and easily startled. There was a look in her eyes, just like the look I sometimes see in yours."

What did he mean by saying that? He had no right to assume . . .

She was a little angry, but at the same time, the look in his eyes made her want to lean in, to trust him, the same feeling she'd had when she nearly threw her arms around him after he protected her from the wolf.

She was being foolish. "You know nothing about me." She barely recognized her own voice, as hoarse and gruff as it was.

She turned away from him and continued walking, even faster this time. She had to get away from this man. He unsettled her. One moment she was annoyed, and the next she felt soft and warm inside, something she'd never felt around a man before. Only her horse made her feel similarly, when he nudged her and snuffled against her shoulder.

But one thing was certain—she could trust her horse, but she didn't trust Steffan.

Someone had hurt Katerina. An animal was only acting on its natural instincts when it attacked and harmed someone. But what kind of human being could harm Katerina? Steffan imagined putting some fear in that person if he ever dared harm her again.

His arm, which had been almost numb since he was injured, was starting to send sharp pains shooting up to his shoulder. Now his whole forearm throbbed. Blood still dripped off his arm, but it wasn't bleeding quite as much as before.

When they reached the bottom of the hill, Katerina stopped and pointed at him. "Wait here." Then she turned and disappeared around the side of an enormous tree. He heard a sound like wood scraping against wood, then she reappeared with a cloth bag in her hand. She set it on the ground, rummaged around inside, and pulled out a roll of bandages.

"We need to wrap that arm." Her face seemed to be made of stone, her eyes never lifting above the height of his injury. She stepped forward. He held out his arm and she began wrapping it, rather tightly, somehow managing not to touch his skin even once.

"Do you have supplies stored away behind every tree?"

"Not behind every tree." Her expression didn't change and she didn't look up, so he was able to study her face.

Her lips and chin were delicate and perfectly shaped. The curve of her cheek was feminine, her skin pale, her eyes mysterious, and her lashes dark. One would never imagine she could stab a giant, raging wolf with a crossbow bolt and then a mere half an hour later wrap a wound with steady hands.

He'd felt a strange tension from her ever since they'd killed the beast. At one moment he thought she might throw her arms around him. The next, she was coldly turning away, refusing to look at him. He wished he could see inside her mind.

"Thank you." He bent his head, trying to get her to look at him. "For bandaging my arm."

She glanced at him. He captured her eyes with his, willing her to reveal her thoughts. She did stare back at him, her mouth going slack. But then she quickly glanced away.

"It's a little tight," she said, pulling out a knife from her bag and cutting the end of the bandage into a smaller strip; she then tied it around the bandage to keep it in place. "But it will be fine until you can get to the healer's house in town. It's on Butcher Street."

A cracking noise, as when a man steps down on a dry, leafy twig, made them both jerk their heads in the direction of the sound.

A strong breeze sent the leaves in the upper branches of the trees dancing and chattering like the rapid waters of a stream. When the wind died down, they both kept still, listening, but heard nothing but a lone bird singing.

Katerina turned and marched off toward the town.

He trotted after her. "Will you show me the healer's house?" He wasn't ready to part from her.

"Very well."

They entered the town gate. Katerina's eyes alighted on each guard in turn. Was she searching for a particular guard?

Katerina moved on. She was nearing her stepfather's house when two large, burly men came out.

Katerina slowed her pace, then halted. Just when she did, the men caught sight of them and hurried toward them. One of the two men was Otto.

By the look on Katerina's face, she was thinking of running from them. Steffan rested his hand on his sword hilt. But instead, Katerina stayed where she was and faced them.

"The Bürgermeister wishes to see you," one of the men said, looking from Steffan to Katerina and back. "Both of you."

Katerina and Steffan continued on with the guards on either side of them.

Soon they entered the mayor's house and were led into a small room where Hennek stood staring at a large sheet of parchment in his hands. He quickly folded the parchment, shoved it into a wooden box on the table in front of him, and slammed the lid closed.

Hennek's cheeks were red, and he widened his eyes when he saw them, then quickly coughed and broke into a smile—a smile that looked brittle and forced.

Steffan's hand went to his sword hilt again.

"*Ach!* So, you have killed the beast!" Hennek's voice boomed and his arms went wide, his eyes focused on Steffan. "My men just reported they saw a beast lying dead in the forest and the two of you walking away from it. I suppose I know what your motive was, eh? The reward?" He raised his brows and jerked his head in Katerina's direction.

"The Beast of Hamlin is indeed dead," Steffan said, though it was strange that Hennek's men had seen the dead beast so quickly after they'd killed it. Perhaps Otto had been closer behind them than they'd thought? It pained him a bit, but by the horror and, yes, fear, that flickered over Katerina's face, he knew what he had to do.

"I did not kill the beast. Katerina did."

"What did you say?" Hennek stared, openmouthed.

Katerina's mouth also dropped open, and she turned to face him.

Steffan swallowed a lump—his pride, no doubt—that rose into his throat.

Hennek sputtered, unable to form a coherent word.

"I cannot claim the generous reward, I'm afraid. Katerina slayed the giant wolf with her crossbow bolt."

The look on Katerina's face—shock, a softening, gratitude shining in her beautiful eyes—was worth the half-truth and blow to his ego.

He smiled and shrugged. "She is a fearless huntress and slayer of giants." Then he winked at her.

Winking might have been a bad idea, as her expression suddenly morphed to a scowl.

Hennek blustered a moment more, then narrowed his eyes at Katerina. "Is this true? Did you kill the beast?"

"We both did. That is, Lord Steffan helped."

"Well, if Lord Steffan struck the fatal blow, he is still entitled to the reward. He deserves your hand in marriage." He glared at his stepdaughter.

"I am sure it was Katerina who landed the killing blow, Herr Bürgermeister."

"You are sure of this? Because I—"

"Quite sure."

"Well then." Uncharacteristically, Hennek fell silent.

Steffan glanced at Katerina. Her eyes met his for a moment. They both knew that killing the beast had not accomplished much of anything. The children were still missing, and there was a second beast. But something kept him from mentioning that fact to Hennek.

Seven

Katerina's heart still pounded. Steffan had proclaimed her to be the slayer of the Beast of Hamlin. He could have downplayed her role in the killing and claimed Hennek's reward. Instead, he'd made sure Katerina was safe from Hennek's badgering—or trying to force her—to wed Steffan. And this, after all the rude and accusatory things she'd said to him.

She glanced askance at him. What manner of man was he? Or did he have some less noble reason for denying his own role in the slaying of the beast? But in this moment she wanted to believe his motive was pure.

Hennek was clearing his throat. For once in his life, he didn't know what to say. No doubt he was confused that someone would give up a reward.

Steffan was saying, "If you wished to give me half the reward—five hundred silver guilders instead of a thousand—I would not object to that."

So he was still a mercenary.

Hennek laughed. "How about I strike a new deal with you. If you are able to rid the town of all the rats, the reward is yours. Is that not a most generous offer?"

"I will accept the reward for getting rid of your rat problem."

Was he willing to allow Hennek to force her to marry him after all?

Steffan glanced in her direction. She did her best to warn him with her eyes. *If you think you can force me to marry you, you will meet the sharp edge of my knife blade.*

He half frowned, half smiled at her harsh look, then winked again.

The man thought he was charming. Kat allowed an uncharming snort to escape her.

"You may yet get to marry a duke's son, Katerina!" Hennek roared with laughter, an exaggerated reaction to his own jest. But his laugh sounded fake and even angry.

Until now, she'd been thinking Steffan was safe from Hennek, that Hennek would want to impress him and send him back to Hagenheim with a glowing report of what a good man the Mayor of Hamlin was. But Steffan wasn't leaving. And if he truly wanted to help her find out what was happening to the children of Hamlin, as he said he did, then there was no knowing what Hennek might do to him. Hennek wasn't just angry that Steffan hadn't accepted the reward for killing the Beast of Hamlin. He was angry that Steffan was still there.

Suddenly she remembered Steffan's arm.

"Lord Steffan was injured," Katerina said, interrupting Hennek. "I shall show him to the healer's house."

"What?" Hennek looked confused.

Steffan raised his sleeve. "The beast took a bit of flesh before succumbing."

A few spots of blood had seeped through the bandage.

"Ho ho! A few more scars to add to your collection, eh?"

Steffan shrugged. "They make for good stories to tell at the alehouse."

"Ah, yes! Of course, of course."

Katerina took two steps toward the door, and as she'd intended, Steffan followed.

Hennek called out nonsensical warnings, laughing at his own inept jests, as they left and went in the direction of the healer's house. She walked in silence, trying to figure out how to warn Steffan that his life was in danger.

———◦◦———

Steffan followed Katerina, who kept up a brisk pace. She turned right down a side street and then left and then right again. Then they went down a street that smelled of freshly slaughtered meat. Past two butchers' shops, Katerina pointed to a doorway.

"You will come inside with me, won't you?"

Katerina opened her mouth and hesitated. Then she stepped forward and knocked on the door.

An older woman answered and invited them in.

"Frau Windmoeller, this is Lord Steffan. He was bitten by the Beast of Hamlin."

The old woman's face was wrinkled and leathery, but her pale, wizened eyes fixed on his arm and she turned and said, "Come in."

They followed her to a room with shelves full of glass vials, leather flasks, brass bowls, and lidded pots.

"Sit."

Steffan lowered himself onto the edge of a narrow bed while Frau Windmoeller sat on a stool in front of him.

She grabbed his wrist, squeezing hard with her bony fingers. "Is this your only wound?"

"Yes." Thanks to Katerina. If she hadn't stabbed the beast with her crossbow bolt, the animal probably would have torn out his throat.

Frau Windmoeller asked Katerina to fetch some things while the old woman unwrapped the bandage. Then Katerina poured water over the wound, which burned and stung even more when Frau Windmoeller used her fingers to rub the blood off. But he would rather bite his tongue off than let Katerina hear him cry out.

The woman peered so close to his arm that he was sure the tip of her nose would touch his skin. Then she fixed her eyes on his face. "We don't want to lose you to a putrid infection like Herr Otfried a few months ago. That beast has poison in its fangs." Suddenly she turned to Katerina.

"Did you kill it?"

"We did," Katerina answered.

"Glory to God. What was it? A dog? A wolf?"

"It was a wolf, but tall and more muscular."

Would Katerina tell her that they'd seen a second wolf just like it? Such a thing would be almost unbelievable. He wouldn't believe it if he hadn't seen it with his own eyes. Katerina opened her mouth as if to speak, but then looked at him and said nothing.

The healer turned back to Steffan. "I shall clean it."

Hadn't she already cleaned it? She uncorked a flask and he smelled strong spirits. She poured the brown liquid over the puncture wounds.

Burning pain seared his arm. He sucked in a breath through his teeth, then coughed in an attempt to mask his reaction. Finally, she started rewrapping the wound.

When the healer had finished with his arm and Katerina had answered her questions about killing the wolf, his arm was hurting worse than ever.

"Take some wine for the pain," the healer said as she put her bandages away. "That will be five silver pfennigs." She stared him in the eye without blinking.

Steffan's stomach sank. He had not one single coin on him. What did he have that was equal the value of five pfennigs? He couldn't give her his knife, as he needed it. He possessed very little else besides his horse.

"I shall bring you—"

He was about to say "a pheasant," but Katerina handed Frau Windmoeller five silver pfennigs before he could get the words out.

Katerina turned and started walking to the door.

"Thank you, Frau Windmoeller." Steffan hurried after Katerina.

"Thank you for paying the healer," Steffan said as he caught up with her. "I owe you five pfennigs."

"You owe me nothing."

They were nearly to one of the main streets when Katerina suddenly stopped and backed up against the brick wall of a warehouse. Her gaze darted in every direction before settling on his face.

"I believe your life is in danger if you come back with me to my stepfather's house." Her dark eyes were intense. Her gaze faltered as she spoke, then bore into his again. "You should go. Just leave here and go back to Hagenheim, and when you do, tell your father that many things are amiss here in Hamlin, and if he cares for the people of Hamlin at all, he should come and look into it."

He took a moment to absorb this information, but she looked so beautiful when her eyes were so intently gazing into his.

Fear flickered in the dark blue depths, bringing his thoughts back to her sobering words.

"Why would I be in danger? In danger from whom?"

She frowned, then said in a hushed voice, "Hennek, of course."

"Why would Hennek want to kill me? I am the duke's son."

"Which is why he wants to kill you. If you discover something amiss here and report it to your father, he may uncover Hennek's wrongdoing."

"Wrongdoing? What is Hennek doing?"

"He must be taking money from the tax coffers. He seems to have almost unlimited wealth all of a sudden, and I don't know where it's coming from. He also takes bribes so that innocent men are found guilty while the guilty go free. I have witnessed it."

"Do you have any evidence?"

She shook her head. "And I can't tell anyone because the townspeople are all fooled by his pretense of being a righteous, benevolent mayor who spends all his time doing good for others and making the town prosper. But he suddenly has so much money he has been giving it away all over town, because he loves the people's praise. I know the people trust me, and normally they would believe whatever I told them, but Hennek has them in the palm of his hand. And if he knew I'd told anyone he took bribes or I suspected he was stealing money, he'd harm Mother and would probably kill me. But I believe I could find some evidence. If I did, could you help me get it to the duke quickly?"

When he didn't answer, Katerina crossed her arms over her chest. "I'm only telling you this so you'll go home and get help. Bring your father, your brother, and some fighting men."

"Why didn't you say something sooner?"

"I didn't know if you would stand up to Hennek or if you were perhaps in league with him. But now . . . I see that you would stand up to him, and that makes you a threat to him."

"So you actually think he will try to kill me?"

"Yes, because he doesn't want you speaking to your father. You don't know him as I do. He is capable of any ungodliness to get what he wants."

Steffan stared at her, thoughts darting through his mind. Then his stomach sank as he gripped his sword hilt. "Did Hennek hurt you? He is the one who hurt you, isn't he?"

Her mouth fell open slightly, then she closed it and her cheeks turned red. "If you don't want to listen to what I'm telling you, it is your choice. But don't say I didn't warn you."

So she wouldn't admit it, but now he knew. His blood boiled. What a despicable man Hennek was. Steffan wouldn't rest until Hennek was stripped of the title of Bürgermeister.

"Perhaps I am overreacting, but I don't think so. Hennek will never come right out and say it, but you will be able to discern his hostility if you listen carefully. He tries to sound friendly and generous and make you think he is good, but there is malice behind his loud jests and laughter."

Her words brought to mind the strange sensation he'd felt earlier that there was aggression behind Hennek's jolly demeanor and words.

"I have to at least go back and get my horse and belongings." Maybe he was in danger, but he had fought real battles, not to mention training as a knight all his life. He wasn't about to be so afraid of the Bürgermeister that he would sneak or run away.

Was she so concerned about him?

She took a step toward the main street, and he laid a light hand on her arm. She flinched and looked up at him.

"You didn't answer when I asked if Hennek hurt you. You are not safe there with him either."

Her jaw hardened. Finally she said, "My longest knife is always by my side, even when I sleep. Anyone who tries to hurt me will regret it. And Hennek knows that."

"What did he do?"

"I will not speak of it with you." She was already striding away, turning onto the main street.

"Katerina, wait."

He put his hand on her shoulder. For the first time she didn't flinch, she only stood very still.

Her shoulder was surprisingly thin and fragile. He made sure his grasp was gentle as he bent slightly so he could look her in the eye.

"You and your mother are not safe with Hennek. Come with me to Hagenheim. My father will—"

"I won't leave my people. At least fifty of Hamlin's children have been either killed or stolen away, and if they are alive, I must find them." She lowered her voice to a fierce whisper. "I cannot leave until I discover what happened to them."

She was so determined, so courageous.

He'd never wanted to kiss a woman so much in his life.

$\mathcal{E}$ight

$\mathcal{K}$aterina's insides trembled at Steffan's warm, gentle hand on her shoulder. But she wouldn't let him know how much she longed to have someone to trust, how she longed to trust Steffan. How had she become so attached to this man in so short a time? Men were not trustworthy. How daft would she have to be to fall into the same trap her mother had fallen into?

But she was practically holding her breath to see what he would say next.

"I am not leaving without you." He leaned slightly toward her. "I shall stay close until we both find out what is happening here."

Did he mean that? Or was he only making her think he cared and wanted to protect her? She would start to trust him, would let down her guard with him, and then what? If he was a good man, Hennek would kill him, but if he wasn't . . . he would only hurt her.

Fear gripped her, rising into her throat and cutting off her breath. Her voice was hoarse as she choked out, "I don't need your help." She hurried away down the cobblestone street.

But what if she was wrong? Her stomach sank at the brusque way she treated him after he had said such protective things. But her fear was stronger. It kept her feet moving at a fast pace and her head from turning to see if he was coming after her.

When he didn't appear at her side as he had before, her eyes stung. Was she actually what her stepfather had called her years ago, when she was too young to understand what he was talking about? *"A temptress and a cruel minx."*

After talking to her priest, she realized she was not a temptress at all, nor was she cruel. But the words seemed stuck in her mind forever.

Steffan, although he'd had opportunities, had not tried to take advantage of her and had not called her names or blamed her for his own depravity. Instead, he had stepped in front of the beast to protect her. Now he was offering to stay close to her to once again protect her.

Her heart pounded against her chest. What should she do? Did she dare to trust him? Fear tried to choke her again as two opposite feelings warred inside her. She stopped, turned around.

Steffan was still standing where she had left him. He was staring back at her.

She took a step toward him and her hands shook. She took another step and another, her knees wobbling. *Bad things will happen to you if you let a man help you. You will hate yourself for trusting him.*

But she didn't stop. She walked all the way back to him, her heart pounding, stealing her breath.

What would she do if he smirked? Laughed at her? She would feel like a fool.

He didn't move, and his expression was sober as he watched her come closer and closer. She sucked in a wispy breath.

"It is dangerous." She stopped and forced another breath into her tight chest. "But if you wish to come back with me . . . to help me discover what is happening to the children . . . I would be glad of the help."

His throat bobbed as he swallowed. "Good. Yes." He straightened his shoulders. "I would like to help."

Their eyes locked for a moment, until Kat had to look away, afraid he could tell that she was having trouble breathing. She said a quick, silent prayer that God would keep him safe from Hennek.

Steffan fell in beside her as they started walking back toward the home she'd shared with her mother and Hennek since she was eight years old.

Would she soon be free of Hennek? Of his cruel ways of oppressing Mother and his even more cruel threats? If God was willing, she would make sure she and her mother never had to cower to him again. She would find a house for her mother and her, and she would provide for them herself. They could live off the game she shot, and perhaps Mother could be a clerk in a shop. Kat also had a hidden stash of money in her room that she got from selling small game, although it wasn't enough yet for a house. The biggest obstacle would be convincing her mother to leave him.

But what about Steffan? She'd always prided herself on never trusting anyone. And yet she was already beginning to trust Steffan—a little. Even though she'd probably regret it. Well, she would never let him take advantage of or use her. Not now. Not ever.

The sight of Johannes hurrying down the street toward them jolted her out of her thoughts. Katerina went to meet him.

"Fräulein, you said to let you know if Bridda said anything else."

"Yes, of course. Did she say something?"

"I asked her where she has been, and she said, 'In the mine.'"

"In the mine?"

"I asked her what she was doing there, and she said she was digging rocks. I tried to ask her what kind of rocks and where this place was, but she started to cry and wouldn't talk anymore. Do you know what it means?"

Katerina shook her head. "No."

Her mind raced. Katerina didn't know of any mines in this area. There were some silver, iron ore, and copper mines in the Harz Mountains, beyond Hagenheim, as well as in the Black Forest, but those were far away.

Kat asked, "Do you know where the closest mine is to Hamlin?"

Johannes shook his head. "Near Keiterhafen there are silver and coal mines, but they have been abandoned for years. She's so young. What could she know of mines and mining?"

"I don't know, but don't tell another soul about this, not until we figure this out."

Johannes nodded. "I understand. And I shall let you know if she says anything else."

"Thank you." Steffan nodded to the man. "We appreciate it."

Since when had she and Steffan become "we"?

———◦◦◦———

Steffan made an effort to smile and look pleased when Hennek met them just inside the front door, but his skin crawled and his hand itched to draw his sword when he thought about this man hurting Katerina.

"Get the arm patched up?" Hennek asked. Before Steffan could answer, he said, "We have the best healer in the Holy Roman Empire. If Frau Windmoeller tells me what herbs to take for an

79

ailment, I know they will work like nothing else. I daresay you have no one whose remedies are as good as hers, even in Hagenheim."

Hennek was eyeing Steffan and Katerina by turns, but Steffan did not answer him.

"God must have been watching out for you two today. That beast has killed so many before you, it's strange that you were able to slay it so easily."

"It was not easy," Steffan said, "and no one else had Katerina to accompany them with her crossbow."

He glanced her way to see how she would take his compliment. A look of pleasure flickered across her face, but it was fleeting.

"Oh yes, our Katerina always carries her crossbow. I'm surprised she hasn't shot herself." He laughed. "Women are given to strong emotions. You had best take care she doesn't mistake you for another wolf and shoot you." He laughed again, this time with no amusement in his eyes, as if his mind was on something else.

"So, how is the arm?" Hennek said, motioning for Steffan to sit while he ignored Katerina. She, who looked as if she was used to being ignored, propped herself against the wall and watched.

"The arm is well." He'd never let on how bad it hurt.

"Did Frau Windmoeller say anything about how she thought it would heal? Did she foresee any problems? Because, you know, the last man who was attacked died of a putrid infection."

Steffan felt a chill run down his spine at the suspicion that that was exactly what Hennek hoped would happen to him. "I should heal well."

"I am glad. Come. We shall have our midday meal together. God is always among Christian men who are eating and drinking in honor of Him. In the meantime, I've sent my men to examine it. If it's the Beast of Hamlin, we'll parade it through town, and you and my daughter will be lauded and praised."

They went into the dining hall, Katerina trailing silently behind, her eyes wary. He thought for a moment she might stay behind in Hennek's little room where his books and papers were kept, but Hennek closed the door behind them and locked it, then dropped the key into his pocket.

During the meal, Hennek repeatedly tried to get Steffan to drink the strong drink he was drinking.

"I like this better," Steffan said, referring to the spiced wine.

"But it's watered down. Try this."

And even though Steffan had already refused repeatedly, Hennek ordered the servant to bring him another goblet and fill it with the stronger drink.

Steffan started to sweat. The smell of the liquor filled his senses, and it was as though he could taste it on his tongue. Memories flooded him, times when he and his friends drank, got into fights, and played pranks on people. Thankfully, he had not shamed himself as much as he might have. And yet he had done things none of the rest of his family would ever dream of doing, and it began by drinking to the point of losing control.

From the age of sixteen, he'd liked the feeling that drinking gave him. At this moment, as the smell of it wafted to him, he became almost dizzy. He wanted it. His hand trembled to take the goblet and bring it to his lips.

Hennek was clearly tempting him. But why? What was his intention? To get Steffan drunk and then what?

Steffan reached out. His hand wrapped around the cup. He could drink one sip to shut Hennek up, but would he be able to stop? Hennek would only keep pushing him to drink more. Not only that, but there was Katerina . . . He didn't want to disappoint her. If he allowed her stepfather to ply him with drink, he might lose her tenuous trust—and that trust had become a precious thing to him.

Steffan was no longer that reckless young soldier who was willing to risk anything, to get drunk and rowdy and do mischievous deeds, to prove he wasn't worthless.

He could still smell it, though, and even though he wished it didn't, it still drew him. But . . . *This is not who I am.*

He pushed the goblet away, and instead took up his cup of weakened wine and drank a long gulp.

Steffan's eyes met Katerina's.

A servant entered the room and whispered in Hennek's ear.

Hennek barely nodded, then said loudly, "Is everyone finished? Let us see what my men have to report about the beast you killed."

They got up and followed Hennek to his office. Just outside stood Otto with his big, beefy arms crossed, another large man beside him. Hennek unlocked the door and they all went in.

The hair on the back of Steffan's neck stood up. Hennek's expression was too smug. The big guards looked defiant.

"What did you find, men?"

Otto grunted, then spoke. "The animal we found dead on the side of the hill outside Hamlin was a young wolf, but not uncommonly big. It was not old enough to have killed the first victims."

Katerina clenched her fists at her sides. "That's a lie. It was not a young wolf, it was two years old at least, and it *was* uncommonly big." She leaned close to Otto, eyeing him with an angry scowl. "*Uncommonly* big."

"Are you calling me a liar?" Otto asked, taking a step toward Katerina.

"Yes."

Steffan took a corresponding step closer to Katerina, ready to step between her and the burly giant.

Hennek held up a hand. "There, there. It is understandable that an inexperienced woman might think a young, small wolf was the Beast of Hamlin. An understandable mistake. But, Steffan, you realized it wasn't an uncommonly large animal, did you not?"

"Herr Bürgermeister, I am sorry to contradict you and your men, but the beast we killed was neither young nor small." Steffan realized it would do no good to argue. Neither Hennek nor his men would ever capitulate. However, he was not going to let Hennek taunt Katerina with a lie.

Hennek made a show of turning his body toward his men. "We shall all go up and see the animal's body, then."

Otto's mouth opened slightly while the man beside him cleared his throat and shuffled his feet.

"What is it, man?"

Otto coughed and said, "We already buried it."

Hennek threw up his hands. "Why would you do such a thing? I don't suppose you'd even be able to find it now, would you?" Hennek gave a slight shake of his head while staring intently at Otto, a movement so tiny Steffan might have missed it had he not been paying such close attention to Hennek.

Otto froze, then leaned his head back. "It was somewhere in the woods. I couldn't tell you where we were exactly. The ground was soft all around, so we just dug a deep hole."

Hennek heaved a loud sigh. "Well, it can't be helped now." He swung his head toward Steffan. "You are satisfied, aren't you?"

"Satisfied?"

"That it was not the Beast of Hamlin. It is an honest mistake.

The wolves in Hagenheim are probably not as big and strong as our wolves. Your wolves are used to a more mountainous region. All that climbing up and down the Harz Mountains will have kept them small and wiry."

Steffan nearly snorted at the ridiculous explanation. But he bit back the sarcastic reply that jumped to mind and merely said, "Perhaps so."

Hennek must want them to doubt their own judgment. He was playing some kind of game, almost as if he were being deceptive for no reason. But there must be a reason, and Steffan was more determined than ever to discover what it was.

Katerina's eyes were narrowed and her chest was rising and falling, but she stayed still and quiet. She was staring hard at Hennek's desk. Steffan followed her gaze and saw a large sheet of parchment, about ten hand-lengths long, lying across the surface.

An idea started forming in Steffan's mind.

Hennek chuckled. "You two thought you killed the famed Beast of Hamlin." He guffawed loud and long, his head thrown back.

Katerina took the chance to sidle closer to his desk.

Steffan started moving toward the door. As he'd hoped, Hennek stepped that way as well, Otto and the other guard following.

Steffan stood in front of Hennek and leaned toward him. "What is your theory about this Beast of Hamlin, Lord Mayor? What I mean is, do you think it is a real creature? Or perhaps some demon spirit that has descended on Hamlin? Is it killing some and spiriting others away?"

"A demon spirit, you say?" Hennek's brows lowered, then raised. "I would not be surprised! But no, a demon spirit is not the culprit. These people are being taken and eaten by this enormous beast. There are witnesses. It is an accepted fact."

Katerina was behind their backs, leaning over Hennek's desk. When Otto turned to look behind him, Katerina quickly straightened and moved to follow. The guard looked askance at her but said nothing.

As Steffan and Hennek stepped outside the room, Hennek waited for everyone to leave. Just as he stuck his hand in his pocket, no doubt to retrieve his key so he could lock the door, Steffan put his arm around Hennek's shoulders and said loudly, "How about that drink you promised me. I need something to soothe my disappointment." He had to think of something quickly, and it was the only thing that came to his mind.

Hennek blinked, then said just as loudly, "Now you are talking sense! A little wine cheers the heart. How much more so the stronger spirits? Come! You will taste my ale man's best drink."

Hennek led the way toward the dining hall, forgetting all about locking the little door.

Steffan forced himself not to glance over his shoulder. He could only hope Katerina was taking advantage of this opportunity and that Otto and the other guard were not paying any attention to her.

* * *

Katerina went around the corner and backed into the shadows. Otto and Herman never looked her way as they made a few grunts and comments under their breath, then went out the front entryway.

Katerina hurried to the door of Hennek's study. She opened it and slipped inside, closing it carefully behind her. She stepped to the large sheet of parchment. She'd seen Hennek peering down at it while he talked to Otto before, but he never left any of his papers out, and he also never left the door of his study unlocked.

Her eyes drank it in, trying to devour every detail, but it made no sense. It must be some kind of map, but there were no names, and nothing that looked familiar. There were several symbols, Xs and lines, tiny boxes with four sides and boxes with three sides, markers for something, but she didn't know what. Some other symbols looked like trees, perhaps indicating a forest, and there was a drawing that looked like a pile of rocks, possibly signifying an outcropping of boulders.

If only there were some words to help her decipher what this was a map of.

At one end was what looked like a gate. Could that be one of Hamlin's gates? She closed her eyes and imagined the east gate. Did it fit with this picture? There was the hill east of town, and yes, there was a rocky area just there. Perhaps this was a map of the area east of town. Yes, that was the very hill where the Beast of Hamlin had attacked her and Steffan, and that was the forest at the edge of which she found little Bridda.

She bent her head even closer to the map. What did these Xs and circles and boxes mean? There was a black space just behind the rock outcropping. Could that be a hole? Could the symbols indicate something underground? A tunnel? A mine?

Katerina's heart pounded so hard it hurt her chest. This could be the place where Bridda had been for the last five months. Were the other children being held there? She stared at the map, trying to memorize every mark and detail, every symbol.

Her foot bumped into a long wooden box on the floor beside Hennek's desk.

Katerina flipped open the lid. Inside were more pieces of

parchment of various sizes, some folded and others rolled up like scrolls. She drew out the one on top, unfolded it, and laid it on the desk. It was also a map, only this appeared to be more detailed, and it seemed to show one long passageway, with side passages, as well as many Xs and the same symbols from the other map.

Where was this place?

Did she dare take this map with her? Would Hennek realize she was the one who had taken it? There would be terrible consequences if he caught her. It was likely he would kill her.

She glanced quickly at the other papers. They appeared to be ledgers, records of amounts of money. Perhaps they were proof of Hennek's corruption. She would have to risk taking the map and some papers since she needed evidence she could show the Duke of Hagenheim.

Her hands shook as she grabbed a handful of rolled-up parchments, including the long, narrow piece of parchment that she had been studying. Her breath was shallow and her knees weak, but Bridda's face rose into her mind's eye. She stuffed the parchments up her sleeve and stepped toward the door.

Voices came from the dining hall. Hennek and Steffan were in there. Should she go into the hall so Steffan knew she was finished in Hennek's study? Or would that look too suspicious?

She thought for a moment, then headed into the kitchen through the door down the corridor.

The cooks, Hilde and Grette, were standing at the door between the kitchen and the dining hall, peering through the crack.

"Are there any sweetmeats?" Katerina deliberately made her voice loud.

Hilde and Grette jumped and spun around, clasping at their throats. "You frightened us nearly to death," Hilde whispered.

"Forgive me." She kept talking loudly. "I believe I found something." She lifted up a cloth and did indeed find a soft pastry, fat with filling. But the words were for Steffan's ears, if only he wasn't dull of understanding.

Nine

Steffan only pretended to drink the strong drink Hennek had poured for them. Perhaps it was because he was so intent on what Katerina was doing, but he wasn't as tempted by Hennek's liquor as he had thought he would be. The smell was still familiar and enticing, but given a choice between getting drunk and Katerina, he chose the girl.

He did his best to nod and smile at appropriate times while Hennek talked on and on about himself. Then he heard Katerina's voice in the kitchen. He focused his gaze on Hennek's face, but he was listening intently to Katerina.

"I believe I found something."

The words were muffled, but there was no mistaking them.

She said something else that was too low for him to make out. Then he heard her say, "I think I'll go hunting."

Other female voices, a bit lower than Katerina's, answered her.

Hennek kept talking. Indeed, he seemed too intent on telling how his leadership had improved life in Hamlin to have heard Katerina. "Except for the rats, which you will rid us of, eh, Lord Steffan? To win the hand of a beauty like Katerina?"

Steffan smiled. "You know"—he pushed his chair away from the table—"I should go now and plot my strategy for getting rid of the rats. I have many ideas, actually."

"Ideas? Won't you share them with me?"

"Oh, poison them, trap them in a net, drive them into the river. Many ideas." Steffan stood and headed for the door.

Hennek was still talking. "You hardly drank anything."

"Thank you! I'm off to find some rats." Steffan hurried out the front door before Hennek could say another word.

Steffan glanced around. As if his words conjured them, a herd of chittering rats was scurrying down the cobblestone street. People scrambled to get out of the way. Steffan waited for them to pass and caught sight of Katerina hurrying around the corner of the narrow street that bordered her stepfather's house on one side. She must have gone out the back door. Steffan trotted after her.

He caught up with her. Her face was lit up and her eyes seemed to sparkle in the sun. He glanced behind him.

"Is anyone following us?" she asked without looking at him.

"No. Wait." He saw movement. It was the man who had been with Otto earlier. "Yes, there is someone. One of Hennek's guards."

"We shall have to lose him. Keep up with me." She suddenly darted down a side street and broke into a run.

Steffan ran just behind her. At the end of that street she hastened down another street, then another and another. Steffan no longer saw the guard following them. But when they reached the town gate, he'd probably be there waiting for them.

They suddenly came to a dead end—the town wall was directly in front of them. But Katerina kept going forward. A narrow alley led along behind the back wall of a house, just wide enough for a couple of people, and Katerina went down it a short way, then looked up at the wall.

An opening was there, about a foot above her head. She started climbing. When she reached the makeshift window in the wall, she stuck her head into it and wiggled and squirmed, then, pushing her feet against the wall behind them, she disappeared from view.

Steffan blew out the breath he'd been holding while he watched her shimmy through the opening in the wall, then he did his best to climb up as well. Thankfully, there were several jutting stones that made good foot- and handholds, and he pulled himself onto the bottom ledge.

This was harder than she made it look. Especially since he was wider than she was, and his arm was still throbbing. He scraped his elbows as he pulled himself through, his sword, which was strapped across his back, scraping the top of the opening.

He tucked his head as he fell to the ground on the other side and landed on the back of his shoulders. At least the opening wasn't as high off the ground on this side as it was on the other side.

"Are you all right?" Katerina squatted by his side. Her face hovered over his.

Steffan lay on his back. "Just catching my breath."

"I may have some evidence of Hennek's corruption from his study. I also found two maps," she whispered. "I'm wondering if they could be of a mine underneath the town."

"There is a mine underneath Hamlin?" He sat up.

"I've never heard of one. But what if there are more children, like Bridda, who are still alive? This could be where they are." Her eyes were wide and her jaw was set.

"Let's go get them." His heart leapt as he jumped to his feet.

Katerina took off at a gentle run and Steffan kept up with her, running by her side.

"I have to warn you," she said. "It appears the entrance to the supposed mine is very near where we saw the beasts. I don't know what those animals have to do with this mine, but I have a feeling Hennek is involved."

"You think Hennek is responsible for the missing children?"

"Yes. And there may be guards near the entrance. It could be dangerous."

Were they foolish to attempt to rescue the children by themselves? Just the two of them? But she was so brave, how could he dissuade her? If he suggested they wait until he could go to Hagenheim and fetch his father and his soldiers, he'd look like a coward. Besides, she might insist on going alone. And he couldn't allow that.

Still, he had to try. It was the wise thing to do.

"I can go to Hagenheim and get help. If your stepfather has guards protecting the mine, and if they overpower us and kill us, we will have failed these children."

She slowed her pace, then stopped, staring out at the hill they were heading toward.

"If you know anyone who's not on Hennek's side who could help us . . ."

She shook her head. "Perhaps you are right." She let out a long breath.

"So you will allow me to ride to Hagenheim tonight?"

"You can't get to Hagenheim in one night."

"No, but I can leave tonight and get there in two days. Will you wait until I come back before you go looking for the children?"

She only looked at him with troubled, downturned brows, biting her lip.

He had his answer. "You have to come with me, then."

"I don't obey commands from you." Her eyes widened along with her stance.

"I won't go to get help unless you come with me."

"It matters not to me if you go get help or stay." She huffed out a breath, uncrossed her arms, and bit her lip again. "I want to do my best for the children. But if we are killed . . ."

Perhaps she wasn't as stubborn as he'd thought. His heart warmed at the intense look on her face.

"Then we shall travel to Hagenheim and get help. Do you have anyone here who could assist us?"

"There is one guard who is very loyal to me and would never tell Hennek. His name is Hans."

Was that the guard whom she seemed so friendly with when he arrived? Why did she trust him so much? A pang went through him. He wanted her to trust him that much.

"But could we at least go and take a look?" She turned her intense look on him. "Don't we need to confirm that there is a mine? Come on."

It probably wasn't wise. But then again, if they couldn't find the mine, how would they find the children? And what real evidence did they have that the children were still alive and hadn't been eaten by the Beast of Hamlin? Besides that, his curiosity was getting the better of him. So as she started walking away from the town wall, he followed her.

After skirting the area around the gate, they made their way toward the hill where they'd killed the beast.

Just before they entered the forest, Steffan glanced over his shoulder. He didn't see anyone following them, but of course, the guard they slipped away from might guess they were coming this way.

Steffan laid his hand on his sword, remembering times he'd used it in battle, when he'd killed and injured men who were only defending their homes. But he shook his head to rid himself of the images. He'd rather remember how he and Katerina had slain the Beast of Hamlin, an act that, no doubt, had saved people's lives.

Even if he and Katerina never received the acclaim for killing it.

They were making their way up, keeping off the path so they would be less likely to be seen or followed. Katerina was quite close to him when her arm brushed against his. She snatched her arm away and mumbled something as she moved farther away.

His heart sank at the way she flinched. Would she flinch away from Hans?

He was jealous. He wasn't sure he'd ever felt that particular feeling before, not over a woman. If he was honest, he might admit that he'd felt jealous of Valten for being the firstborn son and getting an inheritance, and jealous of Gabe when he married a woman of considerable fortune, and jealous of his sister's husband when Steffan's father gave him a castle and land, which came with great honor and power. But this was a different feeling.

This woman had him wishing she liked him, trusted him, admired him.

And it wasn't only because he considered her a challenge. She was beautiful. And intriguing. And she cared more about finding those children than about her own interests. Here he was contemplating the honor and attention he could get from saving these children, but she truly cared about them. She loved the people of her town in a way that reminded him of how his father felt about the people of Hagenheim.

Still, she was quite stubborn. She didn't trust him or like him, and she clearly didn't want him to get too close. She would hate him if she knew all that he had done, all the wrong, stupid things, the bad choices, the ways he had disappointed his family. The ways he'd hurt people.

They were nearly to the spot where they'd been attacked by the wolf earlier and seen the other one run away. He strode forward to get ahead of her. "Be careful," he said.

"Why?"

"I just have a feeling we're not safe here."

She turned her head enough to look him in the eye. "Are you saying you are a prophet?" Her smile was brief, but it still sent a warmth through his chest.

"I'm not a good enough person to be a prophet." He became aware of how near she was as she turned her whole body to face him.

"I should think if you were a bad fellow, you would be telling me how good you are. Besides, where is it written that a prophet must be exceptionally good?"

"Very well. Perhaps I am a prophet." He rested his hand on his sword hilt. He still had the feeling that danger lurked nearby, so he glanced around, listening, checking for any signs that someone or something meant them harm. But he was quite enjoying this less defensive side of Katerina. He didn't want to let the opportunity escape him.

"I prophesy that you will learn more about me, and I shall learn more about you."

"Oh?" She raised her brows at him.

"You shall be surprised to find that, although I am a mighty warrior capable of courageous and mighty feats of valor, I am also quite trustworthy."

"But this does not agree with what you said about not being good."

He sighed. "I have not always been so trustworthy. When I

was younger I defied my father and was often angry. I teased my sisters to tears sometimes, and I was reckless. But almost a year ago, I decided I wanted to be a better man."

"So you were not always a kindhearted prophet?"

He shook his head. He used to think of himself as a kindhearted fellow, but now he realized he'd done many things that were not kind at all. "I never wished to hurt anyone, but sometimes my thoughts and actions were wrong. I trusted people who were not worthy of my trust, and I rebelled against the people I should have been faithful to."

She had a thoughtful look on her face as she stared back at him. What was she thinking? Had he said too much? He wanted her to know the real Steffan, but at the same time, he was afraid she wouldn't like him if she saw all the ugliness of his past.

Perhaps it had been too long since he'd been to confession. He should stop talking, or he might just tell Katerina everything he'd ever done wrong.

"Shall I tell you what I've heard about you?"

He groaned. He knew it was bad, but he was curious if it was the truth.

Ten

Katerina studied Steffan's face. It was a handsome face, even with the scars. Sometimes they made him look dangerous; other times they gave him a vulnerable look. But when she asked him if he wanted to hear the rumors about him, he made a low sound in this throat.

"Mostly that you are the rebellious one of the Duke of Hagenheim's children and that you joined the Teutonic Knights against your father's wishes. But since you are not actually a Teutonic Knight, I suppose that is false."

"It is nearly true." His expression was a bit sad, not jocular or bold, which were his usual expressions. "I am the rebellious son, and I fought with the Teutonic Knights in Poland, with the intent of becoming one of them. But I changed my mind."

"What happened? I recall you telling me that you did not wish to become a monk, which you would have to do to join with the German Order of Teutonic Knights."

"Yes, that's true. Well, I shall tell you something else because I already prophesied you would learn more about me and I about you, and I am hoping since I was right about the first thing, I shall also be right about the second one."

His usual jocular tone and expression almost returned, but was clouded over again when he continued speaking. "I foolishly disregarded my father's words and went to fight with the Teutonic Knights against my father's allies. I was angry and harsh with my brother Wolfgang. But I really decided not to join the order when I saw how their leader persecuted women and innocent people because of his own ambition. And then, when I was asked to fight against my brother and risk killing him, I realized I'd rather die than kill Wolfgang."

She remembered how he'd stepped in front of the beast for her, taking the brunt of the attack to protect her. Perhaps it was true. If he could care about her, a stranger, enough to sacrifice himself for her, he would surely love his brother that much. But then again, she also knew there were people in the world, people like Hennek, who loved the praise of men, who would do something generous or sacrificial for others in order to look like a good person, but who would treat their family with contempt and cruelty.

Was Steffan like Hennek? She didn't have a knife in her hand, and they were alone together. In fact, at this moment they were quite close to each other. He could grab her and try to harm her if he wanted to.

Steffan stood looking down at her. He was glancing all around every few seconds. Was he looking for danger, checking for the second beast they'd seen run away? Or perhaps he was making sure no one was around.

She felt herself stiffen, mentally calculating how long it would take to grab her knife. But instead of looking menacing or suspicious, Steffan had a kind and gentle expression on his face. He wasn't leaning toward her in that disgusting, aggressive way Hennek had. Instead, he was glancing down at his own hands.

"Thankfully," he went on, "I didn't hurt my brother, at least not much."

"Is that where you got your scars? Did your brother do that?" She pointed to her own face, to the corresponding places where Steffan's cheek and brow were scarred.

"Only this one." He pointed to the pale scar just above his left eyebrow. One side of his mouth crooked up in a half smile while his eyelids drooped, giving him almost a sleepy, brooding sort of look. "We were jousting. Injuries happen."

"And your other scar? The one on your cheek?"

Why did she ask him that? She never asked men personal questions. Until now.

"I got that one fighting in Poland with the Teutonic Knights. I was attacking one of Duke Konrad's soldiers and he slammed his sword into my cheek. At the last moment I was able to deflect the blow so that it was mostly the flat side of his blade that struck me."

"That's very fortunate." She didn't like to think what might have happened if the man had struck him with the sharp edge of his sword.

"Now you know more about me. But I won't ask any questions about you until I know you trust me."

"Why do you want me to trust you?"

"I don't think you trust anyone. Do you?"

"Not many people." She couldn't help smiling at the way he accepted her distrust. "Perhaps I'm not the most trusting person."

"I should say you are not."

"I have my reasons. It's safer."

Steffan twisted one side of his mouth into a frown. After a few moments, he said, "Are you sure about that? I think it's safer if you do trust people, as long as they're the right people."

"How do you know who is safe to trust and who is not?"

"Therein lies the problem, I suppose."

Their gazes met and held. It was as if he truly understood her. She wasn't sure she'd ever felt anyone understood her. For the first time in her life, she wanted someone to know her. And she wanted it to be this handsome young man. Her heart fluttered, and she looked away. Was she being ridiculous?

"Some people are not trustworthy." He stared intently back at her.

He understood. Her heart thumped against her chest. What would it be like to sink into his chest and feel his arms around her?

"Shall we go?" She turned away from him, taking a big step closer to the rocks that she suspected were on the map, abruptly ending their conversation.

Steffan came along beside her. He said nothing as they both moved cautiously. This was the spot where the second beast had run away. There were no trees here, almost as if they'd been cleared right around the rocks. She headed toward the rocks and Steffan followed.

Peering around the side of one of the largest rocks, she heard a sound like metal scraping against metal. She froze, listened, but when she didn't hear anything, she continued toward the rocks.

Just then, a hole appeared in the ground in front of her. She stopped short, drawing her foot back so as not to fall in.

The open space was well worn on the edges, the dirt and moss and grass rubbed away. Someone, or something, had been going in and out of this hole.

Katerina heard a man's voice not too far away. He was either humming or softly singing. She strained her eyes and saw one of Hennek's guards. He seemed to be relieving himself beside a tree. Steffan was at her shoulder, and he saw the guard too.

Katerina focused on the opening in the ground. It was too

narrow for them both to squeeze in at the same time, so Katerina braced herself, hands on the sides of the hole, bent forward, drew her knees up, and lowered herself down into the opening.

Her feet touched rock. She slid her hands along the sides of the passageway. A glow came from below. She could just make out a series of wooden rungs below her, and she took one step, then another, down into the darkness.

———•◦•———

Steffan watched as Katerina lowered herself into the ground. He should tell her to stop, but his voice might alert the guard.

As soon as Katerina was in, he went in after her.

The hole was almost completely dark, but he could just make out the rungs of a ladder below him. Katerina's head bobbed below, and he followed her down.

They finally reached the bottom. The floor was uneven, like the floor of a cave, and he caught up with Katerina and placed his hand lightly on her shoulder. This time she didn't flinch or shrink away from him.

They kept walking toward a light that was faint but distinct in the otherwise pitch-black cave. A sound drifted to his ears, a tapping or far-off banging. Katerina had her hand out in front of her, and Steffan kept one hand on the wall beside him.

The cave wound around a bend, growing brighter as they went. Suddenly they could hear voices. A large room opened up in front of them, with torches set into the walls. He and Katerina both plastered themselves against the wall of the cave.

Children, about six or seven of them, were facing the opposite wall. Steffan watched them, hardly believing what he was seeing. They were using picks and chisels, digging something out of the rock.

A big, stout man stood guard. He was so close to where they were standing, Steffan could smell an odor coming from his body—like garlic and unwashed feet. If the man turned his head, he would see them.

Katerina seemed transfixed, her eyes wide and her jaw clenched as she watched the children. Had she seen the guard? *Don't make a sound*, he longed to whisper to her.

But she was silent as she stared at the children. Was she relieved to have found them? Or anguished at what she was seeing?

Was this all of them? This was only a small portion of the children he knew were missing. Were there more? A tunnel at the other end of the large cavern seemed to indicate there might be more to this mine, especially if it extended underneath the town, as Katerina suggested.

He squeezed Katerina's shoulder, finally getting her attention, and motioned toward the dark corridor through which they had come. Katerina stepped back so they wouldn't be seen by the guard.

Most of the children were very small, maybe only seven or eight years old, but there were two children who were taller than the others. One of them turned and looked straight at Steffan and Katerina. His eyes widened, and Steffan put a finger to his lips, praying the boy would not betray their presence.

Katerina glanced at Steffan, then moved back slowly and quietly. Steffan waited for her to go first, watching the guard, but he still seemed unaware of their presence. As they made their way back through the corridor, a cracking noise, as if Katerina had stepped on a stick, broke the silence in the narrow corridor.

She began to walk faster. The tunnel brightened as a light came from behind them. The guard must have been coming after them with a torch.

Steffan's hand slipped off her shoulder as she all but ran, slowing only as they approached the steps leading up. She climbed quickly and Steffan stayed close behind her.

"Who is there?" a masculine voice boomed behind them. Steffan didn't bother to look behind him as he was nearly to the top. He heaved himself up and out of the opening, scrambled to his feet, and he and Katerina ran, plunging into the forest.

They both ran down the hill, dodging trees, leaping over bushes and fallen limbs. Steffan stayed just behind Katerina in an effort to keep his body between her and any arrows that might be directed their way. He hadn't seen the man who'd been guarding the opening, but he was no doubt nearby.

They continued to run until they were at the bottom of the hill. Then Katerina veered to the right and headed toward a small shelter built of wattle and daub and open on the two sides facing away from the hill.

They both were breathing hard. Katerina closed her eyes and pressed her hand against her chest, over her heart. "We found them." She drew in a deeper breath. "Thank You, God, we found them."

"You found them. You are amazing, Katerina. Truly."

She smiled and shook her head. When she'd caught her breath, she said, "I want to go back there, shoot that guard, and take all the children out, this moment."

"I don't think it would be that easy. There must surely be several more guards down there."

"You're right. We mustn't be arrogant and get the children killed. Do you think we could leave for Hagenheim tonight?"

"We could leave as soon as we saddle our horses."

"Let us go."

Just then the sound of a horse's hooves—two horses, at least—came thundering down the hill. Instinctively he grabbed Katerina's arm and pulled her back as he stepped into the shadows of the shelter. She shrank back with him, her body pressed against his side, her hand against his chest.

The horses thundered past, moving too fast for him to recognize the riders.

Katerina moved away from him, pulling her hand away from his chest as if she hadn't realized she'd been touching him. A bereft feeling, of missing her warmth, swept over him.

They moved at the same time, hurrying away from the shelter and running toward the town wall.

"Wait," Katerina said, veering off the path. She went to the tree where she'd fetched the hidden bandages she'd used to wrap his arm. She reached into her sleeve and pulled out some rolled-up parchments, then stuffed them in the hole in the tree.

"Those are the papers you found in Hennek's study?"

"Yes. I don't think anyone will find them here."

"Good idea," Steffan said. Now hopefully they'd be able to prove Hennek's corruption so there'd be no doubt of his guilt.

They headed for the hole in the town wall where they had come through earlier. When they reached it, Steffan could see it was too high for Katerina, but she quickly said, "You'll have to grab my leg and give me a boost. And see that you don't touch anything but my foot and lower leg."

"Upon my honor, my lady, you have my solemn word." Steffan bent and grabbed her calf with one hand and her heel with the other. She wasn't heavy, so it was easy to boost her up to the opening, then help her through by letting her use his hand and shoulder to push against.

A fallen tree was nearby. He dragged it over, stood on it, and was able to grasp the bottom of the opening and pull himself up.

He'd expected her to have run on toward Hennek's stable when he stuck his head through, but she was waiting.

"Grab this handhold across the way." She pointed to the building across the narrow alley. Some stones jutted out, and he reached out and grabbed them, pulling himself the rest of the way through, then dropping to the ground beside her.

Together they hurried down the alley.

Once they reached the street, they slowed to a normal pace. He stayed just behind Katerina, occasionally glancing over his shoulder to check for Hennek's henchmen.

Hennek's stable, where Steffan's horse was being boarded, was just behind the mayor's four-story house. They skirted past the house, not seeing anyone outside, nor any faces through the windows, and entered the stable.

Steffan grabbed his saddle while Katerina also started saddling a horse.

"I'll pack some provisions," Katerina whispered. "Do you think you can risk retrieving your things?"

"Not worth it. It's only two days to Hagenheim, and my father can provide us whatever we need when we get there."

"What have we here?" Hennek's voice was behind them, near the entrance of the stable.

Steffan froze. Four men were with Hennek, two on each side of him, standing menacingly tall and straight. Steffan probably couldn't fight off so many, and he had Katerina to protect. He thought quickly.

"Since the wolf we killed was not the Beast of Hamlin, we are going to see if we can track down the real beast."

"Together? I did not know the two of you were such good friends."

"We are not, but you know what a skilled hunter your step-daughter is." Steffan shrugged and tried to smile. "I talked her into coming with me."

Hennek's face, even in the dim light of the stable, was hard and unflinching.

"I would rather you did not go looking for this beast." Hennek's voice was cold, so different from how he had spoken to him before. "I might not be able to explain to your father about your getting injured while here in my town."

"Oh, Father will think nothing of it. I've been injured many times in battle, and just tilting with wooden swords with my brothers."

"Nevertheless, I wish you to come back into the house with me. It is nearly time for supper."

"We shall not be gone long. Have to take advantage of the waning daylight."

Hennek's face grew darker, his expression completely without mirth or the bluster he usually displayed.

"There is a matter I wish you to help me with. It is more pressing than tracking down a wolf. Put the saddles away." It was a command, not a request.

Steffan began removing his horse's accoutrements and Katerina followed suit. Then they silently accompanied Hennek and his men toward the house.

Was Hennek the one who was behind the enslaved children working in the mines? Judging from the drastic change in his manner, he was, and he must also know they were seen in the mine. Would they be able to escape if they simply ran? Surrounded as they were, their chances were very small.

Inside the house, Hennek led them all into his study. The seven of them filled up the room, with Katerina pressing herself against the wall, shrinking away from one of Hennek's burly men. Her face was pale and her hand, which hung by her side, trembled.

"Get away from that maiden." Steffan said the words without thinking, stepping toward the guard.

"Dieter, Lord Steffan thinks you're crowding my stepdaughter," Hennek said.

The big guard took a tiny step away from Katerina. She had already straightened her spine, her head lifted high, and her cheeks were turning from pale to red, as if she were either embarrassed or angry—or both.

"Now then," Hennek said, "if one of you has the sheets of parchment that I kept in this box here"—he kicked a box on the floor—"I would greatly appreciate you giving them back to me."

The hair stood up on the back of Steffan's neck. *God, help me keep Katerina safe.*

$\mathcal{E}$leven

$\mathcal{K}$aterina flinched when the big burly guard's arm brushed against her, forcing her against the wall. She could feel the blood drain from her face. Steffan ordered the guard away from her. Her face burned, and she was furious at herself for allowing this guard to intimidate her. But a flash of memory had come over her, of the first time one of Hennek's men had tried to coerce her and frighten her. Did her cheeks burn because these men had seen her shrink away from Dieter? Or at the way Steffan came to her defense? Her heart thumped erratically in her chest and she couldn't look at him.

But what Hennek said next made her insides go cold again. Her mind went to the rolled-up parchments she had hidden in the tree.

"You have it, don't you, Katerina?" He stepped toward her.

"Have what?" She forced her mind not to even think about where the map was. "I want nothing that belongs to you." Suddenly her loathing for this man nearly choked her. Anyone who pretended to be good, who made a show of giving to orphanages but stole children away and enslaved them—and she had no doubt now that that was what he had been doing—was nothing but evil. If only she could end that evil.

"You see what I have to put up with?" Hennek looked sad as

he shifted his gaze to Steffan. "I love her mother, but her daughter hates me without cause. I am good to her, I care for her, clothe her, and feed her, and yet she insists on defying me." He let his shoulders droop as he held out a hand, palm up.

Why was Hennek still trying to fool Steffan? Could it be that he didn't know she and Steffan had been in the mine? Perhaps he only knew she had stolen his map. Perhaps he was still holding out hope that they didn't know the atrocities he had been perpetrating.

"Yes, it must be a trial." Steffan spoke the words, but his voice was flat, cautious.

"It is." Hennek's eyes brightened. "It is a very great trial. I treat her with love, while she does things like steal a valuable map and try to turn my wife against me."

Katerina could call him a liar, could defend herself and her mother. But it hardly mattered what Hennek or his men thought.

"Well, if we are done here, I think I'll just go and fetch my horse and . . ."

Would Steffan take his horse and leave? Would he go to Hagenheim without her? Of course that was the wise thing, the best thing to do to save the children. She should not feel hurt. She'd do the same if it were the only way. But . . . would he be glad to be rid of her? She had never said flattering words to him. She had flinched away from him, treated him with disdain, and proven she didn't trust him.

Hennek stared hard at him. "It is my wish that you stay." Hennek's voice held that cool, dangerous tone.

Hennek could not let the duke's son go back to tell his father. She had warned Steffan, and now the warning would come true.

Her heart sank to her toes.

"I am at your command, then, Herr Bürgermeister." Steffan

gave a slight bow. Deference and calm smoothed out his expression. Not a trace of fear or mistrust. What a good pretender he was.

"All the better," Hennek mumbled. Then he boomed, "Let us have a good meal to celebrate you staying another night in Hamlin."

Hennek started moving toward the dining hall, and the guards glared at Kat and Steffan until they followed, then they came very close behind. She glanced at Steffan out of the corner of her eye. His expression was tense; his jaw twitched and hardened. But when he glanced at her, his face softened and he winked, as if to say, "Don't worry."

They went into the dining hall and soon the evening meal was served. Mother did not seem to notice that anything was amiss—or any more amiss than usual. When Kat asked to be excused to go to her bedchamber, Hennek said, "No. I want you to stay." Then he suddenly became loud and jovial. "We're having a pleasant evening! Friends and family, enjoying a good meal together! You are a fortunate young maiden. Other women in Hamlin, in the Holy Roman Empire, would love to have the food you see here. But what's even better, you are spending time with Lord Steffan, the son of the Duke of Hagenheim!"

With that, he laughed raucously, having drunk more wine than she'd ever seen him drink. What was Hennek doing, feeding them and dragging out the evening? She supposed he wanted to enjoy the thought of having the duke's son in his home, at his mercy, one last time. And whatever he was planning to do next, he probably needed all the wine he was drinking to give him the courage to carry it out.

When the meal was finally over, he dismissed Mother, who glanced worriedly at Kat and left the room.

Steffan kept looking at her too. Did he have a plan? But the two guards who stood by the doorway to the hall had been joined by two more, who stood by the door to the kitchen. How could she and Steffan get away from the four huge men guarding the exits? They had no weapons, as Hennek had taken Steffan's sword and her crossbow. They'd just have to wait for a better chance to escape.

When Hennek finally allowed them to retire to their beds, the guards and Hennek followed them up to their rooms, which were side by side. Then, in the narrow corridor, Hennek motioned with his hand, and one of the guards grabbed Steffan by the shoulder and slammed him against the wall. Steffan tried to fight back, but the guard grabbed him by the throat with one hand and pulled out a knife with the other.

"Stop!" Katerina yelled and took a step toward the guard, but one of the other guards caught her shoulders and pushed her against the wall as well, capturing her arms and pressing them into her sides while Hennek held his hand over her mouth.

Fury ignited inside her. She kicked and struggled, but she couldn't loosen their hold.

"Get off her!" Steffan's voice was low and gravelly as the third guard came over and leaned on one of his shoulders, pinning him.

"All is well," Hennek said, directing his nasty smile at Katerina. "I only want my map and other important papers back. One of you has them, and I am guessing it is you." Then he removed his hand from her mouth.

She spat on the floor at his feet. She could scream, but what could her mother or any of the servants do to help them? She'd only be putting them in danger if they tried to come to her aid.

"You can torment me all you want, but I will not give you anything. I never have and I never will." She gave him her own version of a nasty smile.

"I will have my guards search you." Hennek gave her a menacing look.

"You said you were a godly man, Hennek," Steffan said, his tone cold. "A godly man would not allow these men to search Katerina."

Hennek puffed out his chest and fairly shouted, "I *am* a godly man. The whole town will tell you. They know of my good deeds."

"If you are so good, then why are you harassing this young maiden?" Steffan's eyes bore into Hennek's.

"Very well." Hennek abruptly took a step back, his jaw flexing as if he was clenching his teeth. "But you will each have a guard to watch over you. That map belongs to me, and if either of you has stolen it, you will not go unpunished."

As strange as it was, Steffan had hit upon the thing that Hennek cared about, the only thing that could be used against him, to manipulate him, and that was his love of praise, his desire to believe he was a good, godly man. Hennek was truly delusional.

Steffan regarded him coolly. The biggest guard pushed him toward the bedchamber door and Steffan did not fight him. Instead, he stepped toward the door and gazed at Katerina. A flash of conflicting emotions flickered over his face, his cheek twitching. But what could either of them do? They both went into their rooms as they were told.

Steffan lay awake, the biggest and meanest-looking guard standing against his door. Hennek knew they had the map, and probably suspected they'd been in the mine and seen the missing children. He was surely planning some way to kill them.

"Aren't you going to take off your clothes to sleep?" the guard asked.

Steffan's mind went to the dagger in the sheath strapped to his thigh, hidden by his long tunic.

"No, I prefer to sleep with my clothes on."

The guard barely raised a brow and remained unmoving with his back against the door.

Was Katerina being similarly guarded? Steffan would kill that guard if he put one finger on her. He wanted to kill him just for being in her room. And Hennek . . . Stealing children and putting them to work in a mine! No wonder Katerina was so defensive and mistrustful. She no doubt had had to survive much abuse and oppression from the loudmouthed mayor with the fake laugh.

What would Father say when he found out the man he put in charge of Hamlin was actually capable of this much wickedness?

He and Katerina had to escape. But how?

Steffan pretended to fall asleep. He made his breathing deep and harsh—difficult to do when he wasn't actually asleep. After perhaps half an hour, he slipped his hand up to the sheath that held his dagger. He clasped the handle.

He knew the guard had a sword, not to mention his hands were like two giant clubs, capable of beating him senseless. But he'd fought in battles, hadn't he? He'd faced death before. And he was facing death anyway, whether he tried to escape or not, for Hennek could not let them leave this house. He'd probably guessed that they'd hidden the map.

As silently as possible, he turned onto his side and opened his eyes just enough to see the guard in the candlelight. He was leaning into the corner of the room, half his body against the door. His eyes were closed, and it looked as if he might be asleep.

Steffan clutched his dagger tightly. He had to kill him, even though this guard was in great need of repentance, confession, and absolution. Steffan had no choice. It was a matter of kill or be killed.

He leapt to his feet and lunged at the guard.

Katerina pretended to sleep, but the guard at her door was not only still awake, he was watching her closely.

A heavy feeling of sadness revealed just how much she had hoped killing the beast would lead to her freedom. But now that she knew the children were still alive, their freedom was more important to her than her own.

Suddenly she heard a loud crash coming from Steffan's room, just on the other side of the wall.

Her guard's eyes flew wide open and he stood up straight. He snatched open the door. When he did, Steffan barreled in, slamming into him. In the semi-darkness, her eyes locked onto a long knife. The guard was holding on to Steffan's wrist, holding the knife high.

Kat snatched her own knife out of the secret sheath she kept strapped to her leg. She jumped up and came at the guard. She was aiming for the guard's neck when another guard came through the doorway and knocked her down.

Kat struggled with the guard. He pinned her hand to the floor and used his thumb to press the center of her inner wrist so hard her fingers went limp, sharp pains shooting through them, and her knife fell out of her grasp.

She slammed her clenched fist into his face.

He slapped her, and the blow made her vision go dark for a moment.

Her eyesight was clearing when suddenly the man leaning over her was knocked to the side and Steffan was standing over her. He grabbed her by her arms and hauled her to her feet. Just then, more guards ran into the room. Steffan turned and slammed his fist in a guard's throat. The man went down, clutching his neck and gagging.

Steffan's fist smacked another guard's chin and the guard's head snapped back. Then two guards leapt on Steffan, holding his arms while a third guard punched him hard in the stomach.

The guard who had slapped her had risen to his feet and now grabbed her by the arms. She kicked out at him but missed.

"What is this?"

Hennek's booming voice came from the doorway. Kat threw all her body weight away from the guard, trying to free herself, but he only tightened his grip on her arms until she cried out.

The guard slammed his fist into Steffan's stomach again, then punched the side of his face.

Kat clenched her hands, still struggling to free herself, so furious she could barely see.

Another man came up behind Hennek. "Jakob is dead."

Hennek's mouth fell open. "What?"

"He's in the room where Lord Steffan was sleeping. His throat is cut."

"Lord Steffan." Hennek's voice took on a shocked tone. He

shook his head slowly as he stared at Steffan, who was leaning forward after being punched. "You killed one of my best men. I cannot allow you to get away with that, now can I? Come."

Another guard came alongside Kat so that a guard had hold of each of her arms, and they pulled her out of the room.

Steffan was ahead of her, also flanked on each side by a guard. As they made their way down the corridor, he turned his head to look at her. "Are you all right?" His voice sounded strained.

"Yes. And you?"

"Yes."

Blood spatters covered his face. She hoped it was the blood of the guard whose throat he had cut. But a bad bruise was already forming on the side of his face.

They made their way down two flights of stairs and out the front door. Even amid all of the commotion, no one, not the servants, nor even her mother, had come out of their rooms to see what was the matter. Hennek must have threatened them with some dire consequence, or locked them in their rooms. She only hoped he hadn't hurt Mother.

The street was very dark, and it would have been darker if not for the full moon shining over them, climbing its way up to its highest point in the sky. The night air cooled her cheek that burned from the guard's slap. But Steffan had to be in far worse pain. Had they injured him internally?

Hennek must be taking them out of town so the guards could shoot them and hide their bodies.

They walked through town. No one was on the street.

As they reached the town gate, Hennek said, "I regret that I shall never see the two of you again, but a man has a responsibility to protect himself from those who wish him harm."

"You cannot kill us, Hennek." Steffan's voice was almost disinterested. "My father will come and investigate. He will discover what has happened to me and to your stepdaughter. You will never be able to escape my father's justice."

Hennek, one of his creepy smiles plastered on his face, replied, "When your father learns you were mauled by the Beast of Hamlin while hunting for it, he will have nothing to blame me for."

"And how do you plan to make it look like I was mauled by an animal?"

"You will be mauled by the beast, because I control it."

"You control the Beast of Hamlin?"

"It was a brilliant plan. About three years ago I had my men capture a wolf cub, only they ended up capturing two. We kept them in a cage in the woods and fed them the best fresh meat, as much as they could eat. They grew so big and tall and fat that by the time they were full grown, there couldn't have been another wolf in the Holy Roman Empire as big as they were. We also beat them to make sure they hated men, and they stayed fit and strong by wrestling each other in their cage. I had a man train them to come when called. When I was ready to start my mining business, we stopped feeding them until they became ravenous. Then whenever anyone came near the mine entrance, we set the beasts loose and let them do what wolves do—hunt. And kill."

"It was a clever plan," Steffan said, as if he were speaking of a plan to build a new stable.

"And it worked. People stopped coming to this hill, so there was little reason to fear that anyone would discover our mine. And when we were ready for workers to extract the silver, it was the perfect cover for the children's disappearance."

Katerina marveled at how calm Steffan kept his tone. If not

for his tranquil manner, she might have started screaming at this man who had destroyed so many lives.

"And how do you justify that?" Katerina couldn't keep the fury from her voice. "Stealing innocent children."

"They were mostly orphans, from the lower classes. No one missed them, and it gave them something productive to do with themselves."

"That is a horrible thing to say. And less than half the children were orphans."

"They were foolish, and they made it so easy. And there is no shortage of children in Hamlin, after all. I did their parents a service by giving them one less mouth to feed."

"You are despicable." Katerina's stomach twisted at the man's cruelty and lack of remorse. "No wonder you could pretend to be so generous. You were using children to work your mines, slaves you wouldn't have to pay. Why did you not kidnap adults? Undoubtedly they would be better workers and could make a larger profit for you."

"Adults might escape or fight back. The children were too small and afraid."

"Bridda escaped."

"Ah, yes. Little Bridda. She must have slipped away when the guards were sleeping. We are not certain. But that's another reason children are better than adults. They are easily threatened. I told them that should any of them escape and tell their parents where they'd been, I'd kill their whole family."

"Could you not make enough money for your greedy black soul by paying workers?"

"Greedy? I give away so much money the people have begun to call me 'the Benevolent Bürgermeister.'"

"Oh, I know why you don't hire workers." The breath went out of her at the realization. "It's because the land where the mine is . . . It doesn't belong to you, does it?"

"And I suppose you think the mine and all the silver inside it should belong to the Duke of Hagenheim?"

"Yes, because the land does belong to him." Katerina glanced at Steffan, but he said nothing.

"Would the duke do as much for Hamlin as I have?"

"Do you mean making mothers fearful that their children will be carried away and eaten by a beast, so fearful they don't let them go outside their homes to play and never let them out of their sight?"

"Your hatred of me knows no bounds, does it? You are a selfish, ungrateful girl and you always were, trying to turn my own wife against me. Marriage is a sacred covenant. God will avenge me."

"You are evil," Katerina spat out.

Hennek looked at her coldly. "You are ungrateful and contentious, a selfish daughter who has the spirit of rebellion."

"Accusing your stepdaughter does not excuse you, Hennek," Steffan spoke up. "But truly, the fact that you do not think you have done anything wrong . . . it defies reason and logic."

"The privileged son of a duke," Hennek spat. "You know nothing. You are too enamored by this girl's outward beauty to think for yourself. You should have gone back to Hagenheim when you were able. And now I must go and leave you both to your fate. You brought this on yourselves by stealing my property." Hennek pointed his finger at them. "You brought this on yourselves." Then he turned to his guards and muttered, "You know what to do."

Before he even finished speaking, he was hurrying away down the hill, back toward Hamlin.

Coward.

The guards pulled roughly on her arms and did the same with Steffan. And though he wasn't as thick or as wide as the guards, he was just as tall, maybe a bit taller.

But she'd lost her knife in the fight, and she suspected Steffan had no weapon either.

They marched on, heading into the dark forest and up the slanting hill toward the place where they'd found the entrance to the mine. Would they kill them in the mine and hide their bodies there?

Poor Mother. She'd be trapped for the rest of her life in that oppressive, nightmarish marriage to Hennek, the illustrious "Benevolent Bürgermeister" of Hamlin.

But if she and Steffan died, perhaps the Duke of Hagenheim would come to seek out answers to what happened to his son and would find the children and free them. Was that God's plan?

Kat began to pray, *God, forgive my sins and bring my soul to heaven. And Steffan's as well.* Poor Steffan. He didn't believe he was a good person. Did he know Jesus's death on the cross had absolved him from sin?

It was quite dark as they made their way up the hill, so dark she couldn't see her feet, and she found herself stumbling more than once. Finally they came out into a small clearing where the moon was visible overhead. They were almost to the entrance of the mine.

The guards slowed to a halt. They pushed Kat and Steffan in front of them, holding them by their arms. One of the guards went forward and disappeared around the side of the rock outcropping. She heard a sound as if he were moving tree branches—perhaps uncovering something?—then the sound of metal scraping metal.

The same sound she'd heard before. Growling and snarling followed. Kat strained her eyes to see but couldn't make out anything in the dark.

The guards continued to push her and Steffan forward as the snarling grew louder.

She saw bright yellow eyes reflecting the pale moonlight. They were coming closer, one step at a time, until the large, thin body of a wolf came into view.

Twelve

Steffan kept his eyes on the wolf, which was stalking closer, ever so slowly. The guards were no longer holding tightly to his arms. They probably wanted them to run so that the beast would chase them and maul them.

God, help me save Katerina.

"Don't run," he whispered to Katerina without turning his head. "It will chase you."

And she could never outrun a wolf, especially one that looked as hungry as this one.

This was the end. He would die. Katerina would die. And no one would know about the children. No one would save them. The pain inside his chest washed through his whole body. Now he could never atone for all the bad things he had done.

God. Help us.

An image of the guard from Katerina's room flashed through his mind. He had a sword strapped across his back.

Steffan spun around, breaking free of both of the guards, and grabbed the sword handle. With one swift motion, he unsheathed the sword and slashed at the guard.

The guard managed to jump back out of the way. He turned to take a swipe at Katerina's guards, but they were already backing away, leaving Katerina and Steffan between them and the wolf.

"Steffan." Katerina's voice was urgent.

The wolf was much closer now. Its fur shone in the pale moonlight, its eyes bright. The beast snarled again, baring its white teeth.

Holding the sword out in front of him, Steffan moved closer to Katerina. "Get behind me."

Katerina took a step back. The wolf crouched, getting ready to spring at them. Instead of waiting for it, Steffan charged forward with a loud cry. The wolf sprang. Steffan slashed its throat while it was still in the air. The wolf fell on the ground at his feet and didn't move.

He spun to his rear, sword at the ready for the guards, who suddenly swarmed them. One grabbed Katerina, and the other three attacked with their swords. Two of them slammed their blades into his, then someone grabbed his arms from behind and yanked down. The next moment, a sword blade sliced through Steffan's shirt, the point raking down his chest.

But instead of stabbing him through the heart, the men tackled him to the ground and forced his sword from his hand. One sat on top of him, while the other two held his wrists.

Katerina appeared to be throwing all of her weight forward in an attempt to break free from her captor. "You'll rot in hell for helping Hennek."

She struggled some more, then went still. The guard was sneering over her shoulder.

"Let us go free and we will leave this place," she said. "You can tell Hennek we died and you buried us."

Steffan added, "Yes, we'll run away and you'll never hear from us again."

Of course they'd go to Hagenheim and come back with his father's army. And unfortunately, the guards probably knew that as well. But he was desperate. He had to save Katerina and the children who were trapped in the mine.

"What should we do?" one of the guards muttered to the others. "Hennek specifically said not to kill them with the sword."

"We can't let them go," another said. "And we don't have another wolf to attack them."

"Why couldn't we let them go? If they go away and never return."

"Are you daft?"

"Straw for brains," another growled.

"Get us all killed."

"Well, we can't sit on him all night," said the one sitting on Steffan's legs.

"Maybe we could have our way with the girl." The one holding on to Katerina ran a hand down her cheek.

She turned her head and spat in his face. The man slapped her across the mouth.

"I'll kill you!" Steffan struggled to break free, but the men only held him tighter. They weighed too much, and the three of them could hold him down all night if they wished.

"You can't kill anyone," the guard taunted. "And I can do what I want."

He couldn't let this happen. *God, You can't let it!*

"Hennek didn't give us permission to have our way with the girl," the guard with the even voice said. "They're both supposed to die with obvious marks on them from the wolf."

"Then what do you say we do? Stay here in the woods all night and wait for someone to find us in the morning?"

"Lock them up in the mine. Then we'll send someone to find out what Hennek wants us to do with them."

They muttered and mumbled, then hauled Steffan to his feet. They pushed him forward, and he stumbled but managed to catch himself as they moved toward the mine entrance. His chest was bleeding, stinging, as his shirt clung to the blood. And he was pretty sure they'd broken a rib when they punched him in the stomach.

Somehow they had to escape.

———•◦•———

Katerina had to save herself and the children. And Steffan. Though she never would have thought she would have cared about saving him.

But how she was to save anyone at this point was a mystery.

They made their way toward the mine. The first guard squeezed between the rocks and lowered himself down. Then they pushed Steffan toward the hole and he made his way into the mine. A second guard went next, then Katerina.

They made their way through the narrow tunnel as they had done earlier that day, with the guards occasionally shoving them in the back to make them walk faster.

Her eyes met Steffan's. His gaze was sharp—watchful and wary. *God, this feels like certain doom, but You, O Lord, can turn this into victory.*

God had saved her out of other bad situations. Surely He would save her again.

They continued into the mine, encountering another guard, whose eyes widened upon seeing them. Inside the larger cavern, the children were no longer working with their picks. She noticed bundles on the floor, then one moved and coughed, and she realized the bundles were the children lying down, sleeping.

The other two guards who were in the mine left their posts and gathered around the four guards with Steffan and Kat. They spoke quietly.

Kat focused on the children as she counted the sleeping bodies. More now than they'd seen earlier. The children started to awaken and sit up, staring at Steffan and Kat. But it was their eyes that made her heart sink. Their eyes were dull, their expressions nonresponsive. Except for one boy and girl, lying at the far end. Their faces became more alert. They appeared to be the oldest of all of them, perhaps eleven or twelve, and they turned to each other and seemed to be conversing. But the guards didn't notice the children. They were all curiously staring at Kat and Steffan.

"I say we should kill them now," one guard said. "Hennek wants them dead. And we don't want to risk them escaping."

"But Hennek wanted them killed by a wolf, and now they're both dead."

"Then we make it look like it was the beast."

"And just how do you expect we do that? Are you about to grow fangs and claws?"

The guard glared. He stuck out his chest, balled up his fists, and took a step forward.

"Easy, now." The third guard held up a hand between them. "We simply have to send someone to Hennek and wait for his orders. Nobody wants to lose their heads."

When she glanced at Steffan, he was eyeing a sword strapped to another guard's back. But the other guards were too close. If he stole the sword and tried to attack as he had earlier, the guards would be all over him. He'd be killed in a moment. There was no snarling beast now to distract them.

"Wait till the guards spread out," she whispered to Steffan. He didn't answer, still staring at the sword.

————◦◦————

Steffan especially hated the guard who kept grinning salaciously at Katerina. If he was able to get one of the guards' swords, he'd kill that one first.

The guards were deciding who would go back to town and tell Hennek what happened. It would take a couple of hours at most, so a couple of hours might be all the time they had left to live. They would have to take a risk and attempt an escape. They might be killed, but they were definitely dead if they didn't get away.

If he could create a distraction and then kill a couple of the guards, maybe he and Katerina could outrun the rest.

One of the guards left to report to Hennek. Now there were five. The two mine guards went back to their posts, while the other three turned sullen faces on Steffan and Katerina.

"Sit down!" one of the guards ordered.

Steffan glanced at Katerina. She was looking up at him.

"Sit down or I'll turn you over to Ruger."

The short guard who had been eyeing Katerina grinned and took a step toward them. Katerina quickly sat and Steffan sank down, the wall to his back, beside Katerina.

Ruger continued to stare at Katerina. The other guard didn't move or change his expression, just kept his beefy arms folded across his massive chest.

Sitting there waiting to find out how Hennek wanted to kill them, with a crazed guard watching over them, Steffan wondered how God was going to get them out of this predicament.

He glanced around for anything he could use as a weapon. Several feet away he spotted a small pick for mining. He could use that, if he could reach it. He tried not to look directly at it so the guards wouldn't notice.

Thirteen

Katerina shuddered inside at the disgusting guard staring down at her. But she would rather die than let him know she was afraid. Instead, she thought of everything she'd like to do to him, like punch him in the throat and knee him violently in the groin. But fantasizing about hurting the vile, lewd guard was not going to help anything.

Father God, forgive me for my violent thoughts. And help Steffan and me to get the children safely out.

She looked around for a weapon. If she could locate one, maybe she could inch toward it. The guards had been so sure they couldn't escape, they didn't even bother to tie their hands or feet together. They weren't even paying them much attention, as they were engrossed in a conversation about how much Hennek was paying them.

Steffan leaned over and whispered close to her ear, "A pickaxe on the ground, to your right. When I give you the signal, go for it, and I'll snatch a sword."

She nodded even as she shivered. Did she shiver because of the energy flowing through her at the danger they were in? Or because of the way his breath felt in her hair?

She was surely daft, because she even noticed the warmth

of his shoulder pressed against her arm. He wasn't like that vile, villainous guard. Steffan was protective and gentle with her. Why had she mistrusted him? Probably because he came across as arrogant and flippant. But he had also been bold and brave, and at the moment, he was ready to fight his way out. And she would be right beside him.

The streak of bright red caught her eye, reminding her how the guard had slashed Steffan's chest with his sword. In fact, his shirt was gaping open, revealing bare skin and blood. She had to tear her eyes away.

Her heart thumped and stuttered in her throat. But it was only because she wished she had something with which to tend the wound. That was the reason, surely. She had never felt an attraction to a man. Why should Steffan be any different? It was natural she should feel pity for his pain and want to tend his wound, was it not? But they had to escape first.

She leaned toward Steffan. He moved his head closer to her. She whispered, "Perhaps I could cause a distraction, something to make one of the guards turn so you could get his sword."

Before he could answer, one of the guards yelled, "Quiet! No talking."

Steffan met her eye. He whispered, "Not yet."

Kat glanced over at the children. Two of them, the older boy and girl she'd noticed earlier, were sitting up and whispering, then they glanced over at Kat.

One of the guards on that side of the cavernous room said sternly, "Lie down and be quiet."

The two laid their heads back down. Were they plotting how to escape, even as Steffan and Kat were? Or were they simply talking because they'd been awakened?

The guards standing over Steffan and her were still facing them, suddenly very watchful. After several minutes, Kat's traitorous eyelids were becoming heavy. She hated to admit it, even to herself, but she was very tired. Would it be so bad to die? At least she could rest. But she couldn't think like that. Her mother needed her, these children needed her, even the townspeople of Hamlin needed her, if only to be a voice raised against Hennek.

If she died, Hennek might get away with all this.

The minutes passed. No one moved or changed their position. Steffan occasionally shifted his arms or legs. But the guards were more focused on them than ever, even to the point of ceasing to talk among themselves.

Kat's head was so heavy, but she would not allow these men to see her relax her vigilance. But her thoughts were as heavy as her head and eyelids, mired in the danger that surrounded them, worrying she might not be able to rescue the children, as well as feeling concern for the wound on Steffan's chest.

She leaned her head back against the stone and allowed herself to close her eyes. But when she felt her head lolling to the side, she quickly forced her eyes open. She had to stay awake. She pinched her arm, hard, and bit the inside of her lip. Steffan had the long cut on his chest to keep him awake, she supposed. Did the wolf bite on his arm still pain him?

It surely had to be almost morning. Perhaps they weren't to be killed after all. Kat's eyelids kept closing. There was obviously no immediate danger, and she would hear if the guard who'd been sent to Hennek came back. She closed her eyes. How pleasant just to rest her head and her eyes for a moment.

Voices drifted into Kat's mind. Men were laughing and talking a long way away. Her head was resting against something firm but comfortable, but it wasn't the mine wall. It was Steffan's upper arm.

She sat up straight and blinked. The guards stood where they had been before, staring at her and Steffan. Steffan was also looking at her, his blue eyes soft, his expression compassionate.

"Go back to sleep," Steffan whispered. "I'll wake you if—"

"Quiet!" A guard kicked Steffan's foot. Steffan did not even acknowledge the kick, but closed his own eyes and leaned his head back.

Part of her wanted to lay her head against his arm again, but the other part of her was embarrassed that she had slept with her head on Steffan. How could she have let herself do that? She was usually so vigilant. And she normally awoke at the slightest sound. Would Steffan think badly of her?

Her eyelids were growing heavy again. If she fell asleep, would she end up on Steffan's shoulder again? She forced her eyes open. Steffan shifted, his arm brushing against hers. Her heart stammered.

Suddenly she heard footsteps, then Hennek's voice booming, "Welcome to my humble mine!"

The sleepiness went right out of her at Hennek's voice. Even the guards stood straighter, their eyes growing larger. No doubt they had not expected Hennek to come himself.

"How do you like my little business endeavor?" Hennek's grin and tone were as hostile as his words were boastful. "It produces a ton of silver every month. My little workers know the consequences if it doesn't. And that is what got me thinking . . . You two"—he looked pointedly at Kat and Steffan, raising his brows at them—"are more valuable to me if you work in my mines than if I kill you." He thrust his shoulders back. "The thorn-in-my-side stepdaughter who tries to turn my wife against me, and the son of the wealthy and powerful Duke Wilhelm of Hagenheim. And with you healthy, strapping beast killers in my mine, it should produce twice as much silver, maybe more."

Hennek rubbed his hands together, but his eyes were dull and dark.

Kat glanced at Steffan. He was staring hard at Hennek, but his expression betrayed no emotion.

How could one man be so despicable? To profit off the labor of children, to devise this elaborate scheme for something as meaningless as silver. Wealth was worthless compared to a child's life.

But when she heard that he hated her for speaking the truth about him to her mother, her heart expanded and she felt a rise in her spirits. *Yes, and I will continue to speak the truth when I get out of here. I shall speak out against you over and over, and everyone will know you for the evil man that you are.*

"How long do you think you can keep this up, Hennek?" Steffan said the words in a lazy drawl. "I'm just curious."

"As long as I want to. It is the perfect scheme." Hennek's eyes were black and cold. "If I had gotten rid of this stepdaughter of mine a long time ago, no one ever would have discovered my plan. Everyone else in my household is either too loyal or too daft."

"You're just too clever for everyone else, aren't you?"

Hennek's eyes narrowed as he seemed to be weighing whether Steffan was sincere or not. Then Hennek spun around and yelled, "Everybody up! No more sleeping! Your new fellow workers just caused you to lose your last hour of rest. Get up!"

The guards standing near the children started kicking at their feet. The little children on the floor sat up one by one, their eyes barely open. But the two oldest children were wide-eyed and stared straight at Katerina and Steffan and Hennek.

"You too," Hennek sneered at Kat and Steffan. "Get up and get to work. Let's see how much silver you can dig out of my mine."

Katerina got up off the floor and stood beside Steffan. Hope surged. Hennek couldn't resist feeding his pride, but it would keep them from being killed right away.

They both went to the wall. Would they be given one of the little pickaxes? They were small but could certainly be used as weapons. But when they reached the spot Hennek indicated, the guards gave them each a small chisel with a dull, flat end.

The poor children seemed to know their own stations and were already standing or kneeling at them, hacking away at the hard rock. Even in the relatively dark mine, Katerina could see the veins of ore running through the rock walls.

Heat and fury welled up from Kat's gut.

"Get to work," one of the guards ordered. Something pressed her side and she looked down to see the guard was jabbing her with a stick.

She glared at him, but he glared right back. When she turned back to the rock in front of her, Steffan was watching the guard from the corner of his eye. The guard backed away a foot or two and Steffan whispered, "We will escape. Soon."

Yes, Hennek would regret not killing them. He was so greedy and loved to puff himself up, and that would be his demise.

Fourteen

Finally, after many hours of work, Steffan and the rest of the workers were allowed to lie down and sleep. Katerina lay her one blanket near his. He waited, holding his breath. Would the guards separate them?

Steffan lay down quickly, his head near hers. The floor was hard and uneven, but he had slept on the ground many nights. He imagined Katerina, even though she was used to a soft bed, was probably too tired to notice. Her eyelids had been drooping for hours, and she stumbled when she moved.

So far he had made note of every bit of the mine that was within his view. He wasn't sure how, but they would escape. It was only a matter of time. And when his father found out what Hennek had been doing, he would be outraged and would bring swift justice.

A slight pang nipped Steffan's chest to think he had once accused his father of being unjust, to think of how he had defied his father and disobeyed him. For the past year, the truth had slowly dawned on him more and more. His pride had taken a beating, admitting to his brother Wolfgang that he had been wrong. When he began to think that his anger had been foolish and unnecessary, all these last many months, he'd felt adrift.

He had to change the way he thought about many things.

His father was a good man, just and fair. Steffan had been foolish to distrust him. His faults were very hard to admit, even to himself, but he'd experienced what happened when a man deceived himself into thinking his actions were righteous when they were not.

He'd been wandering a circuitous path from Poland toward home for the past year, seeking adventure and fortune, looking for a way to redeem himself. Pride. That was what was keeping him from going straight home. Joining the Teutonic Knights, seeing how warped their leader's motives were, and having to fight against his own brother, whom he loved, perhaps more than any other person in the world, had begun to open his eyes. And remembering the men he had killed in battle, men who were only defending themselves and their land and their families . . . That was certainly the worst part.

Why was he thinking about this now? He had to stay alert to an opportunity to escape and get Katerina and these children out of here.

Poor Katerina. She was probably already asleep. His own eyes were burning, and so was the cut on his chest.

The guards were gathering at one side of the room. Finally, Rugen joined them.

"Did you see those children? I wish the guards would let us talk to them."

Katerina was speaking to him. He rolled over and found himself face-to-face with her. Even though her eyes were red from exhaustion, they gleamed in the torchlight as she spoke.

"Which children?"

"The two older ones, the boy and the girl. I think they will help us."

What could two children do to help? But he didn't want to discourage her. They had to keep their hope alive.

"They may know things we don't about the mine to help us," she said, her teeth starting to chatter.

"That is true. Are you cold?"

"Not very much." Her voice sounded groggy. She wasn't accustomed to going two days and nights without sleep.

"Go to sleep now." He sat up and said loudly in the direction of the guards, "Hennek's daughter needs another blanket. Hennek wouldn't like one of his best workers dying because of the cold."

"It's not cold in here," one of the guards barked back.

"How do you know what Hennek wouldn't like?" said another.

A third guard muttered something as he fetched a blanket from the pile on the floor. He took a step toward Steffan, then tossed it to him.

"Thank you," Steffan said.

He laid it over Katerina, who, even as tired as she obviously was, lay in a defensive position, on her side with her hands in loose fists resting on her chest. Her eyes were open a slit as she watched him.

"Thank you."

"You're welcome." Steffan wanted to be able to say that he would stay up all night and keep watch while she slept, but he wasn't sure how long he would be able to keep his eyes open, since they were in no immediate danger. And just as he'd expected, he soon heard Katerina's heavy, even breathing indicating she was asleep. The guards were still talking as a new group came in and the others left. These new guards looked very sober and attentive. Soon Steffan's eyes were closing and he was drifting.

After two days in the mine, Katerina had convinced a guard to give Steffan another shirt, one that wasn't slashed across the chest, exposing him to the cool underground air. Thankfully the cut had scabbed over and didn't look as hideous as it had previously. When she handed him the new shirt, he gave her a half smile and thanked her.

He drew his old torn shirt over his head with one quick motion. Kat spun around to give him some privacy, but not before she caught a glimpse of taut stomach muscles and bulging arms. When she turned back around, he was fully clothed again.

The guards were allowing them their afternoon rest time, so Kat and Steffan both sat down with their backs against the wall. Kat looked at her palm in the dim torchlight. It was covered in mine dust and blisters. She rubbed the worst blister very carefully, saying a prayer it wouldn't break open and fester.

She had also managed to get close enough to some of the younger children to talk to them. That morning a little girl had hurt her finger with the chisel. When she started crying, Katerina walked over to her and comforted her. The guard yelled at her, but she ignored him, until he threatened to beat the little girl. Then she moved away, smiling and reassuring the little girl that all would be well. The child even smiled back at her. That smile had lifted her own spirits considerably.

Steffan's shoulder was propped against the wall as he turned toward her. He held out his hand as if he wanted to see her palm. Without thinking she laid her hand in his. He held it close to his face and seemed to study it, then brought it to his lips and kissed the back of her knuckles.

She sucked in a breath and snatched her hand away from him.

Part of her wished she had not pulled her hand away, wished she had let him hold her hand as long as he wanted, wished he would kiss her hand again, though it was dirty, and wished she had smiled at him and gazed into his eyes.

But that was foolish. He needed to know he couldn't just kiss her hand. She was right to snatch her hand away from him. Wasn't she?

Steffan whispered, "Forgive me. That was impulsive."

Why would he even think about kissing her hand? They had been living side by side for days now. They had touched each other inadvertently a few times. And she had slept with her head on his shoulder that first night, although not purposely. But he had never tried to touch her or kiss her.

"I suppose you have kissed many women's hands," she said. It probably meant nothing to him. She imagined that was what the sons of dukes did. When they greeted a woman, they kissed her hand.

"I didn't mean to startle you."

"Forget about it. It was nothing." She folded her arms across her chest.

He inclined his head a bit closer to her. "I would never do anything to hurt you. What did Hennek do to you?"

His face was so earnest, she couldn't seem to tear her eyes away from him.

"We've survived wolf attacks, worked together, taken care of each other. We are friends, are we not?"

"I suppose we are."

"Then tell me."

Something inside her wanted to tell him. What could it hurt?

He had never taken advantage of her the way others had tried to. Kissing her hand had been the first untoward thing he had done. The part of her that wished she had let him hold her hand suddenly told her distrustful part to be quiet and let her talk.

"If I tell you, then you have to tell me something you've never told anyone else."

"That is fair."

"Very well then." She had kept this secret for so long. She used to feel ashamed, but she knew none of it was her fault.

Steffan made her feel protected and safe. He accepted her as she was. He didn't treat her as if she shouldn't be bold and strong, as if she shouldn't try to rescue children or kill man-eating beasts. And the fact that no one knew where they were, and they might never get out of this hole in the ground, created an intimacy between them that she'd never known before. Something told her that Steffan would not blame her for what had occurred, as she had always feared would happen if she told someone.

"I was just a little girl when my mother married Hennek." She spoke in a low whisper so no one could hear but Steffan. "She was a beautiful woman with no money. My father was a merchant, but not a very successful one. When he died, he owed a lot of money, most of it to Hennek. Hennek used that debt to persuade my mother to marry him.

"I did not like Hennek from the beginning. He was always forcing himself on my mother, kissing her and touching her when she obviously did not want him to. I would kick him, and sometimes he would hit me, but only when Mother wasn't looking. When we were around others, he would speak of how much he loved my mother and me, making himself look like some great savior of poor widows and orphans for marrying my mother.

"The first time I saw him hit my mother, I screamed, 'I'm going to tell everyone what you did!' He hit me across the mouth and knocked me to the floor. He said if I ever told anyone anything about him, he would kill my mother. He told me he would strangle her with his bare hands, and it would be all my fault. I was about ten years old at the time."

"I'm so sorry," Steffan said. The compassion in his eyes made her lean even closer to Steffan. Her face was only a hand's length from his.

"When I was thirteen years old, he started coming into my bedroom at night. At first he would tell me stories. Then he started trying to kiss me good night, but I would always turn my head. One night he tried to touch me."

A knot tightened in her chest. She'd never told anyone about that, not even her mother. Steffan's face was so full of anger and concern, she had to glance down at the floor, as it made tears sting her eyes.

"The next night I hid a knife under my bedclothes. When he sat down on the edge of my bed, I drew it out and said, 'If you touch me, I will kill you.' He laughed, then grabbed my wrist. I pushed my hand up and the knife point stabbed his chin. He let me go then.

"After that, he stopped coming into my room, but his guards started leering at me, brushing against me, and making lewd comments under their breath. I always pretended I wasn't afraid of them, and if my mother was nearby, I would yell for her and tell her they were frightening me. They mostly stopped after my mother made a fuss and demanded Hennek force them not to bother me anymore. Perhaps some would say they never really did anything to me, did not physically hurt me, but they destroyed my little-girl innocence and sense of safety. It made me always vigilant, always afraid of anyone who got too close."

Steffan clenched his fists and whispered, "How dare Hennek do that to you. And allow those men to harass you, especially when you were only a child. I will kill him."

His reaction was a balm to the part of her that needed a protector.

"There were so many times I wanted to run away," she went on, "but I was afraid of what he would do to my mother if I left. And I thought about killing him. I even made a plan." Kat had to take a deep breath as she remembered that time. "But I didn't do it, because I knew it would hurt my mother. She didn't want to believe bad things about Hennek. It made me sick, but I had to accept that she actually loved him."

"Do you think she still loves him?" Steffan's brows rose.

"Perhaps not as much as she did then. I should have done everyone a kindness and killed Hennek in his sleep."

"If you had, one of his guards would have just taken over this mining business and you wouldn't have discovered what Hennek was doing. The children would still be enslaved. But we are going to escape and take them with us."

Katerina nodded. "Yes, we are."

An almost overwhelming urge to reach out and touch his face caused her hand to twitch. She wanted him to hold her hand, to put his arms around her. But there was still a bit of fear inside her stopping her, keeping her from asking for anything from him.

"I'm so sorry that happened to you."

His gaze was so intense, she looked away, unable to control the chaos in her heart. When he touched her fingers, she didn't pull away. There was still a tiny voice telling her Steffan had some dishonorable motive for getting close to her, but it was stifled by the louder voice that trusted him, liked being close, and wished she was even closer.

"And now it is time for you to tell me something you've never talked about." She smiled, knowing Steffan would not like this part of the bargain.

Just as she might have thought, he frowned and chewed the inside of his mouth.

"I shall hold up my end of the bargain." He cleared his throat and pulled his hand away from hers, straightening a little away from her. "My brother is always trying to get me to talk about this. So here it is. When I was a boy, my brother Wolfgang and I were playing with another little boy. His father was a shepherd who worked for my father.

"This boy said we could not chase the sheep. His father had warned him, and it was the thing his father was the most adamant about. But I, in my arrogant, childish wisdom, convinced him it would be all right if we only chased two of the sheep. I said we would drive them across a stream, just to see if we could, and then we would drive them back and his father would never know. But when we drove them across the stream, the sheep went too far. We tried to stop them, but they fell off a tall outcropping and died when they hit the bottom."

"Oh. That is bad."

"It becomes much worse. I . . . Are you certain you wish to hear this?"

Her heart sank. Would his story shock her or cause her to judge him for his bad choices? But she said, "I'm sure it cannot be so very bad. You were a child, were you not?"

"I was eight years old."

"I will not condemn you for something you did when you were only eight years old." When he still did not speak, Kat said, "Please. Go on."

"The little boy began to cry and said his father would beat him, would kill him. Wolfgang and I told him his father would not do any such thing, but the boy was inconsolable.

"Later that day, Wolfgang wanted to tell Father how afraid the boy was, wanted to tell him what we had done, but I persuaded him not to." Steffan's voice was turning hollow and raspy. "But it was a mistake. A terrible mistake."

Steffan scrubbed his face with his hands.

"What happened?"

"The next day the boy was found beaten to death. The father was gone. No one ever saw him again in Hagenheim." He hung his head and did not look up at her. "So you see what a terrible thing I did. I caused a child's death."

She wanted so much to comfort him, but her hands stayed by her sides. "You did not cause that child's death, Steffan."

"But I did. I actually did." He rubbed a hand over his face again and turned away from her.

"That's a horrible thing to carry around. You were just a child. That man who beat his son to death deserves the blame, and you have to stop carrying the guilt of it." Should she reach out and touch his arm, to console him?

"I deserve to carry it. Wolfgang carried it too, even though it was mine to carry, not his."

"God can give you peace." It was as if the words came out of her mouth before she even thought them. Unable to resist, she lifted her hand and placed it on his arm. "Jesus carried it to the cross so you wouldn't have to carry it. Don't you believe that?"

He turned his head and looked her in the eye. "Who told you that?"

"I heard it from my priest. But it is the Easter story, is it not?"

Was she imagining that he was leaning into her hand on his upper arm? And that his expression was softer as he gazed into her eyes.

"It's easier to believe it when it's applied to someone else." One side of his mouth quirked up.

"I suppose that's true."

"Get up!" the guard yelled. "Get back to work. Your rest is over."

She quickly pulled away her hand, which had begun to feel much too warm and comfortable on his arm, and they went back to work. But something had shifted, something deep inside her was leaning, leaning toward Steffan. And she wasn't sure if it felt good or . . . terrifying.

Fifteen

Steffan sneaked a glance at Katerina as she worked. She had not complained once since they'd been in this mine—four days and five nights. All that time Steffan had been studying the guards and watching for an opportunity to escape. Katerina was doing the same, as they had discussed the guards' patterns, which ones seemed the least adept at fighting and the least likely to kill them, and how they might escape.

The guards had relaxed their rule against Steffan and Katerina talking to the children. The night before last, the guards did not stop the children from gathering around Katerina while she sang them a lullaby and talked softly with them. A couple of the littlest ones even climbed into her lap while Kat caressed and cuddled them. It gave Steffan a very unsettled feeling, however, that he couldn't explain. But every day the desire to set them all free grew stronger.

Then last night Steffan had had a dream that Hennek changed his mind and decided to kill Steffan and Katerina, scared they were going to escape. Steffan awoke feeling a renewed determination to find a way out, thinking that perhaps the dream was God's way of telling him that now was the time to make an attempt.

Later, as they sat eating the midday meal of bread and cheese and dried fruit, he noticed Katerina staring at his face. "You resemble a priest I knew when I was a child."

"An ugly priest?"

"No." Katerina smiled.

Her smiles were like a rainbow after a hard rain.

"No, this priest was kind and always talked to me when Mother would take me to the church to pray. We were very poor after my father died, and once he gave us food." She shrugged. "I liked him. Do you remember your priest when you were a child?"

"Yes."

"Did you like him?"

"Yes."

"When was the last time you went to confession?"

Steffan coughed and raised his brows. She was obviously waiting for him to answer, so he thought about it seriously and cleared his throat. "I have not been to confession for a long time. But I would like to go. Soon."

"Why?"

"Why do I want to go soon?"

"No. Yes. Well, I meant, why have you not been to confession in a long time?"

"Because for a long time I was not sure I trusted God. And even after I decided I could trust Him . . . it had been so long since I'd confessed, it was just hard. Hard to admit . . . how long it had been and how much I had to confess."

"I'm sure you do not have that much to confess."

He raised his brows again. "I cannot tell if you are in jest." Katerina didn't seem a particularly naïve person, but if she thought he didn't have much to confess, then she did not understand what he had done in Poland.

He didn't really want to talk about confession. He was focused on his dream and his increased drive to get them out of there before time ran out and Hennek had them killed.

"Listen." He looked her intently in the eye. "Tonight, when the guards think everyone is asleep, we'll escape. I'll find a way to steal a sword. Once I get that guard's sword, I'll kill him and another guard, then I'll throw you the second guard's sword."

Katerina nodded.

"I have another idea."

Steffan spun around to confront the small voice behind him. The older boy who had been staring at them since they'd arrived was crouching there.

"I am Albrecht. My friend Verena and I have a plan."

Katerina's arm brushed Steffan's as she leaned forward to get closer to the child. "There are fifty-two of us. But the others are not far from here, digging in that passageway." He pointed behind him.

"What is your plan?"

"There is a pit down that passageway on the left. It's where we dump our loose stones and dirt. If the children in the passageway create a lot of noise and force the guards to come see what is happening, we can trip them or attack them with our picks and push them into the pit. There are too many of us for them to kill us all."

"That sounds very dangerous for you," Katerina said.

"No more dangerous than you and this man trying to kill all the guards by yourselves. Besides, it will work. The guards have become less cautious with us. We're only children, after all. They don't expect us to do anything."

"No." Steffan shook his head. "I cannot let you endanger

yourselves. I can kill the guards, and Katerina can help me. While we are fighting the guards, you and the other children can escape. Are there any other openings or ways to get out of this place?"

"I believe there is only one."

"Well, then, let's get to it. I will wait until the fresh guards come, just after we've all laid down for the night, and then I will attack. So listen for a commotion, then stay where you are and wait for us to come and get you."

"We can help," Albrecht said.

"I don't want any of you doing anything that could get you hurt. Do you understand?" His throat constricted and he could barely speak. What was wrong with him?

The boy Albrecht stared back at him. "We will defend ourselves and fight for our freedom."

"You are just children. Let Katerina and me defend you."

Albrecht didn't say anything.

"Be very careful," Katerina said. "Watch over the little ones and make sure they get out. Steffan and I shall do our very best, with God's help, to save us all."

Steffan was still struggling to breathe. He knew why. This boy reminded him of the shepherd's boy. He couldn't let these children die, because then he'd be haunted by all of them as well. He wasn't sure he could bear it.

"You stay alive," he heard himself telling Albrecht. "All of you, stay alive."

"What passes there?" A guard took a step toward them. "You, boy. What are you doing? Go along, back to your place. And you two." He pointed at Steffan and Katerina. "Stop talking or I'll see that you get no supper tonight."

The guard grunted and went back to the rock where he'd

been sitting. These guards didn't really believe it was possible for their prisoners to escape, and hopefully that would work in their favor.

Katerina lay on her blanket and held her breath while the new guards arrived and the old ones left.

Steffan's body looked tense as he lay staring in the guards' direction. His head was on the ground, but his arms were taut and his hand was beside him, as though ready to push himself up. He told her he would wait until he was sure the daytime guards were well away and would not hear his attack.

Katerina prayed, *Help us, God.* Her thoughts were flitting so fast, it was the only thing she was able to say. *Help us.*

The lecherous Ruger was there. But he was short, and Katerina suspected he was the weakest of the guards. Hopefully Steffan would pick him to attack first.

Minutes passed as Katerina clutched her little chisel under her thin, moth-eaten blanket. None of the guards called out anyone to ridicule or harass, as they sometimes did. Instead, though they were facing their prisoners, they were standing close to each other, talking in low voices. She heard Hennek's name once or twice.

Finally, Ruger moved away from the other guards and pulled something out of his pocket, probably the dried meat jerky he often chewed on.

Steffan sprang up from the ground and leapt at Ruger.

Katerina jumped to her feet as Ruger reached behind his back for his sword. Kat held her breath. *Don't let him get his sword out before Steffan reaches him.*

Ruger's hand was on the hilt. He was drawing it upward, just getting the point freed from the scabbard.

Steffan grabbed the hilt as he knocked Ruger onto his back. Steffan was on top of Ruger. But who had possession of the sword?

Steffan raised the hilt up and stabbed downward.

The other two guards shouted, unsheathing their swords as they ran. Katerina ran toward them with nothing but her little chisel.

The children erupted from their beds and yelled, a war cry of child voices.

Steffan straightened to meet the other two guards. Katerina ran closer, ready to pounce on Ruger with her chisel, but Ruger didn't move.

Steffan seemed taller than ever as he met the other two guards. He slammed his sword into the first one and shoved. The first guard stumbled back into the second one, and Steffan quickly took advantage and stabbed the guard in the neck.

That guard's eyes went wide. His hands went loose and he dropped his sword.

The sound of children's screams echoed from the passageway behind them as Katerina swooped down and snatched up the sword, then leapt back so she wouldn't be in Steffan's way.

He clashed blades with the third guard and yelled, "Go help the children!"

Should she defy his order and stay and help him kill the guard he was fighting? But he was a good swordsman, and someone needed to get the children to safety.

She turned and ran toward the passageway. She followed the sound of the yelling and screaming and entered the dark passage.

$\mathcal{S}$ixteen

$\mathcal{K}$aterina had never been in this tunnel, and it was too dark to see where she was going, but as long as she could hear the screams and yelling, she would head in that direction.

She kept her hand on the wall, stumbling over a rock, then hit a sharp curve that had her bumping into the wall, but she kept going. *God, don't let me fall into that pit Albrecht was talking about. And please let Steffan win his sword battle.*

A man's voice ahead made her speed up her pace. He was yelling and cursing.

A dim light flickered. Finally she was able to see where she was going, and the voices were getting louder.

As she rounded another bend, she could see, from the light of a torch, a guard with a child clinging to his back. The child was pulling the guard's hair with one hand and slapping his face with the other, while various children attacked his front with picks and chisels. He stumbled, alternately grabbing at the child on his back and the one in front of him, but they always managed to dart out of his reach. Then the child on his back wrapped his arms around the man's eyes.

The children in front redoubled their efforts to push him, until he got his hand around the throat of one little boy, probably about seven or eight years old. The boy fought, pounding at the guard's arm, but the guard lifted him off the floor and showed no sign of letting go.

Kat rushed forward. Should she strike with her sword and risk hitting a child? Because now the children were grabbing the man's arms, scratching at his hands to make him let go. He cursed and threatened, and then Kat saw the goal: a large gaping hole in the direction the children were pushing him.

The large man continued to stumble closer to it, and the clawing, biting children finally managed to get him to let go of the little boy whose neck he was squeezing. The boy fell to the ground, gasping and coughing and crying. But at least he was breathing.

Two more steps. One more step. Kat reached out and grabbed the child on his back just as the man fell. The child let go at the right moment and Katerina snatched him away from the edge of the pit.

Albrecht and the older girl, who must be Verena, appeared beside her.

"Are all the guards in the pit?" Kat asked.

Albrecht and Verena nodded.

She turned to the children who were gathered round.

"We did it!" Katerina's heart was pounding so hard it hurt, but they were alive!

"Hoorah!" The children cheered and whooped, some hugging each other, others jumping up and down. Katerina embraced Verena and then Albrecht.

"Come," Kat urged. "Is everyone here? We must hurry."

"Are we leaving anyone behind?" Verena looked like a miniature mama as she craned her neck and appeared to be counting heads.

"No one is left in the farthest chamber," one little girl said. "I was the last one out."

"Very good. Let us go." Verena herded them with her hand.

Anxious to see if Steffan was all right, Kat allowed Verena to take up the rear as she hurried ahead.

When they were spilling into the large chamber where she'd left Steffan, her eyes hungrily sought his tall form. When she didn't see him, she called, "Steffan!"

No one answered. Two bodies lay on the floor. But where was Steffan and his last opponent?

Katerina ran forward and searched the ground. "Steffan!"

Then she saw a body lying facedown against the wall. Was it Steffan? She ran toward it. No, it was the guard. She let out a strangled sound.

"I'm here," a muffled voice came from above her.

"Where?"

"Up here."

She looked up and there was Steffan's face emerging from a hole in the wall a few feet above the guard's body.

"What are you doing up there?"

He didn't answer as he disappeared for a few seconds, then his feet reappeared as he lowered himself down. He used the guard's body as a step and emerged, dirtier but smiling.

"Making sure we have money if we need it." He held out a bag and a handful of silver coins. "Hennek must be using the extracted silver from the ore to make coins, silver guilders."

"And you found where he was storing the silver money he was making?" Kat reached out and picked up a piece.

"How badly are you hurt?"

The question, spoken by Verena behind her, pulled Kat's

attention away from Steffan and to the child Verena was talking to, the little boy whom the guard had been choking. Kat knelt beside him. "Are you well? Can you speak?"

The boy nodded and lifted his head. "I was brave, wasn't I?"

"You were so very brave. I'm sure your mother will be so proud when I tell her."

"I don't have a mother."

"What is your name?"

"Dietmar."

"Well, Dietmar, you must continue to be brave, because we must escape from a very bad man."

"The piper?"

"Piper?"

"The man who plays the flute pipe. He's the one who lured us away, then his men grabbed us and put us in a sack and carried us here, to the mine."

So that was how Hennek had managed to take the children without leaving any trace. She had known he was responsible for taking them, but luring them away with something as innocent as playing a pipe . . . Children loved when Hennek played his pipe. He would play in the town square at every holiday, and sometimes on market days. People would smile and compliment his playing and thank him, assuming he was good and gentlehearted for wanting to entertain children. How dare he use that against them!

"Yes, we must go now so the piper cannot get us. Are you ready?"

Dietmar nodded.

She turned and found Verena just behind her.

"Is everyone here? Anyone badly hurt?"

"I counted fifty-two, including Albrecht and me, so that is everyone. No one seems badly hurt. Just a few bruises."

"Were the guards not able to strike anyone with their swords?"

"The children all attacked at once and stole their swords before they could draw them."

"Miraculous." Kat breathed a prayer—"Thank You, God"—as Steffan came up beside her.

"What do we do with them now?" Steffan looked nervous.

Katerina opened her mouth, shut it, then said, "I guess we forgot to talk about that. But we have to get them far away from Hennek."

"We should take them to Hagenheim. But for now we had better get out of here." Steffan looked at Albrecht and Verena. "Can you get them to the opening?"

"Of course." Albrecht turned and spoke to the children. "We're getting out of here, but we have to stick together, you understand?"

"Yes, we will," several of them said.

"This is Steffan and Katerina, and they will help us. But we all have to be brave."

"Yes, Albrecht." Some of the little faces looked eager. Some still had that dazed, frightened look, but they would feel better, surely, once they were out of this hole in the ground.

They started toward the passage that would take them back to the opening through which they had all been forced to climb down. But this time they were climbing up, to freedom.

———— ✦ ————

Steffan hurried to the entrance of the mine so he could help the smaller children climb up the ladder.

The three men Steffan had killed weighed heavy in his chest, but he'd done it so they could escape. They were men profiting off children, and he had little choice. He did not, would not, regret the deaths of these henchmen of Hennek's . . . as he had regretted some other men he'd killed.

He hoisted a little girl up the ladder, and an older girl came alongside her and helped her climb the rest of the way. Most of the children scrambled up the ladder without any help at all, but one particularly small girl started crying when she got to the ladder.

"I'll help you." Steffan placed a hand on her small, frail shoulder.

The girl only cried harder and shrank away from him.

Katerina came forward and bent down to her level. "I will go with you. Don't be afraid."

"I can't," the little girl wailed.

"What if I carry her on my back?" Steffan suggested. Nearly all the children were above ground now, waiting for them.

"That might work."

They continued helping the children up the ladder while the littlest girl clung to Katerina's side with a tiny fistful of Katerina's tunic.

Finally the little girl was the last one left. Katerina bent to look into her face.

"I'm going to put you on Steffan's back. Is that all right?"

The little girl nodded.

Steffan knelt on the floor as Katerina lifted the girl. "Hold on to him. That's good."

Her hands clutched his shoulders. Steffan stood and, leaning forward, grasped the ladder and started climbing. He prayed the wooden ladder would hold their weight and moved steadily up. When he reached the top, hands appeared in the opening and pulled the little girl up and off his shoulders. Steffan pulled himself out and turned to see if Katerina needed any help. But she hoisted herself out before he could offer.

"Which way is Hagenheim?" Katerina was holding a child's hand on either side of her, looking as stalwart as he had ever seen her. But he had a sudden urge to moan. How were they going to get all these children all the way to Hagenheim? Without any carts or horses? With a madman chasing them?

"It's that way," Steffan said.

The children quietly turned in that direction and started walking down the hill.

The sky was clear, and as he and Katerina brought up the rear, the sea of children brought a strange unsettledness to the surface. Hadn't he always said he didn't like children? Now he had fifty-two of them looking to him to save them. Because if Hennek caught up to them again, he would surely kill them all.

"Fifty-two children," he said quietly under his breath, for Katerina's ears only. "We can't hope to outrun Hennek, or to escape his notice, as he'll surely scour the area for us in the morning."

"Maybe we should turn around and take them home. There's no safer place than their own homes with their fathers. But I'm not sure we could sneak them past the guards at the gate."

"Could we boost them through the opening in the wall?"

"Perhaps."

Steffan thought about how they could possibly get that many children quietly and safely through the wall. "No, that's too dangerous. Hennek's guards would surely see us before we could get even the first child home."

"Maybe we just need to get to a town or village nearby where people don't know Hennek and aren't afraid of him. Perhaps we can hide the children there while we travel to Hagenheim and alert your father."

"How do we hide fifty-two children?"

"We will find a way." She looked so brave, and yet he thought he saw and heard a hint of doubt.

"Yes, we will find a way." Steffan reached out and touched her shoulder. "We will. The children are brave, and I won't let any harm come to any of them. Or you either."

She looked askance at him. One side of her mouth rose in a crooked smile. "Our protector?"

He shrugged and nodded.

"You don't sound like the prodigal son I've heard so much about."

He winced. "What have you heard?"

"Only a little carousing, drinking, and breaking women's hearts, that kind of thing."

Steffan's chest grew heavy again. "It is true. I drank too much and was not the son my mother and father raised me to be, but I did not carouse with women."

It was a pathetic protestation, perhaps, but he wanted her to know he had not broken any hearts, not by making false promises to any young woman or fathering illegitimate children, as dukes' sons were so often known for doing.

"No women?" She was still looking at him out of the corner of her eye.

"No."

She turned her gaze forward and nodded.

Katerina was so good. She was brave and strong and determined.

"Why did you stay?"

"What?"

"Why didn't you leave and get away from Hennek?"

"I told you, I couldn't leave my mother."

"You could have married Hans. Surely he would have protected your mother too."

"Hans? He's been my friend since we were children. Besides, he's been planning to marry a maiden named Hilda."

His heart expanded inside him at this news.

They were nearing the road, but it was probably close to midnight, judging by the position of the moon, so they were not likely to encounter anyone. They allowed the children to walk down the hard-packed dirt ruts. As they walked, he imagined what Hennek would do when he discovered they had all escaped.

"What is the closest village of more than a hundred families?"

"The closest village of that size would be Keiterhafen, just east of here, maybe five miles."

"We should be able to make it there by morning, then."

"Children walk much slower than we do."

"We can carry the little ones and let them rest when we must. We can make it."

"Hopefully."

Albrecht and Verena were leading the children, who were all strangely quiet, while Steffan and Katerina brought up the rear.

One of the little girls was lagging behind, the same little girl he had taken on his back up the ladder. When she was very near to him, he scooped her up and held her in his arms. Looking into her eyes, he was reminded a bit of his little sister Adela. How old must Adela be now? Nearly grown, he would imagine . . . oh yes, nineteen. It had only been a year since he'd seen her, but she still remained a child in his mind.

"What's your name, little one?"

"Johanna," she whispered. Her body was stiff, and she was holding herself away from him.

"If you're tired, I can carry you. Is that all right?"

She only stared back at him.

"Do you want me to put you down?"

Johanna did a slow cringe, pulling her arms into her body and dipping her chin to her chest, her bottom lip protruding. Then she whispered, "Yes."

Steffan lowered her to the hard dirt road. He was being impulsive again. Of course she wouldn't want a scary-looking man picking her up, especially after what she'd been through. He should have asked her first.

"She just doesn't know you very well yet." Katerina gave him a gentle smile.

One of the little girls who was holding Katerina's hand grabbed Johanna's, and they walked beside him.

As slow as their pace was, he was not at all sure they would make it to Keiterhafen by morning.

After they had turned off the north road onto the road that led east, a child just ahead of them stumbled and fell. He got up slowly. Another child, a little girl, started crying, a soft wailing. Another said, "Where is my mother? I want my mother."

This was not good.

"Let's take a rest," Katerina said. "We'll lie down in this nice soft grass off the road and take a nap, shall we?"

She was so brave. Could she tell he was more afraid of taking care of these fifty-two children than of battling a hundred guards with swords?

$\mathcal{S}$eventeen

$\mathcal{K}$aterina nearly stepped in goat dung and called out, "Watch where you step."

Steffan herded the children, watching until every child was on the grass and either sitting or lying down. Then he started walking toward her. Why did her heart thump at the way he was looking at her? He sat down near her and propped himself on his hands.

Her mind wandered to what he had said earlier, admitting the excessive drinking and that he hadn't been the best son but saying there had not been any women. Did she believe him? Her first thought was that if he was going to admit all the other things, why not admit that too? He hadn't lied to her before, that she knew of.

Her eyes started closing on their own, her head nodding.

She forced her eyes open and slapped her face lightly. She had to stay awake.

A little boy was whispering in Steffan's ear. Steffan got up and walked with him to the edge of the woods. He stood guard while the little boy went into the trees. A few moments later he came back out and smiled at Steffan.

When Steffan sat down beside her again, he said, "Go to sleep and I will keep watch. After an hour or so of rest, we will continue on."

"I shouldn't."

"Yes, you should. There is no sense in both of us staying awake."

Perhaps he was right. "I shall stay awake and let you sleep the next time we stop for a rest."

"Of course." One side of his mouth went up. Did he wink? She wasn't sure.

She lay down on the grass. She probably wouldn't be able to sleep anyway, but she would close her eyes.

"Katerina?" Steffan's voice drifted into her dream of lying in a meadow in the sun.

Katerina opened her eyes to see him kneeling beside her in the dark, with only the pale moon to see by.

She sprang up. "I'm awake."

"We need to get everyone up and keep moving."

"Of course." Katerina felt a little sick. No doubt the children would feel even worse to be awakened from their short rest, but they had to do it. They had to be cruel, at least for tonight, in order to save them.

She and Steffan called softly to the children to wake up, having to gently shake some of them. Albrecht and Verena helped as well. When they finally had all of them back on the road, they moved forward at the slow pace of the youngest children, who looked as if they were sleepwalking, their eyelids nearly closed.

One little boy walked with his head practically resting on his own shoulder. When he gradually came to a stop, Steffan knelt in front of him, said something in a low voice, then picked him up and held him against his chest, the boy's head on Steffan's shoulder.

The rest of the children plodded along, but how long could they last?

Two hours later, Katerina carried one little girl in her arms.

Steffan was now holding two, and Katerina was already seeing a bit of gray in the sky, brightening up the night. Was it already dawn? How would they escape Hennek now? They were still quite a way from Keiterhafen, and several of the children had been stumbling, unable to keep their eyes open or lift their feet high enough to avoid the dips in the road.

How much farther could they go without rest and sleep?

The sky grew lighter. Her arms burned under the weight of the little child sleeping on her chest. Her shoulders ached and her eyes hurt as if they'd been scratched by grains of sand. But they had to keep going.

She hadn't realized she'd slowed her own pace until Steffan's broad shoulders were in front of her. If he could keep up his pace while carrying two children, she could surely do it with one.

The other children marched on like little tired soldiers.

The sun was over the horizon now, shining through the trees at their backs. She kept walking, though her feet and legs ached and her stomach felt sick. Still no sign of life, besides the occasional hare that flew swiftly in long leaps over the road in front of them. Soon Hennek's men would discover the dead guards and missing children and come after them.

Sounds drifted toward them from the opposite direction as a man came into view driving a donkey loaded with sacks.

Her spirit rose. She could ask this man how far they were from Keiterhafen.

Steffan slowed, peeking over his shoulder—and over the child's head that rested on that shoulder. He waited for Katerina to catch up to him.

"Don't ask the man anything about Keiterhafen. We don't want him to be able to tell Hennek that's where we were going."

Yes, that was wise. "But don't we need to know how much farther it is?"

"It doesn't matter how much farther it is, we have to keep walking. Or find another place to hide."

It was true enough.

Steffan quickened his pace as the man was getting closer. He was nearly to the front of the group of children when the man said, "Where are all you children going? So many of you?"

Steffan said in a loud, cheerful voice, "We are headed to Hagenheim. Can you tell us if we are on the right road?"

"As a matter of fact, you are not. This is the road north to Keiterhafen. To go to Hagenheim, you need to go east."

"Thank you, sir," Steffan said quickly. "Are you headed to market?"

"My master, the Baron of Rotterfurt, sent me to market at Keiterhafen, and I am now returning with the goods he bade me buy."

"All the way from Keiterhafen? You must be tired."

"It is only about two miles."

Two more miles! Katerina's heart sank.

Steffan nodded and smiled and conversed with the man a few more moments. Then Steffan bid him fare well and began to walk again.

The man looked slightly chagrined at not getting to talk longer. Katerina did not even acknowledge him, but kept walking with her bundle.

When they were out of sight of the stranger, the little girl in Kat's arms, apparently awakened by the voices, lifted her head and yawned.

Just then another little one started crying as two others stopped and simply collapsed on the ground and lay down on the hard dirt.

"Can you walk?" Kat pushed the hair out of the little girl's face. She nodded and Kat put her down.

"Let me carry you," Kat said to the crying child.

"The Piper is going to get us," she said, sobbing.

"No, Steffan and I won't let the Piper get you." Steffan must have seen the two children collapse on the ground, because he'd put down the ones he'd been carrying and was walking toward them.

"I don't think the children will make it two more miles. Not without another rest." Kat felt the tears sting her eyes, but she blinked them away. She had to be strong.

"They have to make it. They can and they will." Steffan scooped up one child, then the other. Neither one even seemed to awaken as he settled them, one on each shoulder.

Katerina bent and lifted the crying child into her arms.

"I'm tired," one of the children said.

"I'm tired too."

"I'm thirsty."

"I'm thirsty too."

"Let's sing a song." Katerina made her voice as cheerful as she could. "What's your favorite song?"

No one responded, so she asked, "Does anyone know this one?" and began to sing a well-known troubadour ballad. Steffan joined in, his voice deeper than she might have guessed. Soon some of the children began to sing along. Katerina sang as many of the verses as she could remember, then fell silent.

"I'm hungry."

The voice was so forlorn, tears stung Kat's eyes.

O God, don't forget us. We are grateful to be free, but please have mercy now and help us.

"We do need to find water," Steffan said softly. "I think there might be some down this ravine." He pointed off the road.

Kat hadn't even noticed the ravine. She stepped closer. It wasn't terribly deep, but it was steep. Steffan started climbing down, sliding the last ten feet.

"There's a little stream down here," Steffan called, "but keep walking with the children until the ravine gets less steep."

She kept the children moving. "Let's sing another song. Do you know this one?" She started singing, "Under the linden, on the heath." She sang of crushed flowers and grass and a nightingale's song. If only her life were so peaceful, had ever been so peaceful.

Would these children ever find their way back to their secure and pleasant life, at home with their loving families? Some of them were probably like her when she was a child, left with no father, caring for herself and her mother rather than the other way around. And many of them were orphans.

She finished that song and started singing of King Wenceslaus, the saint, and of his good deeds for the poor and needy. After that song, she started one about the crusaders, "*Palästinalied.*" Steffan joined in from the ravine below, and the sounds they were making quite cheered her. She suddenly didn't feel as tired anymore.

Katerina stepped off the road to peer down and saw that the ravine was growing more gradually sloped. She readjusted the little girl in her arms, propping her on her other hip, and kept walking, a bit faster now.

Steffan carried the tune well. Their voices seemed to blend as he sang the man's part and she sang soprano, the lyrics all about seeing the Holy Land where their Lord once walked.

Soon Kat spied the water below, in spite of the forested ravine.

"This looks like a good spot," Kat called down to Steffan. "Should I let the children come to you?"

"Send them down." Steffan climbed up most of the way and helped the younger children. The older ones were able to go down without help. Kat followed at the end.

The children were kneeling and drinking out of their hands from the little fast-moving stream. Kat joined them. After she drank so much she felt a bit queasy in her stomach, she splashed her face, rubbing her cheeks with her fingers. The children were already lying down on the grassy bank, their eyes closed.

Kat sat near the littlest ones. Gazing up toward the road, she suspected no one could see them, unless they got completely off the road and gazed down, and even then they might not notice them through the thick foliage of the trees.

"Do you think we are safe enough here to stay for a while?" Katerina asked Steffan, who was sitting near her.

Steffan seemed to be thinking, then he said, "I'll go see if I can buy some bread. You rest."

"You need rest too."

"I'll be all right. But when I come back and they've eaten a bit, we shall have to force them all to get up again. It may seem cruel, but we have to get them to the town and hide them."

"Yes. I understand."

Steffan met her eye a moment, then turned to go up the bank. "Steffan."

He stopped and faced her.

What should she say? Be careful? Stay safe? "Thank you."

He smiled. "I'll be back as soon as I can."

Steffan was not at all the spoiled and privileged duke's son she'd thought he was. And he had never been unseemly with her, not even when they were alone together. Did that mean he didn't find her attractive?

"Ack." Why was she thinking like this? With tears flooding her eyes? She was just tired, that was all. But should she stay awake and keep watch over the children? She should pray that Steffan didn't get caught and that they would find kind people to help them in Keiterhafen. But she could lie down at least. She could pray lying down as well as sitting up.

Kat glanced around, making sure all the children were resting and still, then pillowed her head on her arm and started praying.

The next thing she heard was Steffan's voice, so familiar and comforting.

Kat opened her eyes and Steffan was standing over her. "Are you all right?"

"Yes, of course." She sat up quickly, despising how groggy and slurred her words sounded.

Steffan started rousing the children and handing them bread. Some clutched their bread to their little chests and then fell back to sleep.

Steffan gently lifted one boy by his arms and sat him up, tapping his cheeks with his fingers until the boy's eyes opened.

"Eat your bread," Steffan told him, but in a kind tone. "We have to get to the town and to safety. Be brave. That's good."

Kat followed his example, waking the girls and insisting they eat their bread. "When you finish, drink some more water." The water was cold and would help them wake up.

Finally, they were all awake and began climbing back up the stream bank. Once they were all on the road and walking, Kat fell in beside Steffan.

"Did you have any trouble finding bread?"

"I bought some from five different bakeries, so as not to look suspicious. But at the last shop, the woman had such a kind face—she reminded me of my mother—I asked her if she might have room for some orphans I'd found on my travels."

"What did she say?"

"She said yes. Her children are all grown and she would be happy to look after them. Also she said she has a stable where I could sleep. She even showed me where it was. I told her I would go fetch the five orphans and come back. I was afraid if I told her I had forty-seven more, she would become suspicious of me. But when we go back, I'll show her the others and explain. I'm sure she'll let us all stay in her stable, at least for now."

Kat's heart soared, then caught in her throat, keeping her from speaking. She had to swallow before saying, "That is wonderful."

"Yes, I charmed her with my smile."

And your kind blue eyes and handsome face and perfect manners. "No doubt she also was impressed by the silver coin you used to pay for your bread."

"Perhaps."

"But I'm very happy you found a place we can hide. It was very resourceful of you."

She looked at him out of the corner of her eye and found him looking at her the same way.

"Are you complimenting me? Commenting on one of my many good qualities?"

Kat shook her head. "You are resourceful, that's all I said." She was too afraid to admit that she did indeed see other good qualities in him. He would gloat too much if he knew. Besides, she was already trusting him more than she was comfortable with.

But barring any sudden changes, he had shown himself to be determined, brave, noble, kind, protective, and sacrificial, concerned more about these children who were no relation to him than about his own gain. He could easily have taken those bags of silver coins and left her and the children to fend for themselves.

The children kept walking, and soon travelers became more frequent. They'd already met three or four more on the road, all of whom had raised their brows at so many children and asked about them. Steffan successfully deflected the questions, but . . .

"Should we try to get off the road when people come?"

Steffan's mouth was more tense than usual. "I wondered the same thing. But it's probably too late now. Hennek will eventually discover that we came this way. We just have to have the children well-hidden before he reaches us."

They would need a lot of God's favor for that to happen.

Eighteen

When the town wall was in view, Steffan motioned for Katerina to help him herd the children off the road. A small copse of trees would help hide them.

"We're almost there, children," he said, then lowered his voice as he leaned closer to Katerina. "We should go in a few at a time. Do you think Albrecht and Verena can take care of some of the children while we take others into town?"

"We can," Albrecht said, chiming in from just behind Katerina.

"Very well. Here is the plan. Katerina and I will take about ten of the youngest children, and I'll show her where the stable is. Albrecht, you and Verena watch over the rest. Then I'll come back here and take another group until we're all inside the stable. Then I'll take the five youngest to Frau Goschen and they can stay with her."

Albrecht nodded, then went to relay the plan to Verena.

Steffan and Katerina gathered the children who looked the most tired and got back on the road. They would surely be noticed with so many children, and he would also surely be noticed coming back in with even more children. But just then, a crowd of travelers came along. Steffan hurried through the gate in the middle of the crowd. The guards didn't seem to even notice them.

They walked down several streets to the small bread shop.

Behind it and down a tiny alley, they came to the stable. No one was around, so he ushered Katerina and the children inside.

In the dim light, they directed the children to the clean stalls. They lay down on the hay and seemed to fall asleep immediately. His own eyes burned from lack of sleep, but he'd gone without sleep many times during battles and when he had been traveling with the Teutonic Knights. He could go as long as he needed to.

"Lie down and sleep with the children," he said to Katerina. "I'll go and fetch the rest."

"I feel guilty sleeping while you are doing that."

"You are needed here, to protect the children. So lie down and sleep. You'll awaken if there's danger."

She acquiesced and lay down beside the children. She stared up at him with just a wisp of a smile, her eyelids already starting to droop.

Steffan hurried away, his heart racing as it always did when she showed a bit of trust in him.

Katerina heard the soft sound of a horse chewing. She opened her eyes. Where was she? Dim, muted light was visible at a crack in the wooden wall beside her. Was that the light of morning or of the coming night? Her heart beat fast as she sat up and glanced around.

Hay surrounded her, and several children lay asleep nearby and breathing heavily. Had they slept here all day? The last thing she could remember was Steffan coming back with the remainder of the children, then lying down in the middle of the stable, placing his body between them and the only door.

Kat stood and saw he wasn't there. Had he abandoned them? The children were not his responsibility; they were hers. She was from Hamlin. Steffan was a duke's son from Hagenheim. Why should he care? But she would never abandon these children. She didn't want them to feel like she had, alone and afraid.

Kat yawned and stretched out her stiff back. She had to find food and water for the children and ensure they had a place to stay the night. Had they gone undetected all day? Or did the owner of this stable know of their presence?

Kat started counting the little sleeping forms, lying close together like puppies around the warm stable. Forty-seven. Where were the other five children?

Her heart began to pound. Had someone snatched them? Taking them to do hard labor for someone as sinister as Hennek?

Albrecht sat up and rubbed his eyes. "What is it?"

"Five children are missing."

His eyes flew wide. "What? How many did you count?"

"Forty-seven."

Albrecht blew out a breath and shook his head. "The other five are in the house with Frau Goschen. The woman from the bakery?"

"Oh yes. I forgot." Kat sighed and held a hand over her heart. "I'm sorry."

"It's all right. Do you need anything?" He yawned.

"No, no, go back to sleep." Katerina went back to the place where she'd been sleeping and sat down and rested her head in her hands. "I can do this," she whispered. "I can take care of these children." She didn't need Steffan. She didn't need anyone. She never had needed anyone. She'd become too dependent on Steffan, and now he was gone. Well, it was a good lesson for her. How foolish she had been to think he would stay, and so foolish to let him take the lead and rescue them. She—

"Is anyone hungry? We've brought bread and cheese."

A woman, plump and smiling, stood inside the door of the stable holding an apron full of bread, and crowding behind her stood five more women.

The women all came inside and started bending down and talking with the children and handing them the bread from the woman's apron. Coming in behind them was a man carrying a large basket. Steffan.

The air rushed into her lungs. Steffan had not left them at all.

This was the same feeling she had each time Steffan had protected her. A wave washed over her. Her knees actually went weak as Steffan gave out the small rounds of cheese to the children.

Kat stood back while the children went forward to receive the food. She watched as they took the bread. Some of them immediately bit into it. One little boy sniffed it first. One girl clutched the bread to her chest and took some cheese with her other hand and went to sit down.

"Katerina." Steffan was motioning for her to come to him. He had no idea she had just been thinking he'd selfishly left her and the children to fend for themselves.

She moved through the sea of children and made her way to Steffan.

"Katerina, these are friends of Frau Goschen. They want to help us by taking in some of the children."

"Oh." Kat nodded at them as they introduced themselves to her, each of them smiling and looking like friendly, kind-hearted mothers. Kat could feel the tears damming up behind her eyelids.

"Do you know which of the children are orphans?" Steffan was speaking in a low voice by her ear, so close his breath rustled her hair. "One of the women is childless and would love to adopt a few of them."

"*Ja*, that is me, Frau Gruber." The closest woman grasped Kat's hand. "I have longed for a child for five years now, but we are still childless." The woman's eyes were swimming in tears, then one dripped from each eye.

Katerina had never been able to see someone cry without crying herself—a silly thing that she had always been able to conceal before, but now, as her own tears fell, she had nowhere to hide her face. But she wiped the tears from her cheeks.

"I shall go get Albrecht and Verena. They will know."

She looked for the two older children while the women went back to talking to the children and handing them ladles of water from a few buckets they had brought.

"Albrecht, do you know which of the children are from the orphanage?"

The boy hesitated and drew his brows together.

"It's all right. There is a woman here who wants to possibly adopt some of them. But we won't let her take them if they don't want to go."

"Very well." His expression changed.

"Come and you can introduce her to them."

They went back to where the woman was talking with a little boy. Albrecht said, "This is Berthold. That is Margret. Over there is Hans. This is Christobel and Caspar—they are brother and sister—and that is Dietrich and Helena and Anna. Over there is Fronika."

"Is that all? Only nine orphans?"

"I am also an orphan." Albrecht crossed his arms over his thin chest.

Perhaps the fact that he was an orphan and had lived at the orphanage explained why Albrecht was always putting himself in charge of the children and taking the lead. He was used to taking care of other children, and unused to anyone taking care of him.

"And Verena?"

"Her mother lives near the orphanage."

"I would like to take all the orphans," Kat heard Frau Gruber say to Steffan.

Steffan looked around until his gaze rested on Kat.

"I have a large house," the woman said. Her lips were smiling while her eyes pleaded. "And I have servants who can help me with the children."

Albrecht bent and talked to each of the children, asking them if they wanted to go with the woman, telling them he believed she was safe and that they would be treated well. The children all agreed to go, and Frau Gruber took hold of one of their hands, her face aglow. Albrecht watched them filing out of the stable.

"You are to go with her too, Albrecht," Steffan said.

Just then the woman turned and looked at Albrecht.

"Go on, Albrecht." Katerina motioned for him to go.

"No, I should not."

"Why not?"

His expression was troubled, then hardened. "She doesn't want me. I'm too old. Mothers and fathers only want young children and babies."

"Nonsense! You're not that old. You must go or . . . you will hurt her feelings. Go on!"

"Come." Frau Gruber's expression was gentle as she looked

him in the eye. "Albrecht, is it? You can be my helper. Come, Albrecht, and if you do not like our home, you can come back here."

"Yes, Albrecht, come!" Some of the younger children began to call him, smiling as if it were a game and they wanted their friend to come and play.

The invitation proved too irresistible. He started toward them.

Verena was staring after him now, her lips slightly parted. Albrecht turned and saw her. He ran back to her, and they threw their arms around each other. They said words that were too quiet for Kat to hear, then Albrecht hurried out with the rest of the orphans, following Frau Gruber.

When the women had taken as many children with them as they could accommodate, Frau Goschen agreed to take the few who were left back to her house.

"What will you do now?" Frau Goschen asked Steffan.

"I'll buy a horse and ride to Hagenheim and get some help from my father. Then I'll go back to Hamlin and arrest Hennek and all his guards and anyone who helped him or knew of his scheme."

"When?" Frau Goschen asked.

"Now, if you'll sell me a horse." He gave the plump woman, who was probably old enough to be his mother, his heavy-lidded smile, but there was something strange about Steffan's appearance. His cheeks were flushed, but the rest of his face seemed pale.

"I will give you a horse."

"I wish to pay for the horse. I doubt that I will be able to bring it back to you."

"Very well, then."

"I shall go too." Katerina took a step forward.

"No, you stay here to help look after the children."

So he was planning to leave her here? But more importantly . . .
"You can't ride hard for two or three days when you've had no
sleep."

"I slept today."

"How long?" Was she being silly? Or worse, enamored of him?
But something told her it was far more foolish to let him leave
without her.

"I slept a few hours."

"Barely three hours, I would guess."

Frau Goschen spoke up. "It will do these children no good if
you fall asleep atop your horse and fall off and break your neck.
You should sleep a full night before you go."

Steffan's jaw hardened, though his eyelids stayed half closed.
"You two are worse than my mother."

"We are encouraging you to be sensible." Frau Goschen's
hands were on her hips. "I raised three men, and I know how stubborn you all are. But you will not be able to stand against the both
of us. And if you think on it, you will see that we are right."

"She is right." Kat adopted Frau Goschen's calm but firm tone.
"It is sensible to sleep first, and also sensible to take me in case
you have trouble."

"Oh no." Steffan held up his hands and shook his head. "You
are not coming with me."

"Why not? I can ride as hard and as fast as you can."

"Can you?"

She wasn't sure she could, but she wasn't going to admit that
to him. "You need me, in case something happens to you."

"What could happen to me?" Steffan gestured broadly with
his hand, his brows lowering.

"You could get attacked by robbers or fall in a ditch, or your horse could break its leg."

"It is true," Frau Goschen added. "No man is immortal, and you cannot help if your horse steps in a hole and breaks its leg. It has happened to my husband's brother. He had to walk for days in the rain and nearly died of a putridness of the lung."

Hearing Frau Goschen speak of putridness reminded Katerina of Steffan's injuries. "You also need to let a healer look at your wounds."

"He has wounds?"

"Yes, on his arm and his chest."

"I shall take him at once. We only have one good healer in town and—"

"I am well. I don't need a healer."

"Nonsense. It can't hurt to let her look at you." Frau Goschen took hold of his arm and pulled. "Come."

Steffan threw up his hand. "Very well. But we are wasting time."

Frau Goschen shook her head. "Come." Over her shoulder, she said to Kat, "I'll be back soon for the children." She pulled Steffan with her out of the stable.

Katerina sighed in relief. The flushed look on his face had worried her, but she'd been too afraid to make a fuss over him.

She sat on the floor with the children who were left. They talked quietly with Katerina as they ate their bread and cheese. They were quiet, but their eyes had lost that dazed look and they seemed less afraid. They even smiled. Katerina felt much better too, but they weren't out of danger yet. Hennek was surely looking for them, and he had too much to lose to give up.

She didn't want to frighten them, so she put on a smile and they talked lightly about their favorite foods and their favorite feast days. Soon, a couple of the more adventurous children began to pet the friendlier horses in the stable and to jump about. Others asked when they would see their mothers.

"Soon, very soon," Kat answered with a smile. "Only a few more days."

Just as she was beginning to think it should be time for Steffan to return, he appeared in the doorway with Frau Goschen. Kat quickly read their faces. Steffan's expression was humble, while Frau Goschen was frowning. But as soon as she saw Kat, she came toward her.

"It is a good thing you mentioned Steffan's wounds, Fräulein," Frau Goschen said. "The healer saw the beginning of a putridness in the wound on his arm, and possibly on his chest."

Kat's throat seemed to close up. She tried to swallow but couldn't get past the constriction.

"The healer is making up some of Steffan's healing salve. She assured us she will have it ready before sundown," Frau Goschen said. "Now, don't worry, Fräulein Katerina. He will be well."

"Shouldn't he stay more than one night?" Kat asked. "To rest and heal?"

Steffan folded his arms across his chest. "You all are making too much of this. I can ride in the morning."

Frau Goschen shrugged her shoulders. "He will not listen," she said as she shook her head. "I left the children with the servants, rolling dough for pasties. Come," she said, addressing the children who were left in the stable, "and you can help too."

The children all hurried out with Frau Goschen.

Kat and Steffan were left alone in the stable—the first time they'd been alone for days. Steffan lightly kicked at the hay on the floor. Finally, he slowly turned and looked her in the eye.

He didn't say anything, so Kat said, "Why do you want to leave me here?"

"To look after the children."

"You already found these women to look after them. Obviously you don't want me to go with you. Do you think I'm not tough enough to keep up with you?"

"It's going to be very difficult, Kat." His voice had softened.

"I know that. But I want to come."

His expression seemed to freeze. He stared into her eyes. "Why?"

Her heart thumped against her chest and her breath shallowed. She looked away and shrugged. "I want to make sure you get to Hagenheim. And with two of us, it's more likely we will arrive. Without being stopped by Hennek's men or . . . robbers."

She glanced up at Steffan again. His brows were raised. "I should see to buying you a horse, then."

So he was agreeing?

"I met a horse trader on this street earlier. I believe he had a perfect gelding. I shall return very soon, in less than an hour."

Before she could decide to thank him or tell him she wanted to see the horse first, he was out the door.

Why did he call her Kat a few moments ago? And then, the way he looked at her, when she said she wanted to go with him. It had felt so . . . close, as if he were feeling the same tender feeling she was. Could she have imagined it? Or was it pity, seeing her own tender look but not reciprocating it?

"Oh, let it not be pity," she whispered, plopping down in the hay and realizing the women had left her a bundle of food and a cup of water.

Her heart fluttered, but this time in fear that Steffan might think she loved him. She started eating the bread and cheese, squeezing her eyes closed. She didn't love him, did she? She had better not. He could not possibly . . . How could it work out if . . . ? Where would they live? What would they do to support themselves?

How foolish she was being! Of course he did not love her. Perhaps she should let him go alone to Hagenheim and keep some distance between them. But her argument had been true. Anything could happen, and the two of them would more likely reach Hagenheim if they traveled together than if he went alone. And if she was not ready to let him go on an adventure without her, then why should anyone judge her? He was handsome and capable and . . . she trusted him.

Her cheeks heated and fear filled her stomach like hot coals. She cared for him, and it was terrifying.

Nineteen

Steffan knew he should leave Katerina in Keiterhafen. He should sneak away tonight and ensure she was safe with the women who had taken in the children. He would never forgive himself if something happened to her while they were riding to Hagenheim. And he wasn't worried anything would happen to him. Of course he'd get to Hagenheim all right. He'd been riding alone for a year now, ever since he left the Teutonic Knights and Wolfgang and his sister-in-law in Poland. But . . . he wanted her with him. He couldn't understand it. Was it because she wanted to go and he didn't want to say no to her? Or was it because he didn't like the thought of not seeing her for several days?

Perhaps it was best if he didn't examine his motives.

He quickly found the gentle but young and vigorous gelding he'd noticed earlier and paid the horse breeder what he asked without haggling, then walked him back to Frau Goschen's stable.

When he entered, Kat was sitting in the middle of the stable holding her face in her hands. When she heard him, she quickly pulled her hands away.

"Here's your new horse."

Katerina stepped toward the animal, smiling. Steffan lay down on the hay and watched her as she rubbed the horse, talking softly to him. She was so gentle and kind to animals and children, but he had no doubt she would cut a man to ribbons if he laid a hand on her, and she had no trouble facing down a wolf and stabbing it straight through. She reminded him a bit of his sister-in-law Mulan, even though the two were not very similar in appearance. Katerina's hair was not black and her eyes were blue instead of brown, and she was taller and broader in the shoulders, but both women were fierce and strong. He imagined the two would be great friends.

His eyes were closing on their own. He was more tired than he'd realized, and the cut on his chest was paining him. Frau Goschen came into the stable and started talking to Katerina, asking her if she'd like to take a bath. She responded rather enthusiastically. Well, enthusiastic for Katerina.

"We'll let Steffan sleep," the woman said, and he was grateful, though he badly needed a bath himself. Perhaps he would be able to take a quick bath before they rode to Hagenheim in the morning.

Katerina was up before the sun the next morning, saddling her horse alongside Steffan, who was saddling his. She knew she'd soon be galloping east, getting dusty from the road, sweaty from the exercise, and dirty from resting on the ground. But at least she'd had a bath the day before, which had quite refreshed her. Steffan had taken one after he'd slept an hour or two, then she'd slept in the house in a makeshift bed on the floor while Steffan stayed in the stable.

She'd noticed he looked flushed again just before she left him. And this morning he was moving a bit slow.

"Are you well, Steffan? Did you apply the healing salve to your wounds this morning?" She turned to watch him.

"Yes. Why would you ask?" He adjusted his saddle and didn't look at her.

"Are you sure you are well? Let me see your face."

There wasn't much light in the stable before dawn, but when he turned to her, she could see the frown. She stepped forward and raised her hand to his forehead and pressed the back of her hand to his skin.

Her heart beat hard as she realized how close she was, that she was touching his brow and gazing into his eyes. He bent his head toward hers. Would he kiss her?

She held her breath. His eyes were searching hers. Had he seen her staring at his lips a moment before?

What was she doing? He must think her wanton. She jerked her hand away and took a step back.

He blinked and raised his hand to her cheek. "Thank you for caring." With the back of his fingers he caressed her skin very lightly, then let his hand fall to his side. "I did feel a bit feverish last night, but I am well this morning. Must have been the lack of sleep, and it was a very warm day yesterday."

He went back to readying his horse as if nothing had happened. She did the same, because nothing *had* happened. She'd been concerned about him having a fever or being ill, that was all. Nothing more. But her heart still thumped erratically. What would it have felt like if he had kissed her? Would she have been horrified? Would she have berated him? Or would she have liked it, only to feel like a fool when he went back to Hagenheim and she never saw him again?

Her heart finally went back to beating normally. Soon they

were on the road east to Hagenheim, riding their horses at a fast trot. No doubt Steffan didn't want to tire them out too soon. Katerina was determined to show him she could keep up, no matter how fast he went, so she made sure to stay alongside him and not behind him. Once or twice she even overtook him to see if he wanted to go faster, but he never picked up the pace.

They had been riding about two hours when she noticed Steffan seemed to be slowing down. When she glanced at him, his shoulders were slightly bowed. Maybe it was a military tactic to conserve his strength. Was she imagining that they were moving slower and slower? She urged her horse to move faster and looked back at Steffan. His face was definitely flushed. Had the fever returned?

"Let us stop here," Kat said.

"Why?" He had a stubborn look in his eyes.

"I need a rest."

Steffan guided his horse off the road. The sun was halfway up in the sky, and it was warm. They dismounted and Steffan took a drink, then ran a hand over his cheek.

"Steffan, are you feeling all right?"

He blew out a breath. "I think I should have used some more of the healing salve this morning."

"I thought you said you used it. You did bring it, did you not?"

"Frau Goschen made sure I brought some."

"Thank You, God, for Frau Goschen. Do you need any help?"

"I can do it." He was already taking out the container from his saddlebag. Without a word, he turned his back on her and drew off his shirt. Then he started smearing the salve on his chest, then his arm.

Her cheeks flamed as she took a quick look at his muscular

back and shoulders before turning away. She pressed a hand to her eyes and had to suppress a giggle at her foolish reaction to him.

When had she ever giggled? She couldn't remember.

But this was serious. What if the healing salve didn't work?

She opened her mouth, then closed it. How could she say this without making him angry? "Perhaps you should go back to Keiterhafen now, before you get sicker."

He started shaking his head. "I am not sick."

"It's the only thing that makes sense, Steffan. If you go back, Frau Goschen can tend you and I can go on to Hagenheim to fetch Duke Wilhelm."

"No. I am well enough, but I just need to remember to keep applying the salve. I shall be well in a few hours. Let us ride on."

"In a few hours? It surely will not work that quickly. What if you become so ill you cannot ride? I shall have to stay with you until you are better, and then no one can go fetch Duke Wilhelm."

"Do you think me a child? I will not become as sick as that." But his eyes were red-rimmed.

"Truly, you do not look well."

"I can make it to Hagenheim, and we have an excellent healer there, should I need one."

Perhaps she was making too much of it. Perhaps he was well enough and she shouldn't worry. "Since we are stopped, we may as well rest for a few moments."

She lay down on the grass, closed her eyes, and pillowed her head on her hands. Steffan did the same. She could sense his eyes on her.

"You are very worried about me," Steffan said.

She opened her eyes. He was smiling at her.

"I am worried you may be sick. You slowed down a lot."

"I slowed to save the horses."

"Your cheeks are still flushed. Do you feel feverish, as you did last evening?"

"I think I could have a fever." His smile grew wider.

She felt her own cheeks grow hot. He was trying to lure her over there to touch his forehead again. Would he try to kiss her if she did?

Part of her was outraged that he would use a possible illness to get her to come closer. The other part made her catch her breath at the thought of him wanting to kiss her.

She pressed her hand to her own burning cheek. This was preposterous. This was not how Katerina of Hamlin behaved or thought. But would it hurt to kiss him, one innocent kiss?

A memory flashed before her eyes, of Hennek saying, *You know you want me to kiss you* as he bent over her.

She'd shoved him away, but she could still see his fat, slobbery lips.

But Steffan was no Hennek, and he was not hovering over her.

"You look well to me." She gave him her best frown.

When he had brushed his hand against her cheek, she hadn't flinched. She was not repulsed or angry. And she couldn't stop thinking about kissing him.

Was this good? Or bad?

After trying to sleep while her thoughts went around and around in her head, she opened her eyes. Steffan's breathing was steady and heavy, indicating that he had fallen asleep.

How sick was he?

But it was good he was sleeping, was it not? She knew precious little about caring for wounds. She should rest so that she didn't fall behind later because she was so tired.

189

Kat opened her eyes and realized she'd fallen asleep too.

Steffan lifted his head off the ground. "I hear horses," he whispered.

They both scrambled to their feet and stood still, listening. Steffan's hand was on her shoulder.

The horses' hooves were getting closer, and it sounded like several.

"Get the horses." Steffan turned and rushed to where their horses' reins were tied to a tree nearby. He untied them in a moment and led them farther off the road into the trees.

They hung on to their horses' reins and put calming hands on their heads. Steffan stared hard toward the road. When the horses and riders galloped past, Katerina thought she recognized one or two of Hennek's guards.

"Hennek's men." Steffan rubbed his chin.

"It was a good thing we took a rest when we did, was it not?"

He turned toward her and his jawline softened as he gazed into her eyes. "It was a good thing."

He lifted his hand and caressed her cheek for only a moment, as he had early that morning. "Thank you," he said.

"For what?"

"For trusting me."

"What makes you think I trust you?" But Katerina couldn't suppress the smile that drew up the corners of her mouth.

He lifted his arm and wrapped it around her shoulders.

"Because you let me do this."

She froze, her gaze caught by his. A voice in her head said, *"You're being foolish, like your mother, who trusted a man such as Hennek and even fell in love with him."*

Steffan is nothing like Hennek.

Kat slipped her arms around his back and pressed her cheek against his shoulder. Steffan wrapped his other arm around her. She took a deep breath, reveling in the feel of his shirt against her cheek and her arms around him. He was so warm. In fact, oddly warm, as she realized she could feel heat emanating from the cut on his chest.

She squeezed her eyes closed, wishing she could shut out the feeling of dread that was sweeping over her, remembering the man who had died after getting bitten by the Beast of Hamlin.

Steffan had been bitten by the beast.

She lifted her hand and pressed it to his forehead, then his cheek. "You feel warm."

He placed his hand over hers, keeping it pressed against his cheek.

She took a step back, forcing him to let go. She turned away from him, her heart pounding harder than ever. She went over to her horse, unsure what to do.

Now he would think she was weak and silly. She trusted him, but getting too close was still frightening. Would she always be this way?

Twenty

"I can make it to Hagenheim," Steffan repeated. "I'll keep re-applying the salve every time we stop. It will cure me. You will see."

"Then let us go to Hagenheim. And pray that Hennek's men do not circle around and find us." But her hand was shaking as she reached for her horse's bridle.

Steffan was still thinking about how Katerina had let him put his arm around her, then had placed her head against his shoulder. His heart had soared. He'd been afraid to move, afraid he would scare her. It hadn't lasted long, but it gave him hope that she was beginning to trust and care for him.

They mounted their horses and set out for Hagenheim, riding a bit slower now that they knew Hennek's men were ahead of them. And now that they were riding slower, they were able to converse more easily. Katerina asked him questions about his family, and he told her about the adventures he'd had in the last year since he left Poland. She told him about the funny things that she and her friends had done when they were children, ways she had outsmarted Hennek, and how she had bribed Hennek into allowing her to study under one of the priests in Hamlin.

He'd never heard her talk so much, but he liked it.

"Father Bogdan always encouraged me in my studies, telling

me I was more clever and studious than any boy he'd ever tutored. I did enjoy learning. What about you? I'm sure you must have had an excellent tutor."

"I only enjoyed being outdoors and learning about fighting, improving my skills of sword fighting and jousting, that kind of thing. I'm sorry to say I refused to do my assignments most of the time."

"I'm sure that's only because you just enjoyed battle skills more than science and mathematics."

Steffan sighed but didn't comment further. He should have obeyed his tutor, if for no other reason than so that he wouldn't have to admit to Katerina that he was a terrible student.

They rode on in silence. Steffan was listening for Hennek and his men. They went on for the rest of the day, stopping to rest the horses, get water, and reapply the healing salve to his chest and arm. Each time they stopped, she looked at him longer, smiled at him more, and just seemed . . . less guarded. But he was getting better, feeling less feverish and probably looking less feverish, so she had no reason to press her hand to his forehead. And he was purposely allowing her to decide how close she wanted to get to him.

Soon they mounted their horses again and started back down the road. Unfortunately, the clouds were growing dark and the wind was picking up. A storm was brewing.

———◦—◦———

Katerina hated storms. The lightning, the thunder, the wind, the stinging, drenching rain. And it was all coming down on them hard. Soon their horses were struggling in the thick mud.

They'd hardly encountered anyone on this road for hours when they saw a man traveling toward them, riding on a mule.

Steffan hailed the man, practically shouting to be heard over the wind and rain. "Can you tell us if the road to Hohendorf is near?"

He must have been thinking of waiting out the storm at his brother's castle in Hohendorf.

"Straight down this road, but turn south when you get to the fork beside the large tree with the broken branch."

"Large tree with the broken branch?"

"About a mile from here. You will see it."

"How far is Hohendorf from there?"

"Two or three miles, I know not."

"Thank you."

"Will we spend the night with your brother?" Katerina asked.

"Yes, if the rain doesn't let up. There's too much risk of the horses losing a shoe or breaking a leg."

As they continued down the road, she prayed that the children were still safe in the homes of the women in Keiterhafen, hidden from Hennek, although it seemed likely he had followed them there. Many people had seen them traveling on the road—a man, a woman, and over fifty children. Hennek would surely hear of it.

A streak of lightning flashed. Ahead was the broken tree and the fork in the road showing that Hohendorf was still at least two miles away.

More lightning flashed as they rode the rest of the way to Hohendorf. The rain continued to pour down in sheets, and the castle suddenly loomed ahead of them at the top of a large hill.

A few villagers stood in doorways, and they all stared at them.

She and Steffan faced the castle mount and urged their horses up the road leading to the castle.

Katerina watched Steffan out of the corner of her eye. He was as wet as she was, but he was sitting tall and straight in the saddle. She prayed silently that the healing salve had done its job before it had been washed away by the soaking rain.

Hohendorf Castle was taller than she'd imagined, with towers rising high above the trees of the dark forest all around it. The rain gave it an even more unearthly appearance, as if fairies and trolls might emerge from behind the trees.

At the door they were met by a guard and a middle-aged woman who gave them a quizzical look.

Steffan stepped forward, his hand over his heart, looking very chivalrous and knightly even with his hair dripping with rainwater.

"I am Lord Gabehart's brother, Steffan Gerstenberg of Hagenheim, and this is Katerina Ludken. Are the lord and lady at home?"

The woman's brow creased. "Lord Gabehart and Lady Sophia are not here. But I am the head house servant."

"Can you tell me where Lord Gabehart and Lady Sophia have gone?"

"To the Polish estate of his brother Lord Wolfgang for a visit. But you are welcome at Hohendorf Castle. Please, come in." She and the guard stepped back and welcomed them in.

"We would like to stay the night," Steffan said.

"Of course," the house servant said.

"And perhaps get fresh horses for our journey tomorrow, if you can spare them."

The guard nodded. "Of course. You are Lord Gabe's brother. Whatever you need is yours."

"And now let us get you some dry clothes and a warm place to rest."

They followed the woman through a cavernous entry hall and a long corridor, and Katerina took the opportunity to say, "Lord Steffan needs a healer to look at his wounds and help him apply some healing salve and bandages."

Steffan, who was walking beside her, frowned down at her.

"We have a servant here who serves as a healer. I shall send her to him."

"Thank you," Katerina said at the same time Steffan said, "That is not—"

Steffan cut his remark short and pointed a finger at Kat. She only smiled and raised her brows at him. She longed to know if his wounds were getting better, but thought it best not to offer to take a look herself.

At the end of the corridor they went up some winding stone steps. The woman stopped in front of a door. "Fräulein, this chamber is for you. You will find dry clothing inside the trunk against the wall."

"Thank you very much." Katerina went into the room but did not shut the door. Instead, she listened and peeked out as the servant and Steffan stopped at the next door.

"Lord Steffan, here is your room. I shall bring you some of your brother's clothing, unless you think it won't fit you?"

"I think it will. Thank you."

The woman was coming down the hall in her direction. Katerina shut the door.

She quickly found a long linen chemise and a lovely silk dress that laced up the sides embroidered with flowers around the neckline and sleeves. She stripped off her wet clothes and left them by the door and donned the clothes from the trunk, which smelled of dried lavender and pennyroyal.

She sat unbraiding her hair and squeezing out the excess water when a servant girl opened the door and came in. "I am to start a fire for you." She knelt before the fireplace. Her hair was pulled up into a knot on her head. She looked to be less than twenty years old but more than fifteen.

"Our Frau says you are to come down for supper in half an hour, and you may have a warm bath tonight after the servants are free from supper duties."

"Thank you."

The girl glanced over her shoulder at her. "You are very beautiful. But you have probably heard that many times before. Are you married to Lord Steffan?"

Katerina sucked in a breath and started coughing, as a bit of saliva went down the wrong way. When she was finally able to speak, she said, "Thank you, but no, I am not married to Lord Steffan, or to anyone."

"You are very fair of face. You should make the young lord marry you and not travel the country alone with him, if you don't mind me saying so."

Katerina crossed her arms over her chest. Her first impulse was to tell the girl she had no reason to say such a thing, that she was only traveling alone with Steffan to save a group of children from an evil man. But it served no purpose to be angry with the young woman.

"I would never try to force Lord Steffan to marry me. We are working together on a special quest. He can marry whomever he pleases. I'm only interested in helping my town of Hamlin." But was that true? Was she *only* interested in helping the children and people of Hamlin? Perhaps she did also have a slight interest in helping make sure Steffan stayed well and made it to Hagenheim alive, for his own sake as well as for the children. But she didn't have to tell this young woman that. Soon the servant had the fire crackling and giving off a bit of heat.

"Lord Steffan is quite handsome," she said, getting up off her knees. "If I were as pretty as you are, I would certainly try to make him marry me." She smiled, curtsied, and left.

She was outspoken for a servant girl. But she was right about Steffan being handsome. Kat had always thought so, even when she thought he was arrogant.

A memory of Steffan came into her mind of him holding her hand to his cheek. How sweet he had looked, his blue-gray eyes gazing into hers. Her hand tingled just thinking about it. Was he feeling well, or might he have another fever after riding in the rain? Perhaps she should go and make sure he was reapplying his healing salve.

Kat went to the door and looked out. No one was in the corridor, so she slipped out and went to Steffan's door. She knocked lightly.

Her stomach roiled queasily. Why had she come to Steffan's door? What would he think of her? Perhaps he hadn't heard her knock and she could go back to her room and he would never know that she had been there. She turned and started back down the corridor to her room.

The door opened. "Katerina? Is everything all right?"

She turned around and faced him. He wasn't wearing shoes, but otherwise he was completely dressed in a snow-white shirt that laced up the front, loosely tied over his chest. His hair was still wet and hung over one side of his forehead.

He motioned with his hand. "Come in."

When she slowly started walking back to him, he smiled. Her stomach turned a flip. She stepped into his room and he shut the door. Was it wise to go into his room?

"I just wanted to make sure you were putting the healing salve on your wounds, that you didn't forget . . . to do that."

"We have to go to supper soon, but sit." He motioned to a chair.

Kat was not sure she wanted to sit, so she stood, staring up at him. Stupidly remembering the servant girl's words about him being handsome and how she should marry him.

"So, did you? Put on the salve?"

"Yes, the healer came and looked at it. She insisted on using her own supply of it and rebandaged me." He pulled up his sleeve to show the bandage on his arm.

"Oh good. I should go back to my room then." She started toward the door.

"I don't mind if you stay."

"I don't want the servants to talk. One already asked me if we were married." Why had she said that? Why would she ever say the word *married* to Steffan? Her cheeks heated.

"You do not care about that, do you?"

She turned to face him again. He was clearly amused, grinning, with one brow cocked up.

"Or were you horrified that anyone would think you would marry a brute like me?" He was still smiling.

"I told her no, that we were on a quest together."

He nodded, his smile fading. "Of course. Did you tell her we were only friends?" He leaned toward her, quite close to her.

She swallowed, her eyes staring at his shirt. A bandage was just visible where the lacing was not cinching very tightly. "No,

I . . ." She had to swallow again as she found herself leaning away from him. "I don't remember what I said." Then she laughed. Could he tell she was laughing because she was nervous? Did she seem as daft as she felt?

"I'm very sorry you can't meet Gabe and Sophie. I know they would love you."

Love her? She tried to take a deep breath, but her chest was too tight.

"And I think you would like them too."

"I am sure I would like them. If your brother is as . . . amiable as you are."

"I am amiable?"

"Yes. Sometimes."

He smiled. "Remember when you told me I was not welcome in Hamlin and I should go back to Hagenheim, that day in the bakery? You did not think me amiable then."

"I didn't say that!"

"You certainly did."

Her face burned as she remembered . . . she'd said exactly that. "I did not know you. I thought you were an arrogant son of a duke who was only meddling."

"Is that supposed to be an apology?" He laughed good-naturedly.

"I realized later that you were not . . . what I thought, that you were brave and . . ." She swallowed again. How could she escape this?

"And . . . that you could trust me?" He was staring very intently into her eyes, his voice a gruff whisper. "You know I would never hurt you."

"I know." She couldn't look into his eyes anymore. She put

her arms around him and buried her face in his chest. His arms immediately surrounded her, holding her gently but firmly.

She closed her eyes. She didn't want to think. For once, she only wanted to feel as she let her hand rest over his heart, feeling the bandage underneath. Her heart thumped in her chest. His words, *I would never hurt you*, reverberated inside her. No one could hurt her as long as his arms were around her.

She remembered how he'd protected her from the Beast of Hamlin, from Hennek's men. No one had ever protected her before. No one. It felt so good.

But what would happen now? When he said he would never hurt her, he probably didn't mean hurting her heart. Would he hurt her without meaning to?

She should let go and push out of his arms. Yes, that's what she should do. She would pretend she was only a friend embracing another friend. It meant nothing. She took a surreptitious breath, breathing in the smell of his shirt—herbs and his own unique smell—and loosened her hold on him. She took a tiny step back, but the expression on his face . . . She couldn't help herself. She reached up and pressed her palm against his cheek.

His eyelids instantly lowered. Her heartbeat quickened. His hand was on her face and he was bending close, so close. She put her other hand behind his head and kissed him.

Lips touching lips . . . What was she doing? Her heart was beating in her throat. She thought she'd never be able to kiss a man. But Steffan . . . He was so gentle and protective. She would have been daft *not* to kiss him.

"I'm sorry, I shouldn't—" Kat pulled away and turned her head.

Steffan gently pulled her back, and she kissed him again. Yes, *she* was kissing *him*. He was letting her kiss him. She was in control. But the kiss became too much, so she pulled away and pressed her face into his shoulder.

She could hear his breathing, feel the strength in his arms holding her. But her cheeks flamed hot at what she had done.

"Katerina." His breath was in her hair, his voice sending shivers across her shoulders. "You're wonderful. Have I told you that you are brave and beautiful and . . ." He sighed, pulling her closer.

Fear gripped her, constricting her throat. What was she afraid of? Was she afraid because she had kissed a man she didn't love? No, because she was fairly certain she did love him. Was she afraid he would take advantage of her now? No. Was she afraid that he didn't love her enough to marry her and that she would be humiliated?

Yes. That was it.

She couldn't let him know what she was thinking. So she stood motionless, letting him hold her, letting herself enjoy this while she could. Because it couldn't last.

A knock sounded at the door. Kat jumped. Steffan kept his arms around her.

"Who is it?" Steffan said to the closed door.

"Supper is being served," the voice said.

"Thank you. We will be there."

Kat gently extricated herself from his arms. She couldn't look him in the eye and kept her head down.

Steffan took her hand in his and gently squeezed it. "Shall we go?"

She glanced quickly up at him. His gentle expression made her heart skip a beat. What was she to do now? This was more frightening than two Beasts of Hamlin. She squeezed his hand and let him walk her to the door and down to supper.

Steffan and Katerina were the only ones at the table in the Great Hall for supper. He and Katerina talked about their journey thus far, about the children and how they might get back to Hamlin once they had defeated Hennek. And even though their kiss was never far from his mind, neither of them even alluded to it. He was too afraid of offending her in some way, or embarrassing her, or otherwise causing her not to want to ever kiss him again.

It was a pity he was seated at the head of the table and therefore he wasn't close enough to Katerina to hold her hand. Would she let him?

Near the end of the meal, he asked for one of the guards to come so he could ask him some questions.

"How many guards did Lord Gabe leave here?"

"Most of his guard accompanied Lord Gabe and Lady Sophie to Poland to visit Lord Wolfgang. There are only six left here. Will you need us to accompany you and the lady to Hagenheim?"

"No." He'd already thought about this. "Our enemy's name is Hennek Grymmelin, the Bürgermeister of Hamlin. He could come here looking for us, and he will have many men with him. You need every guard to help defend the castle. You should warn all the male servants as well. There is no knowing what he might do if he thinks we have been here."

"I understand. But perhaps you should take at least one soldier with you."

"Yes, perhaps one guard would be good."

"Very good. Our lord would want us to protect his brother and his lady."

He glanced at Katerina. She kept her gaze on the table in front of her. Was she about to tell the man, most emphatically, that she was not his lady? He could certainly imagine her doing so. But she remained silent.

"We could each use a fresh horse and provisions."

"Of course."

Soon he and Kat were heading upstairs. They would need as much sleep as they could get before sunrise.

He walked her to her door, his heart thumping. She was so quiet and avoided holding his hand on the way back to their rooms. Was she sorry she had kissed him?

"Sleep well," she said as she pushed open her door, not meeting his eye.

He caught her hand and kissed it. "Good night, my Katerina."

She met his eye for the briefest moment, then disappeared inside her room and closed the door.

So she was being demure now. Perhaps that was wise. But he would not forget that she had kissed him. And his hope was strong that she would eventually kiss him again. And even though he didn't deserve her, he was becoming a better man, was he not? And someday, with God's help, he might come close to deserving her.

Twenty-One

Katerina was dressed and ready before the sun was more than a gray bit of light chasing the darkest part of the night away. A knock came at her door and she opened it to Steffan.

They walked side by side, so close their arms were touching, so she slipped her hand under and over his arm. He smiled down at her.

"Did you apply your healing salve?"

"I did. The healer came early to wrap the bandages."

"That was kind of her."

When they reached the stable, where people might see them, Katerina let go of his arm and kept her distance. Their saddlebags were full of provisions and the stable groomsmen were saddling their horses. Kat and Steffan mounted their fresh horses. Soon they were galloping down the castle mount with one of the Hohendorf guards.

It was a long, hard day. The new guard spoke very little, and his presence kept Steffan from talking very much either. But Kat caught Steffan staring at her several times with a look on his face that she had seldom seen—a slight smile on his lips and a softness about his eyes. Sometimes it made her blush, as it caused her thoughts to go to their kiss. And that made her wonder what the future held. Which made her think, *How can this end well? It can't*. And then she chided herself into staying focused on what was important: rescuing the children.

They arrived in Hagenheim just before sunset, tired, hungry, and thirsty, as they hadn't taken time to avail themselves of their provisions for the last several hours.

They rode their horses through the Hagenheim Castle gate. This castle was as broad and spread out as Hohendorf Castle was high. *This is where Steffan grew up.* Was he nervous about seeing his family for the first time in more than a year? But then . . . she'd also be meeting his family. The duke. The duchess. Would they be able to look at Steffan and her and know that she'd kissed their son?

She said a quick prayer and kept her eyes straight ahead.

———◦◦◦———

Steffan rode toward his home with Kat and the guard from Hohendorf. Would Father and Mother be angry with him for waiting so long to come home? Father's guards stared, and he recognized most of them. Then one broke into a smile as they approached. "Steffan? Is that you?"

A memory flashed in Steffan's mind of getting drunk with this man and taking all the other guards' clothes while they were asleep and hiding them in a field. His stomach sank at the remembrance.

"Yes, and this is Katerina of Hamlin. It is urgent that we speak to Father."

One guard hurried inside the castle while another called for a groomsman to take their horses to the stable.

Steffan dismounted and then assisted Kat down from her

horse. Two of the guards opened the doors, and he escorted her inside.

He'd never noticed before how high the ceilings were as they walked past the Great Hall to Father's library door, where he suddenly appeared.

A lump formed in Steffan's throat as Father started toward him.

"Son. Steffan." He grasped him in a tight embrace. Steffan had to clear his throat to chase away a sob.

"Father." He hugged his father back, but a wave of shame crashed over him, of all the bad things he'd done, of the way he'd left over a year ago, practically sneering in his father's face. But this prolonged embrace . . . His father had forgiven him, even though he didn't deserve it, hadn't even asked for forgiveness yet.

He cleared his throat again. "Father?"

Finally the duke loosened his hold and stood back, looking at Steffan's face. "It is good to see you, son. We've missed you."

"It is good to see you too." He coughed. "Father, this is Katerina of Hamlin, the stepdaughter of Bürgermeister Hennek Grymmelin."

Father gave Katerina a serious smile. "I am pleased to meet you, Fräulein Katerina. I pray all is well in Hamlin."

"No, Your Grace, I am sorry to say all is not well. We need your help."

Katerina looked grim and serious . . . and beautiful.

"Please, come into my library so you can speak freely."

They went into the place where his father wrote letters and met with various people who had business with him. They all sat, but on the edges of their seats.

"Go ahead. What is the trouble?" He looked from Steffan to Katerina.

Katerina began the story while Steffan's mind flitted from

Katerina to the rest of his family. Soon he would be able to see his mother again. Would his shame outweigh his joy? But he attuned his mind to the present moment and listened to his Katerina speak in a clear voice about why they were there.

When they had entered the castle, Katerina had tried to walk as regally as she could, but since she knew nothing about being regal, she decided to remember that she'd killed the Beast of Hamlin and rescued fifty-two children, and that helped her hold her head up high.

Duke Wilhelm was tall and broad-shouldered, very much like Steffan, but with gray hair mixed with dark brown. Though he must have been over fifty years old, he was quite handsome, and there was a strong resemblance between him and Steffan.

She had watched as the two men embraced. Tears pricked her eyes at the way they held on to each other. This was how good fathers treated their sons. And the way Steffan kept clearing his throat told her more than words could.

Then the duke had led them into a room full of books and shelves, chairs and a desk, and he had asked them to tell him why they were there. Katerina was explaining, "The mayor of Hamlin has kidnapped fifty-two children and trapped them in a mine underneath the town of Hamlin, where he has been working them as his slaves."

"He has kidnapped fifty-two children? When did this happen?"

"Over the course of the past year."

"Why have I not heard about this?" Anger hardened the duke's expression.

"Hennek did not wish you to hear of it. He warned the people not to speak of it to outsiders, and people who had heard about it thought it was a myth or fairy tale. The Bürgermeister and his men were using two large wolves that they had captured and held in cages to attack anyone who came near the entrance to the mine. He made everyone think it was the Beast of Hamlin that had taken the children and killed and eaten them. But actually, he and his men had been stealing children off the streets of Hamlin and putting them to work in an underground silver mine."

Duke Wilhelm was gazing at her very intensely.

"Steffan and I were captured by Hennek's men and placed in the mine, but we escaped with the children."

"And where are the children now?"

"We left the children at Keiterhafen with some kind women who took them in and promised to keep them safe."

"And what do you believe Hennek will do if he finds the children?"

Kat turned to Steffan and let him answer.

"He will kill them."

Duke Wilhelm said, "We must go at first light to Keiterhafen and then on to Hamlin. I will have my men prepare for the journey."

Kat breathed a sigh. She was eager to get the children back together with their families, and now she had a powerful ally in the Duke of Hagenheim. But Hennek would not back down without a fight. For him, everything was at stake.

Steffan had not seen his mother yet. His sister Adela, who was now grown up and quite pretty, took charge of Katerina and they went off to get her a change of clothes. Then, while Father discussed the trip with the captain of his guard and what they were going to do to rescue the children, Steffan went in search of his mother.

As he reached the top of the steps and the corridor that led to his mother's bedchamber and solar, there she was, coming toward him.

"Steffan!" She ran the rest of the way to him, and he caught her in his arms.

"Mother. I'm so sorry. I'm so sorry."

Mother was crying and laughing at the same time. She clasped his head in her hands and looked into his face. "I'm so happy to see you, Steffan, my son."

He hugged her close and buried his face in her long hair. She must have been getting ready for bed, because her hair was hanging loose.

"They told me you were home and I could hardly believe it. I'm so pleased. Are you hungry?"

"Always feeding us." Steffan gazed down at his mother. As a child he'd thought she was the most beautiful woman he'd ever seen. She was still quite beautiful, but now with wrinkles around her eyes and a crease on either side of her mouth. Her hair had a lot more gray than he remembered.

"How are you, Mother?"

"I am well. You look well and strong. Are you?"

"I am quite well, Mother. I want to tell you that I'm sorry for all the bad things I did."

She touched his cheek. "You are forgiven, my son. I love you."

"I want you to know that I've changed. I don't want to do foolish things anymore."

"I want to hear about these changes. Will you tell me? Or do you want to wait to talk to both your father and me?"

"I am here." Father ascended the final step and stood only a few feet away.

Steffan swallowed the lump that rose in his throat. "I want to say that I am sorry I defied you, Father, and I regret I was so wild and unrestrainable when I was a boy. I led Wolfgang to do many bad things. But I mostly regret . . ." He clenched his teeth to stop the tears. "That I joined with the Teutonic Knights against your wishes, and that I killed innocent people and fought against my brother."

Mother put her arms around him, and Father came closer. He clenched his teeth harder.

"I'm so proud of you, son." Father put his hand on his shoulder. "I'm so proud of you."

Steffan cleared his throat and brushed away some wetness that had pooled in the corner of his eye. How could Father say he was proud of him? His other brothers had done noble things. Even his sisters were noble and brave. What had Steffan ever done that was noble and brave? Even killing the beasts and rescuing the children had been as much Katerina's doing as his.

"It takes a brave man to admit he was wrong." Father's voice was quiet. "I have never been prouder of anyone than I am of you now."

Steffan coughed and cleared his throat again. "There's one more thing. When Wolfie and I were children, something very bad happened, and it was my fault. Do you recall Heinlin, the boy who was beaten to death by his father? I was the one who convinced him to chase the sheep. He didn't want to, but I persuaded him and Wolfgang to do it. It was my fault the sheep fell over the cliff. And it was my fault we didn't tell you about it, Father. Wolfie tried to talk me into it. He told me we should tell you how upset Heinlin was and that he was afraid of his father. It's all my fault. And I'm sorry."

Steffan's throat ached. Mother rubbed his shoulder, and her face was downturned, but he knew she was crying.

"You were a child, Steffan. But I understand how you must feel, that you've carried this burden for a long time. And I'm glad you're laying it down now. Your mother and I have already forgiven you. You just have to believe that God forgives you too."

Mother embraced him, hugging him tight, and Father also put an arm around him.

"We must have a feast," Father said, "for my son was lost, but now is found." His voice choked on the last word. And if Steffan's eyes weren't exactly dry, then neither were his father's, so he wasn't ashamed. Besides, no one saw except Mother.

Katerina glanced over her shoulder at Steffan. He was talking with his father as his younger sister, Adela, took her to her room to find her some clothes to change into.

"Here is a chemise for you to sleep in tonight," she said, draping a thin linen underdress over Kat's arm, "and here is a dress for tomorrow."

"I can wear the clothes I have on tomorrow. I'll be riding back to Keiterhafen in the morning."

"Riding out again?"

"Yes, we left some children there. They were taken from their homes and now the man who took them wants to kill them."

"Oh! That is terrible! I am certain that Father will kill that man for you. My father never allows injustice. Is that why you and Steffan came here?"

"Yes. I—"

"Oh! Mother will be so happy to see Steffan again! I hope he is not as angry as he used to be."

"He used to be angry?"

"Yes, at Father mostly. He and Father used to get into arguments all the time. And Steffan teased my older sisters and made them cry sometimes." Adela chewed on her lip.

"He doesn't sound like a very good brother. But perhaps he has changed."

"Yes, Wolfgang told my mother and father that he had changed. Something happened, I'm not sure exactly what, when they were both soldiers fighting in Poland."

Katerina talked with Adela while she picked out one of her own dresses for her to wear and helped her lace it up. It surprised Kat that she and Adela were the same age, as Adela seemed so young and innocent and unburdened. Steffan's sister was so pretty, with her light-colored hair—the same color as Steffan's—and her sweet smile and carefree manner. As Katerina listened to her, she wondered how she, Katerina, would have been different if she'd lived a privileged life as a duke's daughter. Would she have been irritable and demanding, like some of the wealthy burghers' daughters she knew? Or would she be like this girl—guileless and kind, friendly and open?

What she said about Steffan made her heart ache. Life must have been painful for him if he was as angry as Adela said. He didn't seem very angry now. Now he seemed remorseful and eager to prove himself.

"I hope Steffan is having a good talk with your mother and father."

"Oh, I am sure they are. He's been away so long, I'm sure they will be too happy to argue with each other. Do you think Steffan has changed, like Wolfgang said?"

"Well, I didn't know him before, but he doesn't seem very angry at all." *Not nearly as angry as I have been.* In fact, she had goaded him greatly in the beginning, throwing unfair accusations at him, and he had borne it with hardly a single heated word back at her. "I think perhaps he has changed since he went away a year ago, based on his manner to me."

"Oh? Have you spent much time with him?"

"Yes. At least, for the last week or two."

Adela finished lacing up the back of Katerina's dress. "Can I braid your hair? I love braiding other people's hair."

"Of course. Thank you." Kat sat on a stool while Adela went behind her again and started brushing out Kat's long brown hair.

"What do you think of my brother?" Adela asked.

"Steffan is very brave. He never gives up. He feels remorse for things he's done wrong, and he's very protective of people who are in danger. He is kind and strong and determined. He's also amusing when he wants to be, but not in a cruel way."

"I hope he doesn't drink too much, like he used to."

"No, I don't think he likes to drink anything stronger than wine, and he refused to drink in excess with my stepfather."

"I am glad to hear that." Adela was gently tugging on her hair as she braided it. She said softly, "You haven't met my mother yet, have you? I have a feeling we are all going to love you. All done."

Adela came around and grinned as she took Kat's hand. "Come. I want you to meet Mother."

They walked out into the corridor just as a woman was emerging from another room down the hall.

"Mother! You must meet Katerina. Have you seen Steffan yet?"

"Yes, we were just talking, Father and Steffan and I."

The woman had a softness about her that reminded Kat of her own mother. She smiled at Katerina and came toward them. "Katerina, I am Rose, Steffan's mother."

Kat dropped a curtsy. "Your Grace, it is my pleasure."

"I've been talking too much," Adela said with an apologetic smile. "But I'm sure Mother and I would love to hear, Katerina, how you came to be riding all the way from Hamlin with my mischievous brother."

"Oh, well, it is a rather lengthy tale. Lady Rose will want to spend time with Lord Steffan."

"He is changing his clothes now," Steffan's mother said. "He will be downstairs soon. But come into the solar where we can sit and be comfortable. I would very much enjoy hearing this tale."

They all walked up the stone staircase to a large room with rugs on the floor and chairs with cushions. When Adela and Lady Rose were seated and looking expectantly at her, Kat considered for a moment how she might shorten the tale.

She told them briefly how Steffan had come to town offering to help kill the Beast of Hamlin, explaining how they had killed not one but two beasts, then said, "Lord Steffan and I were captured by a dangerous and wicked man—my stepfather. Lord Steffan was very brave and helped us escape—he and I and fifty-two children whom the mayor of Hamlin was holding as slaves."

Lady Rose shook her head, her eyes wide. "You have been through quite an ordeal, my dear. Are you all right?"

"Yes. But you would be very proud of Lord Steffan. He stayed awake for two days and nights to make sure we all made it to safety. And now the children are with some families in Keiterhafen who are guarding them until we can get back there and take them home. But we must hurry, because my stepfather is looking for them."

"Do you mean Steffan did all that?" Adela's eyes were big and her mouth hung open. "I can hardly imagine. You are both so brave."

"Yes, you certainly were," Lady Rose said, taking Katerina's hand. "My dear, thank you for coming here so that the duke can help you save those children. I am sure I have much to thank you for." Her eyes were watery as she spoke, then she hugged Kat. Kat returned Steffan's mother's embrace, imagining that the gentle woman somehow knew that Katerina had kissed her son. But of course she couldn't know. It was not as if it were written across her face. But did she know Kat had fallen in love with him?

When Lady Rose pulled away, she held on to Kat's shoulders and gazed intently into her eyes. "You are very brave and very beautiful."

"Thank you." Kat had to blink back the tears, suddenly missing her own mother.

"And now the servants are preparing a feast, and I believe the Minnesingers will be playing downstairs soon. Katerina, wouldn't you like to rest for an hour or so?"

She was perhaps more tired than she'd realized. "That sounds lovely, actually."

Adela tugged on her arm again. "Let me take you to my room. You can sleep on my bed and then you will feel like dancing!"

Katerina laughed. She couldn't imagine dancing in front of Steffan's parents, but she didn't want to contradict Steffan's sweet and lovely sister.

The evening was enjoyable, though she did not dance. Instead, she sat at the table with Steffan and his mother and father, Adela, and Steffan's brother Valten and his beautiful wife, Gisela. The Minnesingers did play and sing, and when it was getting late, Steffan reached for her hand under the table. She let him enfold her fingers in his, enjoying the thought that he wanted to hold her hand as much as the actual holding.

He looked sad when Adela motioned to Kat and said, "Time for bed," and Kat let go of his hand before anyone could see.

The next morning at dawn they were all saddling up—Katerina, Steffan, Duke Wilhelm, and twenty of his soldiers. The duke had decided that Valten would stay and help protect Hagenheim.

Lady Rose embraced first Katerina, then Steffan. She let go of her son as the duke wrapped an arm around her. "We must go." Then he bent to kiss her lips.

What would it be like to be loved as Lady Rose was by the duke? Katerina wished she knew, and she wished her mother knew. But instead, her mother had married Hennek and suffered through his accusatory, bragging, hypocritical abuse. Life seemed so unfair sometimes.

But she didn't have time to dwell on that.

Steffan helped her mount the horse Duke Wilhelm had provided for her, boosting her into the saddle, his hand clasping hers for a moment as he stared up into her eyes. Then he went and mounted his own horse.

She was glad no one asked her if she was uncomfortable riding with so many men. She took it as a compliment that they didn't try to talk her into staying in Hagenheim. Truthfully, it did make her uncomfortable to be the only woman riding with these strange men. But Duke Wilhelm was a good man and would not allow anyone to harm her. Still, she was thankful Steffan stayed close to her, even though they were not able to talk freely.

The first night on the road, they camped in a fallow field beside a stream. Duke Wilhelm invited her to sit between him and Steffan as they gathered around their fire and ate. She liked to think that if the other men weren't around, Steffan would have tried to hold her hand. And she would have let him.

While the other men were mostly talking amongst themselves, Duke Wilhelm asked them questions and Steffan and Kat told him more details of the past week's events.

The duke's expression was very intense as he listened to her, his eyes only leaving her face to glance at his son.

"Your son is very brave and noble. He protected me several times. He placed himself between me and the giant wolf that was attacking us. And he helped the children escape who had been trapped so long in the mine they hardly remembered what the sun looked like. He killed three guards and carried the children out. He was tireless in seeing that they were safe."

"Katerina is the one who deserves the praise," Steffan said. "She was determined to save the children. I was only helping her. She risked her life constantly."

"You are too modest." Kat's eyes met his and they exchanged a look that made her heart flutter. But when she glanced back at Duke Wilhelm, he seemed to have taken note of the look as well. Her cheeks heated and she stared down at her feet.

She slept near Steffan and Duke Wilhelm, and she felt as safe as she had at any time in her whole life. The guards also seemed like good men. They did not eye her salaciously, did not send crude grins her way or look her up and down the way Hennek's guards did, and they did not even try to talk to her. Duke Wilhelm had treated her like a daughter, even though he had only known her for a day.

Anyone who thought wealthy, powerful dukes were arrogant and conceited had never met Duke Wilhelm.

And with that thought, she drifted off to sleep.

Twenty-Two

Steffan kept thinking about Katerina's words praising him for being brave, and it was as if a deep wound were being healed, even more so when his father said again, in front of Katerina, that he was proud of him. But Steffan wanted more than anything to be able to prove himself somehow, to redeem himself in his father's eyes and prove his worth to Katerina. He had told her about the bad things he had done, and he wanted to show her that was not the kind of man he intended to be in the future.

After almost a full day of riding, they made it to Keiterhafen and stopped within sight of the gate.

"Father, let me go in first. Too many men riding into town will attract Hennek's attention. Let me go to Frau Goschen's home and see that all is well, then we can all take charge of the children and get back to Hamlin."

Father seemed to be thinking about it. Finally, he said, "I will let you go in and speak to Frau Goschen, but then come back here. If you aren't back in an hour, we're coming to find you."

Steffan nodded, then urged his horse forward, slowing to a walk as he went in through the gate.

A man on the street up ahead, tall and broad, caught Steffan's attention. Was he one of Hennek's men? The closer he got, the more he was sure he had never seen him before. But he could still be one of Hennek's guards.

He checked his surroundings, then headed to Frau Goschen's home. He went around to the back and knocked on the kitchen door. He encountered a servant, a young man.

"Is Frau Goschen at home?" Steffan asked.

The man stared at him a moment. "Yes."

"And the children? It's all right. I am Frau Goschen's friend."

"Yes."

"No problems, then?"

"No."

"Very good." Steffan went inside, brushing past the young man, and went through the corridor. He hadn't gone very far when he heard a childish voice yell, "Steffan!"

He turned and spotted one of the boys from the mine, one of the little ones whom he had carried part of the way to Keiterhafen.

Steffan squatted and waited for the boy to walk to him.

The boy was shy now, walking slowly. Steffan hugged him. "Where are the others? Have you been a good boy? I think you've grown since I last saw you."

The boy grinned. "We are playing with Frau Goschen's puppies. I told her that my mother likes puppies and would let me take one home."

"Puppies, eh?"

"We are all ready to go home. Are you here to take us back to Hamlin?"

"I certainly am. Just as soon as the Duke of Hagenheim gets here."

The boy whooped and jumped up. Then he grabbed Steffan's arm. "Come and tell the others."

"I can't stay long," Steffan said, "but I'll be back." But his last few words were drowned out by children's squeals and yells when the rest of the children saw him and came running. They jumped on him, some clasping him around the ankles and knees, until he collapsed on the floor and started tickling them.

Much laughter and squealing ensued, until Frau Goschen and another woman started clapping their hands to get the children's attention. They quickly quieted so that Frau Goschen's voice could be heard.

"Our friend has returned, I see." Frau Goschen affected a serious, scolding expression, but her eyes were twinkling.

"Were you afraid I'd leave you with these little rapscallions forever?" Steffan chucked a little girl under the chin and ruffled a little boy's hair. His heart expanded and filled his chest at seeing them so lively and happy. When had these children become so dear to him?

"All right, children. It's time for your midday meal. Anka will take you to the table." She clapped and shooed them off down the corridor with the woman who had been waiting behind her. When Steffan stood up, she said in a low voice, "I suppose this means the Duke of Hagenheim is nearby?"

"Yes."

In a whisper, she added, "Your Bürgermeister, Hennek Grymmelin, has been asking all around Keiterhafen about a large group of children who ran away from Hamlin."

Steffan's blood quickened. "He is here, then?"

"He and his men. I regret that I do not know any of our town's officials well enough to go to them and explain the whole story. I was afraid, lest whomever I told be corrupt. They might betray us and hand the children over to Hennek Grymmelin."

"That is wise." He had to find Hennek quickly, before he discovered the children. No doubt he'd be surrounded by his men, but perhaps . . .

"Frau Goschen, do you have something I could use to disguise myself? Perhaps some padding to make me look different? A walking stick and a large cape?"

"You should not be thinking of trying to find that bad man." The plump woman shook her finger at him. "You are far too handsome and distinct for anyone to mistake you for someone else."

"Handsome?" That made him smile. Did Katerina think him handsome? Distinct? What did she mean by that? "Do you not think I could disguise myself?"

"How will you cover up that scar over your eye? You have one under your eye as well. You're taller than most, and your hair is unusual as well. You will need to cut it."

"Will you do the honors, Frau Goschen?"

"I do not approve of you going after this bad man without the duke and his soldiers."

"I will be careful. I need to at least locate Hennek before Duke Wilhelm and all his men scare him away, so we can capture him. Can you cut my hair?" Katerina wouldn't mind him with shorter hair, would she? "Can you make it not look bad?"

"I have been cutting hair since I was a girl. I will make it look good." She gave him a knowing smile.

Soon he was sitting on a stool next to a window in the main room of the house. Using shears and a razor, she began cutting the hair he'd been growing for the last year. He knew it had gotten long, but he'd seen no reason to cut it. He'd had so very little money, he'd thought a haircut was an unnecessary expense. And he was too vain to just chop it off himself.

"How much are you cutting?" he asked as hunks of his light-colored hair landed on the floor around him.

"About a hand's length. You do want to look different, do you not?"

He grunted.

"Worry not. That pretty maiden, Katerina, will still think you very handsome. I daresay she will think you even more handsome with a nice haircut."

He grunted again. Was he so easy to read?

When she was finished, she handed him a looking glass. He did look better, less ragged and unkempt. "You did well, Frau Goschen."

"I know. Now come and let me find you some clothing to cover that handsome frame."

She found him a walking stick that had belonged to her father, she said. He practiced leaning on it, making himself look shorter.

"Now, keep this hood over your head and pulled low so people cannot see your eyes. And I see you have a week or two of beard. That is good. But we'll need to make it look gray so you don't look so young."

She went into the kitchen and made a paste with white wheat flour and water, then spread it on his beard, sprinkling in some additional flour. She even put some on his skin. Oh yes. He would look very handsome when Katerina came riding into town with Father and his army. But at least Hennek wouldn't recognize him, and that was the purpose.

Steffan took the looking glass from her hand. "I'm not a bad-looking old man."

Suddenly the front door opened with a bang and a familiar voice, high and anxious, came from inside the house. It was Albrecht.

Steffan gave Frau Goschen the looking glass and hurried into the corridor leading to the front door. Albrecht glanced at Steffan, but then ignored him, saying, "Where is Frau Goschen? I need to speak with her."

"Albrecht, it's me, Steffan."

His eyes widened and he stared. Steffan smiled, which seemed to help him recognize him, because he exclaimed, "Steffan! Oh, thank God. I need your help. Hennek has found our house. He has found the children. I managed to escape. I ran and came here for help."

"It's all right. We will save them. Can you tell me how to find the house where you were staying?"

"I know it," Frau Goschen said behind them. "It is on Hoherstrasse, and it's not far. Go right, then right again past the Red Boar Inn."

"I have my sword, but I need a helper, and he'll need some weapons. What do you have, Frau Goschen?"

She hurried away and came back with her husband's crossbow and arrows and a knife in its sheath.

"Being a baker, he doesn't have a lot of enemies," Frau Goschen said, as if to apologize.

"These are enough. I thank you. Now, Albrecht, I'm going to need your help. I need you to stay out of sight. Frau Goschen, can you get him a hooded cloak that will cover most of his face?"

"Yes."

"And, Albrecht, I'll need you to help me by keeping the weapons nearby until I need them, but you'll have to stay out of sight. You're tall, but Hennek and his men still might realize you're one of the children."

Albrecht's eyes were shining as he gathered up the crossbow, the daggers, which he stuffed in his belt, and one of the swords.

But something about his face ignited a memory, and a cold shiver snaked down Steffan's spine. Could it be that he was about to get this child killed, as he had little Heinlin? The memory of it was so painful, he wished he had a strong drink to dull it.

No, he would not lead this boy into danger. "I've changed my mind. You have to stay here."

Albrecht's face fell.

"It's just that I . . . I don't want you to get hurt, and you know how evil Hennek and his men are."

"I have an idea," Frau Goschen said. "I will have my servant Klaus go with Albrecht. The two of them can stay out of sight but be there to guard your weapons. Is that good?"

Steffan nodded, even though he wanted to order Albrecht to stay far away. But he sensed that would hurt Albrecht's pride, who had shown himself so brave.

"And you should round up as many men as you can to defend this house, and get word to the other houses as well, but do it discreetly. You don't want to attract Hennek's attention."

So many children's lives were at stake. Should he go and fetch Father? No, he didn't have time to wait. Hennek had already discovered some of the children and would no doubt discover the rest soon.

Steffan had to stop Hennek from killing the children. He wasn't sure he could live with himself if he allowed them to die.

He took a deep breath, hiding his sword under his cloak, and set out toward Frau Gruber's house.

Twenty-Three

Steffan prayed as he walked. *God, I know I have a lot to confess. I've not been a very good person. But please let me save these children, not because I'm good, because I'm not, but because You are good. Bring about justice for these children and for Katerina, because You are a God of justice, and this man is evil.*

Albrecht and Klaus were keeping to the far side of the street, each of them carrying weapons in a pack on their back, too lumpy to show what was in them. As soon as Steffan spotted the house, they turned down a narrow side street and disappeared.

A guard was standing outside the front door—Otto.

Steffan remembered to disguise his walk by limping and using his walking stick. Otto was staring hard at him as he approached. Steffan said in a jovial voice, "I am Herr Obenfettel, the leader of the town council. I have learned that the Bürgermeister of Hamlin is staying at this house, and I wish to welcome him."

"How did you know that?" Otto narrowed his eyes at him.

"Bürgermeister Hennek Grymmelin is an old friend, and he sent word to me. Did you not know?"

"You have to wait here." Otto turned and went inside the house, locking the door with a grinding of metal on metal as soon as he closed it.

Steffan hurried to the corner of the house and turned down the narrow alley, where there was just enough room between the house and the one next to it for three men to walk abreast. And at the other end of it were Albrecht and Klaus.

Steffan tried the latch on the first window he came to. It wasn't locked and turned with ease. He looked inside and saw a small sitting room that appeared empty. He climbed in, knocking over a small table and all that was on top of it, making a loud crash.

Albrecht handed him the loaded crossbow through the window. He already had his sword strapped to his back under his cloak.

Heavy footsteps approached, then crashed through the door. Steffan used both hands to aim and fire the crossbow.

The heavy bolt speared two men, one behind the other, sending them backward to the floor. When two more guards stepped over them to get to Steffan, he wielded his sword, clanging blades first with one, then the other, then leaping to the side to avoid being run through by one while crossing blades with the other as he placed the second guard's body between him and the first one.

Hennek's voice boomed through the house, "What is happening?"

Steffan aggressively thrust forward and stabbed his opponent in the neck, but took a cut to the arm in the process. He didn't have time to think about that as the other guard began attacking. But Steffan could see fear in his face as he beat the coward back against the wall and managed to take his sword away from him. The man's face turned ashen, and he fell to the floor as though dead.

Fainted. How could he kill an unconscious man? He turned away from him.

Hennek arrived in the doorway with Otto. "Get him!" Hennek shouted.

But at the same moment, a man's voice from the other side of the house cried, "The children are escaping!"

The plan had been for Albrecht and Klaus to sneak in the back during the fighting and commotion and help the children escape. They must have succeeded.

Hennek ran back the way he had come. Otto looked after Hennek, as if unsure whether to follow him or attack Steffan. Steffan looked down and saw that the crossbow had been reloaded. Klaus and Albrecht must have done it before they went to get the children.

Steffan snatched up the loaded crossbow as Otto roared, unsheathing his sword. But when he saw Steffan take aim, he turned and ran down the corridor.

Steffan ran after him, but the big, burly guard was faster than he looked. Steffan was afraid of missing him. He saved his arrow for when he would have a better shot, as Otto disappeared around a corner.

Steffan proceeded cautiously, lest another guard be waiting to ambush him at the end of the corridor, but no one was there, and the house was eerily silent. Then he saw the servants on the floor. They were tied up and knocked unconscious, it appeared.

He hurried out the back way, hoping to catch up with Hennek and Otto—and hoping they were not catching up to the fleeing children.

He lurked around the back alleys looking for Hennek and Otto. He had left his sword back at the house, having dropped it when he picked up the loaded crossbow. He had only the one arrow and a dagger hidden in his tall leather shoe.

He hurried down one alley and then the next, avoiding the main streets. The only house he knew of was Frau Goschen's, and since that was where Albrecht and Klaus were taking the children, he decided to head there and be sure they were safe.

He brushed past a woman pouring out a pan of dirty water into the street.

"Pardon me, Fräulein, but did two men pass this way?"

"I haven't seen anyone." She eyed his crossbow, but he hurried down to the corner and turned into an alley that followed the town wall. And just ahead was an old tower built into the wall.

The gate just inside it was open. He climbed the steps to the top, where he was able to look down on the streets of the town. There below him, not far from the tower, were Hennek and Otto. They were standing in an alley and peeking through a window into a house. He could only see the roof of the house from his vantage point, but if he was not mistaken, it was Frau Goschen's.

Steffan ran down the steps, his heart pounding and sweat trickling down his face. He shrugged out of his cloak since he no longer needed a disguise.

He rounded a corner and there was Otto, sword drawn in one hand, his other hand boosting Hennek through the window. Otto turned and saw him just as Hennek disappeared through the window.

"It's Steffan!"

Steffan aimed the crossbow at Otto. A drop of sweat dripped into his eye just before he pulled the trigger mechanism and shot the bolt.

He blinked away the offending drop in time to see Otto dodge to one side and the bolt sail past him, landing in the middle of the town square, harmlessly on the ground.

Otto charged him. Steffan turned, dropped his now-useless crossbow, and ran.

He ran as fast as he could, his heart pumping hard as he sucked in air. He headed straight to the house where he'd left his sword. He could hear Otto behind him, crashing into a woman carrying an armful of copper pans, sending them clanging to the cobblestones, letting Steffan know that he was right behind him.

Steffan made it to the house. He ran through the open back door, down the corridor, and into the room where he'd left his sword. He snatched it off the floor, then dove out the window, landing on his shoulder. He rolled, jumped to his feet, and ran back the way he had come, back to Frau Goschen's house.

As he ran, he glanced over his shoulder and saw Otto not far behind.

Steffan ran into the large cobblestone town square that opened up just outside Frau Goschen's front door. He held up his sword, pointed at Otto, and yelled, "This man is trying to steal away the children in Frau Goschen's house!"

People stopped what they were doing and stared. Otto also halted. The burly guard lowered his sword and glanced around with an angry glare.

"He works for an evil man who, even now, is inside threatening to harm her children!"

The people began muttering and looking at each other. A couple of men stepped forward and said, "What is going on here? Who are you?"

"I am Steffan, the son of Duke Wilhelm of Hagenheim." He paused while another murmur went through the crowd. Then he pointed at Otto. "Help me stop this man!"

Suddenly Frau Goschen appeared at the front door, her eyes

wild. She said, "That's not true. No one is trying to steal children from this house."

Frau Goschen was saying the words, but her body was stiff and her tone was tense. Then Steffan caught a glimpse of Hennek just behind her.

Steffan started walking toward Frau Goschen. Fear shone from her eyes, but she said nothing.

Otto was walking toward the house as well, but since Otto was closer, he would reach Frau Goschen first. Steffan increased his pace, but so did Otto.

"The children are safe with me," Frau Goschen said, no doubt because Hennek was holding a knife to her back—or worse, to one of the children's necks.

Steffan changed course and ran straight toward Otto, striking with his sword just two steps from Frau Goschen.

Otto's sword met his as their blades clashed again and again. Otto bested him in strength, but Steffan was a bit faster. Still, it seemed impossible to disarm him. Every time he made a move to try, Otto's grip stayed strong.

Otto started his own onslaught, pushing Steffan back. Steffan had to be careful not to lock swords with him, or else Otto might use his extra weight to shove him to the ground, which would mean certain death for Steffan.

Suddenly he heard the shouts and screams of children coming from behind Frau Goschen. The sound must have drawn Otto's attention for a moment, because Steffan was able to slip his blade past Otto's and nick him in the chin with his sword point.

Otto's expression was full of rage, and he began to beat at Steffan's sword indiscriminately, slashing and slicing. Steffan jumped forward and back, side to side, throwing Otto off-balance.

Finally, Otto struck to the right as Steffan jumped out of the way and quickly stabbed Otto's sword arm just above the wrist.

Otto's arm moved down in a defensive gesture, giving Steffan the chance to strike his hand, knocking Otto's sword to the ground.

They were quickly surrounded by men dressed in the colors of the Duke of Hagenheim. They grabbed Otto and subdued him. When Steffan looked up toward the doorway, he could see the children beating Hennek's face and head. Two were on his back and shoulders, and others were kicking his legs and biting his arms and hands.

Steffan's father strode toward him as his soldiers apprehended Otto and Hennek.

Twenty-Four

Katerina started running toward the children, but by the time she got there, they had Hennek on the ground, curled into a ball, his arms over his head. Frau Goschen was yelling and shaking her fist at him, looking as if she would have hit him if the children hadn't covered him completely. They had him so well in hand that she looked back at Steffan and saw that he was embracing his father, while Otto was being dragged away, obviously injured.

Some of the duke's men came and dragged Hennek away from the children, who seemed reluctant to stop pummeling him. One girl, who was probably about nine years old, kept screaming at him. A little boy, one of the youngest ones, stuck his tongue out at him. But Albrecht and Verena just watched as the guards apprehended him. They turned to each other, and triumphant smiles broke out on their faces. They hugged, then hugged the children, smiling and congratulating each other.

For his part, Hennek seemed relieved to be away from the children, who had given him a bloody lip and scratched his face and arms rather badly.

When Kat joined the children, they all cheered, and she cheered with them, kneeling to hug them.

"We did it, Katerina," one of the little ones said. "We stopped the bad man from hurting Frau Goschen."

"Yes, you did. I am so proud of you. You're so brave and strong, all of you."

The children beamed back at her before talking and laughing with each other and Frau Goschen. Perhaps getting the chance to fight back a little bit would help them be able to move past this terrible event in their lives.

Kat straightened and looked around for Steffan. He was surrounded by his father's men, who kept asking him questions. He had lines of sweat running down through the powder from his hairline to his beard. The healing salve must have done its work, as he seemed to have all his strength back. She only hoped he didn't reopen his wounds during the strenuous sword fight.

Finally, the men left off asking him questions, and he came striding toward her.

"I'm so glad you didn't get yourself killed," she said as he approached, "though you do look as if you dunked your head in a flour barrel."

"Oh. I nearly forgot my disguise." He looked sheepish as he ran a hand over his beard. "I need to shave this off. It's starting to itch."

Should she hug him? There were too many men around so she just smiled and said, "I'm pleased you were able to defeat Otto. How do your wounds feel now?"

"As good as healed." Steffan gave her a half grin. "And these children. Are they not nearly as fierce as I am?"

"Absolutely." She looked down at them as they played and jumped and danced around, as if they were normal, happy children who had not been torn away from their families and treated abominably.

Kat suddenly noticed a red line of blood marring Steffan's sleeve. Her stomach twisted.

"Your arm." She took hold of his wrist, lifted his arm, and pushed up his sleeve. "Is it bad?"

"Just a scratch."

"It doesn't look deep, but you should be sure and put the salve on it and bandage it."

"I will." His smile was gentle as he stared down at her. He brushed the back of his hand over her cheek, in his now-familiar way, his gaze settling on her lips.

A movement out of the corner of her eye drew her gaze to Duke Wilhelm walking toward them.

"I think it might be best to take Hennek back to Hamlin and put him on trial there," the duke said. "I will question the town council and anyone else who may have been helping him in his schemes."

Katerina said, "I have some papers hidden that may prove Hennek has been stealing money from the town treasury—or at least he was stealing before he started making so much money from the silver mine."

"And have you lived in Hamlin all your life, Katerina?"

"My family has lived there for three generations at least."

"You must know a lot of people there."

"I do."

"I will need someone who could help me discern who among the men of Hamlin are wise and of good character, to help me form a new town council. Would you be willing to help?"

"I would, yes." Katerina did know as much as, or more than, anyone in Hamlin about which men would make good advisors to the new mayor of Hamlin, especially after growing up in the same household with the corrupt mayor. Certainly anyone who colluded with Hennek—or was deluded by him—would not. Katerina paid attention and knew them all.

It meant a lot to her that Duke Wilhelm asked for her help and her opinions. That was more than most leaders would do. Not only was she a woman but she was very young. Still, she was well-educated. Very few men in Hamlin had the education she had had, thanks to Hennek's desire to boast about how generous he was to his stepdaughter.

The duke nodded. "Now I suppose we should find provisions and lodging for the night."

They proceeded to do just that after sending some men to tend to the family and servants at Frau Gruber's, whose injuries were not serious, and drag the remainder of Hennek's men off to the town's dungeon for safekeeping.

Steffan wanted to sleep in the stable with the other men, but the mayor of Keiterhafen adamantly insisted the Duke of Hagenheim and his son, and Katerina, sleep in his home. Steffan and Father were sharing a room, and Katerina was in the room across the corridor from them. After a good meal at the Bürgermeister of Keiterhafen's table, he and Father were preparing themselves for bed.

"Don't you want me to send for a healer?" Father asked him when they were alone. "Just to make sure your wounds are on the mend?"

"No, Father. I thank you, but I will just keep putting the salve on them. I am much better now."

"I am glad you are well. And I am very proud of you, son. I always believed you would do great things, right wrongs, and find your own way and purpose in life. A good purpose."

How could Steffan have been so angry with his father all those years? He'd felt slighted, and he felt his father didn't understand him, didn't care what he wanted. And he'd been so angry about being a younger son, without a place or an inheritance or a title.

"I must have seemed so foolish, always defiant and angry."

"You were young and frustrated. Most men feel that way, I think, at some point when they are young."

"You surely never felt that way. You were the oldest son of a duke. You knew exactly what you would do for the rest of your life."

"Not true. I was told whom I would marry. I was saddled with responsibilities, the pressure to lead, whether I wanted to or not. My father died when I was about your age and I had no choice but to take over, get married to my betrothed, and be the best duke I could, with no one to tell me how."

"I had not thought about it that way."

"But God was with me. I made mistakes, but I married a wonderful woman and had eight perfect children."

They both smiled at him calling Steffan and his siblings "perfect."

They talked for a few more minutes about new happenings in Hagenheim and the news of his siblings. Then Steffan said, "Katerina is the one who discovered what was happening to the children in Hamlin. Is she not a brave and exceptional young woman, Father?"

"She is indeed." Father was looking at him with knowing eyes.

"She is clever and wise beyond her years, and has made it her business to know everything about her town and its people. And she is very fair of face and form, do you not think?"

"Of course. Who would not think so?"

"Do you care for her?"

"Yes." It made his palms sweat to admit that.

"And she cares for you, I am sure."

"Why do you say that?"

"Do you not think she cares for you?"

"I . . ." He remembered her kiss. But she had made no effort to be near him since she and Father and all his men had arrived in Keiterhafen. Perhaps the kiss was only a fleeting fancy.

Father was still waiting for him to answer the question.

"I think she may care for me. But . . . I am not sure." Steffan had done so many terrible things in his life. "I know I don't deserve her."

Father raised his brows.

"She is a very good maiden who has done nothing but good in her life, while I have done many bad things and hardly any good, as you well know. I thought I could redeem myself if I could save these children and do a great, heroic thing, but I realize nothing can make up for what I did wrong." He turned away and faced the paneled wall of the wealthy mayor's home. He did not wish to talk about this anymore. Why had he said so much? He began counting the panes in the tall mullioned window to distract his painful thoughts.

"Katerina knows you have a good heart. An evil man is not sorry for what he has done and rarely if ever believes he is bad. You are not an evil man, Steffan. And Katerina is wise enough to recognize that."

Perhaps he wasn't evil like Hennek, but . . . "What have I done in my life that makes me worthy?"

"You aren't worthy because of what you've done, son, because no one can ever do enough to be truly worthy. You're worthy because God gave His Son to make us worthy."

What Father was saying was hard to grasp. In his mind he'd always been the lowest of his family.

"And you helped Katerina save fifty-two children." Father smiled.

It was true. He did help Kat save the children.

"You have a good heart that desires to do good. And if Katerina loves you, why not allow that to influence you to do more good deeds?"

"I am not certain she loves me. She does not hate me. That is all I know." And he could not have said that when he first met her. "Katerina does not give her trust easily, and she has good reason for that."

Katerina was tired and sore, her backside hurting from being in the saddle so much. She dreaded the day's journey tomorrow, but she was excited to think of bringing the children home to their parents, who would be so overjoyed to see them.

Had Duke Wilhelm thought of how he planned to take the children back? The little ones certainly could not ride on horseback the whole way. Most of them had probably never been on a horse. Perhaps she should go speak to him about it. He'd said that if she needed anything, or thought of anything the children needed, to tell him.

She opened her door and stuck her head out. Had they gone to bed already? A line of light streamed out from the crack of their door, which was not completely closed. She heard low voices, and then she heard her name.

Katerina held her breath and stepped out into the corridor. She crept closer to their door, trying to listen in.

"You can win her over," Duke Wilhelm was saying, his voice barely discernible.

Her heart tripped and thumped wildly in her chest. She couldn't let them catch her eavesdropping, but she desperately wanted to know if they were speaking about her.

Steffan made an undecipherable sound. ". . . didn't trust me . . ."

Duke Wilhelm mumbled something, his voice too low to hear. ". . . one never knows . . ." Then he cleared his throat. ". . . that I will need to appoint a new mayor of Hamlin. And since you have shown yourself to be brave and responsible, and I see so much more maturity in you, I have decided to appoint you, Steffan, the new Bürgermeister."

Katerina's heart jumped to her throat. Her first thought was how happy this would make Steffan, to know he had won his father's respect enough to be granted such a position. But the very next moment she felt a pang . . . of jealousy? Resentment? Envy? She would be a better mayor than Steffan, but a woman would never be granted such a position. Yet truly, Steffan couldn't know as much about the duties of a Bürgermeister as she did.

Her heart thudded heavily. She didn't like these ugly thoughts. She moved as noiselessly as she could over the smooth floor of the corridor back into her room and closed the door.

She didn't want to think these things about Steffan, didn't want to be envious or resentful. Steffan would make a good mayor. He would never take a bribe, never cheat the town or steal money. And it must mean so much to him that his father had so much confidence in him.

She had to be at peace with this, had to get her feelings under control, had to be pleased for Steffan. He would be living in Hamlin. That was good, was it not? She would be able to see him often. That was what she wanted, wasn't it? And if Steffan had any tender feelings for her . . . But perhaps everything would be different when he was the Bürgermeister.

Steffan couldn't speak for a moment. All the breath left him. Finally, when the air came rushing back, he said, "Father, I'm so honored that you would think of me as the new Bürgermeister."

"You will be a very good one. You are honest and good-hearted."

He'd never imagined himself as a mayor. Could he do it? He had always rather imagined himself as a knight—though that was not likely to ever happen now. Or the captain of a guard, perhaps even the captain of his father's guard, though that might be a bit strange, since most of his father's men knew him as a mischievous, immature boy.

Also, how would Katerina feel about him being mayor? Would she be pleased? Proud of him?

"Father . . ."

"Yes, son?"

"I'm not sure I am the best person to be mayor of Hamlin."

"Do you not wish to have the position? Is there a reason why you don't want to be Hamlin's mayor?"

Steffan thought about it a moment. "I have never desired such a position. I don't think I would like writing proclamations and having meetings with the town council. I'm a soldier." He didn't enjoy killing people either, but . . . "I enjoy protecting people." *Especially Katerina.*

"I will give this some more thought. And we should both pray and see if God will show us what His will is." A slow smile sneaked onto Father's face. "Don't give up on Katerina. If you want her, fight for her."

Almost as soon as they lay on their beds, Father was asleep. But Steffan lay awake thinking about Katerina, of her kiss, and how long it would be before he could talk with her again.

Twenty-Five

Katerina was glad to have the sun shining on her face the next morning, and even more pleased to be heading home to Hamlin with the children. The anticipation of seeing them reunited with their families thrummed in her veins. All but the ten orphans, who chose to stay in Keiterhafen with Frau Gruber and her husband. The woman seemed more than happy to have such a large number of children so suddenly. And her husband was smiling as they waved fare well.

Katerina rode her horse close to the children, who were riding on carts pulled by mules. She looked after them and even let them take turns riding in the saddle in front of her. Meanwhile, Duke Wilhelm's guards rode in a circle surrounding Hennek, whose hands were tied together and to his horse's pommel.

"I am innocent of these accusations," Hennek said several times. "It is a misunderstanding. I have been wronged, and I demand to be freed." But no one paid any attention to him.

They had been on the road only a few minutes when Steffan steered his horse to ride by her side.

"How are you feeling?" she asked him before he could say anything.

"I am well."

"Your wounds are not paining you?"

"No, no pain. The healing salve has done what it is famous for."

This was what she would have said to him if she had not over-heard his conversation with his father last night, and she was determined not to treat him differently. It stung that Steffan, an outsider, would be made mayor of Hamlin. But it shouldn't. And she shouldn't be angry or resentful of him. It wasn't Steffan's fault. She should be angry that men never thought women capable enough to be mayors or leaders.

But the truth remained that she resented the very thought of Steffan being mayor, sitting in the same seat that Hennek had occupied for more than ten years. Men born to privilege, they thought everything should be easy for them. And it was! They were given land, towns, wealth, even people. It was their birthright, and they felt entitled to it.

But it was hard to be angry when she noticed the way his mouth looked slack and soft when he looked at her, while his brows were low and intense. He'd washed the flour out of his hair and had shaved—thank goodness. She liked the rugged way he looked with a couple of days' stubble, but the beard made him look bedraggled. Clean-shaven was his best look—sweet and a bit boyish, a good combination with his height, muscles, and broad shoulders. But she truly did not care about muscles or broad shoulders. She cared about Steffan's heart, his kind ways, his gentleness to the vulnerable, and his fierceness against oppressors.

"Are you glad to be going back to Hamlin?" he asked.

"Yes. Are you?"

He seemed to consider for a moment, then said with a smile, "Yes."

Yes, of course you are. You are about to become mayor.

"I know your mother and father were glad to see you again after such a long time away."

"Yes, they were." His expression grew much more sober and he stared down at his horse's neck. "They have always been better parents to me than I deserve."

"Are you not pleased they were glad to see you?"

"Yes, of course. I told them I was sorry for defying my father and fighting on the side of the Teutonic Knights."

"All is forgiven now, I suppose."

"They forgive me for the things I did to them. I only hope God can forgive me for the terrible things I did, for killing innocent people just because I wanted to be a knight."

He looked so sorry. It was a terrible thing. And Steffan would have to deal with it for the rest of his life. But at least he wasn't like Hennek. Steffan was admitting what he had done. Hennek never admitted any wrongdoing, even now that he'd been caught.

"Steffan was a knight?" one of the children exclaimed in a childish squeal.

Kat turned to the children riding on the cart next to her. "Listening to other people's conversations when they are unaware is very impolite." But her words convicted her, after what she'd overheard, and stayed to listen to, last night.

The children only giggled.

"When we stop again, I'm going to tickle all of you," Steffan warned.

That ignited a few more laughs before the children started tickling each other, resulting in a grouchy reprimand from one of the guards, which scared the children into silence. Steffan caught their eye, grinned, and winked.

"You are not a bad person, Steffan."

He looked a bit startled at her declaration.

"I mean, you are kind to children, you admit when you're wrong, and you respect other people's feelings and wishes."

"Does that mean you trust me?" He gave her a slight smile. "I know you trust me a little bit."

"Perhaps. A little bit."

"Were you worried about me when the healer said my wounds were putrid?"

"I was."

"Would you have mourned me if I'd died?"

She let out a long sigh. "You are teasing me."

His horse had come quite close. He reached out and touched her cheek, ever so softly and briefly, with the back of his hand. Her stomach fluttered. Did anyone see what he did? Did he not care that all these men would be teasing him? But perhaps this public display meant . . . something.

Steffan rode beside Katerina, although she seemed a bit less amiable than usual. What would happen now?

Now that Hennek was out of the way, she could stay with her mother and not have to worry about him or his men harming her or anyone else. She wouldn't need him to protect her.

It did not take very long to reach Hamlin, now that they weren't walking or having to carry the children. They had sent a few men ahead to announce that the children were coming home.

Mothers and fathers ran out of the town gate when they were still a long way off, crying when they saw their child, some of them for the first time in more than a year. Many of the children cried too, but their tears soon dried and they were smiling and embracing their families, laughing and talking. Children were so irrepressible and hardy.

As they were nearing the gate, Steffan saw Bridda and her father coming to meet them. When Bridda saw the other children being reunited with their families, she started crying. But she seemed to lock eyes on Verena and her mother, and when she saw Verena's smiles, she began to smile too. Verena caught sight of Bridda and ran joyfully to her. The older girl knelt beside her and they embraced. Verena's manner was lively and happy, and soon Bridda was looking just as lively. Verena took hold of Bridda's and her own mother's hands and skipped through the gate and into town.

Steffan was asked to help bring Hennek into town and secure him in the underground jail of the town hall. He left Katerina talking with Father and the children's families.

Steffan and several of his father's men walked through town with Hennek, his hands tied. Steffan had never seen the man looking so disheveled. Word must have already spread about what the mayor had done, because people hurled insults at him as they passed.

Soon so many people were shouting that Steffan could hardly tell what they were saying. But Hennek's face showed surprise, anger, even hurt. Did he really think his actions would not be judged as wrong? He excused himself for everything and blamed others for his actions, even claiming God's complicity in his schemes.

They made their way to the jail. Steffan and another guard checked all the bars and scoured the rock-walled cell for anything that might help him or could be used as a weapon. Satisfied he could not escape, they searched Hennek again for weapons, then locked him in the cell, leaving two guards to both keep Hennek in and keep others from breaking in and harming him. There could hardly be a greater anger than that of a father—or mother—whose child has been mistreated.

As Steffan went to find Father and Katerina, his chest felt heavy. They might never again get to work side by side to right wrongs. He might never again be the one who would protect her from harm. Would he ever enjoy her company and her smiles again the way he had in the last few days?

———•○•———

Katerina talked with the children's parents until their questions had been answered, then she and Duke Wilhelm made their way to her home. But when they started down the street, a large herd of rats started coming toward them.

Duke Wilhelm's soldiers leapt in front of Katerina and the duke and began slashing the little vermin with their swords, clearing a path. The rats skittered and screeched and actually changed their course.

"I had heard of the rat problem," Duke Wilhelm said as they continued on their way, "but I never imagined so many rats in one place."

"No one has figured out why they are here or how to get rid of them."

"We shall have to come up with a solution, then."

While they walked, the duke asked her questions. Who were the men she would recommend to serve as town councilmen? What did she think were the most pressing needs of the townspeople now that their children were safe? What did she think should be done with the silver mine? Were there any men who were respected or held important positions but were not trustworthy? Katerina answered him, thankful he was so interested in helping the town make a fresh beginning.

When they arrived at Katerina's house, servants came to take their horses.

"Just a moment," Steffan said, taking four leather pouches from his saddlebag. "Here are the silver coins I took from the mine. They belong to Hamlin, to the townspeople." He handed them to his father.

"Thank you, son. These coins you discovered will be a great help to the town. Well done, son."

Steffan nodded and started toward the house.

Mother welcomed them at the door, looking cautiously happy when she saw Duke Wilhelm. When her eyes met Katerina's, she broke into a teary smile and opened her arms.

Katerina hugged her mother amid sniffles from both of them. Mother spoke first. "You are home. I was so afraid I'd lost you forever."

"I'm so glad to see your face again. We are safe now."

Mother kissed her cheek, then stepped back to look at her.

"Mother, this is Duke Wilhelm of Hagenheim. And this is my mother, Ayla Grymmelin."

"It is my pleasure to meet you, Frau Ayla. You have a very brave and wise daughter."

"Your Grace, the pleasure is mine, and I am very proud of Katerina. There is no maiden to compare with her."

"She has been telling me some very interesting things."

"I am sorry for what my husband has done. I knew he had

done some dishonest things, but my daughter, who is as clever as any man, has discovered much worse things than I ever imagined, I'm afraid."

Mother's bottom lip quivered, but after a moment, it stilled. Did Mother finally understand? She was finally admitting the truth about that awful man.

"I know you will be forced to appoint a new mayor," Mother went on, "so I will leave this place as soon as you say."

"You do not have to leave as yet. I will not punish you for the sins of your husband. And though I wish you had sent word to me when you realized his corruption, you were his wife, and I understand why you did not. You were his victim as much as anyone else."

Duke Wilhelm said this last part with a kind and gentle voice. It brought tears to Mother's eyes as well as Katerina's. *Victim.* As much as Katerina hated that word being applied to herself or her mother, by very definition they were victims. But they would not be any longer. If Katerina had the power to stop it, they would never be beaten up, either by words or by fists, ever again.

But it might not be in her power, so she prayed, *Lord God, please be willing to lead Mother and me away from abusers like Hennek. God, give us both wisdom and clarity . . . and healing.*

The servants brought them some food for a light meal, and as soon as they were gone, they discussed who might be a threat to the town and to their safety.

"My men report that there were five dead bodies in the mine, and I'm assuming they were all Hennek's guards."

"Yes, I'm sure they were, but I will identify them, if you wish," Katerina said.

"I don't think that will be necessary, but I thank you for being willing to do that. My men will have them buried after their families have claimed them, if they wish to do so. In addition to those, there were several dead and injured of Hennek's men in Keiterhafen. You saw and identified all of them, I believe. And who else do you think might be left in the city who might wish to do harm to you?"

"There were many of the town guards who were loyal to Hennek, but I know one guard who was not loyal to him. His name is Hans."

Duke Wilhelm had his men go find Hans. In the meantime, Katerina gave the duke the names of any other of Hennek's guards who might still be alive and in town, and he sent men to find them and bring them in so he could question them.

While they waited for Hennek's men to be rounded up and accounted for, Katerina and one of the duke's men went and retrieved the parchments she had hidden in her hollow tree just outside town. At the same time, Duke Wilhelm went into Hennek's office and found more evidence of wrongdoing—bribes, blackmail, and thievery—as well as evidence of simple incompetence. Katerina and Steffan consulted with him and shared in the discoveries.

As they combed through papers and parchments, written lists and ledgers, once or twice Steffan's hand brushed against hers or their shoulders bumped into each other. Her heart would pound and all her senses would be focused on how near Steffan was, the way his head bent slightly closer to her than was necessary, or how reluctant he seemed to move his hand away from hers. But his father was in the room, so she pretended not to notice.

After a couple of hours, they questioned the guards that Katerina suspected of being loyal to Hennek. They all seemed eager to renounce Hennek's evil deeds, most insisting that they knew nothing of the mine. And probably most of them were telling the truth. It was a secret too big, and too profitable, for Hennek to share with many people.

When Hans arrived, she noticed Steffan watching him, his eyes going back and forth between them. Was he jealous?

After Hans and the duke were introduced, Hans took her hand and said, "Katerina, I'm so thankful you are safe. Everyone is astonished at what Hennek did to the children, but so glad they are all home, thanks to you."

"It was not only me. Steffan helped to free them. I could not have done it without him."

Steffan met her eyes and held her gaze with his. "Katerina is the one who found them. She deserves the praise."

Her heart fluttered at the warm gentleness of his voice contrasting with the intensity in his eyes. What was he thinking? Was he surprised at her clasping Hans's hand? No doubt he was, since it had taken Steffan so long to gain her trust. But she and Hans had grown up together, her childhood friend, almost like a brother.

She didn't have time to dwell on what Steffan was thinking, as Duke Wilhelm began to ask Hans his opinions about which guards should and should not be allowed to guard Hennek.

Twenty-Six

Steffan watched as Hans grasped Katerina's hand in a familiar way. She smiled at this Hans, looking him in the eye, and stepped toward him, rather than flinching away as she always had done with Steffan.

Hadn't she said Hans was to marry another girl?

He listened to the conversation about who should be dismissed from the guard, or at least not allowed to guard Hennek in the jail, but Steffan had very little to offer. He didn't know the guards as Katerina and Hans did.

But he liked the way Father listened to Katerina. Father was actually a very wise man, listening to Katerina and Hans, making decisions about what would happen next, what punishments would be meted out, how to move on from Hennek's poor leadership.

Later, during the evening meal, Steffan managed to sit beside Katerina. When he had a chance, he said, "Hans seems like a good man. Did you say that he was getting married soon?"

"Oh, no, he is not getting married after all." Her brows scrunched in a compassionate expression. "It's so sad, but he caught his future wife with another man. I can't imagine any woman doing such a thing to someone as kindhearted as Hans."

"Yes." Steffan's heart sank. Did she like this Hans enough

to marry him? She certainly trusted him, and he was relatively handsome, if one liked the whey-faced look.

"You do not mind me participating in the discussions about the future of Hamlin, do you?" Katerina's eyes were big as she took a sip from her goblet and gazed at him over the rim.

"Of course not."

"I didn't think so." She smiled in a teasing way.

"Who knows Hamlin better, or loves it more, than you?"

Duke Wilhelm called to Steffan. He was forced to lean away from Kat.

"Yes, Father?"

"What about this plague of rats? Perhaps our beast slayers could come up with a plan to get rid of them."

"We will, Father." Steffan raised his brows at Kat.

"I do recall you promising to rid the town of its rats." She was smiling now, a challenging glint in her eye, which was a very beguiling sight to behold.

"Did I? Well then, I had best get to it."

"Do you know what you will do? How you will get rid of them?"

"I have an idea or two."

They discussed a few ideas, talked and laughed and teased each other, but always he was aware that they were not alone, even though no one seemed to be paying attention to them. Apparently Father was interested in speaking with the men from the town council, the ones with whom Hennek had always been at odds, the duke having already dismissed the others.

When they'd all finished eating, one of the men said, "Duke Wilhelm, will you favor us with a song? We all know you play the lute, and I brought mine."

Father's face showed surprise, then he smiled. "I think I would enjoy playing a few songs. I thank you." He took the musical instrument and began strumming the strings. Soon he was playing a familiar ballad, and the men all began singing the words.

———

"Your father is not as I imagined a duke would be." Katerina smiled.

"Are you disappointed?"

"Not at all. He is humble and kind and wise, conscientious, determined to do what is right and fair. I had always heard great things about the Duke of Hagenheim, but to actually meet him . . ."

"You must be surprised I am his son."

"Why? No, you are the kind of son I would expect Duke Wilhelm to have."

"Me?"

"Yes. You are noble and kind, brave and protective. You do not shrink from rescuing a band of children from a dangerous man intent on killing them and you."

"You think I am noble and brave . . . and those other things?"

"Perhaps I should not have told you, for I am sorry to say that you are a bit prone to arrogance and I do not wish to tempt you to indulge in that fault."

He squinted at her. "Sometimes I cannot tell if you are in jest or in earnest."

She smiled and leaned closer. "Someone has to tease you. A bit of your own medicine, yes?"

And speaking of temptations, his lips looked so inviting. Would she—should she—ever kiss them again? No. If he wanted to kiss her, he would. She would not throw herself at him. She leaned away from him just as his father ended the song.

The duke said, "Katerina, do you have a favorite song I could play for you and your mother?"

"Mother's favorite song is '*Stella Splendens*.'" But she rarely heard it because even though Hennek liked to play his pipe in the town marketplace, he said music in the house was too loud and was the din of the devil.

Duke Wilhelm began to play the song, and Mother's expression was so happy. But then her eyes got watery and her chin trembled.

When the song was over, Mother said, "Continue to play and sing, whatever you like, but please excuse me. I must retire to my room, and I bid you all a good night."

The men all returned her good night wishes, nodding respectfully to her as she left.

Katerina turned to Steffan. "Please excuse me as well. I shall see you tomorrow, I am sure."

His eyes bored into hers, then he took her hand and kissed it. "I bid you a good night, then, Katerina."

Was it her imagination, or did his fingers linger on her hand, even as his voice lingered over her name?

She hurried away before she could imagine any other sentimentalities.

Once upstairs, she knocked on Mother's chamber door. "It's Katerina."

Mother opened the door. Her smile was genuine. "My darling, come in."

"Mother, I just wanted to see how you were doing. Are you well?"

"Of course. I am not so fragile."

"But are you sad about Hennek? I was worried you would not believe all the terrible things we've told you that he's done."

"Oh, I believe them. I am grieved over the children being taken and mistreated. It is horrendous, and I am ashamed I never tried to speak out against him."

"I was afraid you still loved him, and I didn't want you to be heartbroken over him."

"Not to worry, darling. The truth is, I've known for a long time that he was not a good man. In fact . . ." Her eyes were glistening with tears, but she was smiling. "I am glad I no longer have to live with him. We are free, darling, and I'm ashamed I stayed with him for so long."

"No, don't be ashamed." Relief flooded Katerina, buoying her spirit. "We are free, and that is good! But you should not blame yourself. It was not safe for you to leave. Hennek would have done terrible things to you, to me, if you had defied him."

"He threatened to hurt you if I ever left him." Mother sighed. "I did love him. I didn't want to believe that he was capable of such depravity, that he was cruel. Even when the truth was right in front of me, I wouldn't believe it. For a while. But when I saw him goading you, saying one thing and doing something else, pretending to be a righteous, godly man when he was stealing from the town . . . I stopped loving him. I only feared him. But I'm sorry I ever married him, and I'm sorry for the ways he hurt you, Katerina. I never should have allowed—"

"Mother, you did the best you could. You have nothing to be sorry for, except that you fell in the path of a very bad man. You are too kind and gentle. Of course you did not believe that the person who promised to love you was actually dangerous."

"But will you forgive me anyway, for not knowing what was happening? For letting him fool me into thinking he was good when I should have known better?"

"Yes, Mother, I forgive you."

"I should have protected you." A tear fell from one eye, then the other, and ran down her cheeks.

"I forgive you." Katerina put her arms around her mother and they held each other tight. "All is well now. Duke Wilhelm is here, and he will make sure we have a man of good character to lead our town. We shall build our town's defenses and rid ourselves of the evil within."

———

Steffan made his way through the early-morning vendors set up in the town center, for today was market day. The spire of Hamlin Cathedral was a beacon up ahead, easily seen above the rooftops, drawing him to his destination.

Steffan went inside the church and sought out a priest. Finding none, he went into the garden behind the church. A very large rose bush, with vines climbing up the brick wall, was in full bloom, displaying red roses amidst the greenery of the vines. Steffan drew near to the bush and broke off a particularly perfect bloom. He would give it to Katerina, but would she even want it? Perhaps she hated flowers. He did not know that about her.

"Good morning."

Steffan stepped around the bush and found a man dressed in priestly robes cutting blooms and putting them into a basket.

"Good morning. Are you the priest?"

"I am. How may I serve you?"

"I would like to confess my sins. Will you hear my confession?"

"Of course." He smiled, showing wrinkles in his cheeks at the corners of his mouth. He moved slowly and his expression was mild. "Would you like to go inside, to the confession box? Or we can sit here, if you are not opposed. I do not think you will be overheard."

Steffan glanced around. It was a small, rather isolated garden. "We can sit here."

The priest motioned toward a bench and they both sat. "When was your last confession?"

"A few years ago. I'm afraid I have a lot to confess."

"You may take as much time as you need. Unburdening oneself is very important."

Where should he start? He decided to start at the beginning, and he told the priest about the little boy, Heinlin, who had died because of him. Somehow it was a bit easier to tell the priest, whom he did not know, than it had been to tell Katerina, whom he wanted to like and admire him. He told of how he had felt jealous that his older brothers seemed to have been provided for, and even his sister's husband was given an inheritance, and yet Steffan, the third son, would receive very little as an inheritance.

"I never should have been jealous. And I was rebellious. I rebelled against my father in a particularly terrible way."

"Tell me."

"My father sent my younger brother and me to fight on the side of his ally, Duke Konrad of Poland, but I deserted my brother and our fellow soldiers, joined with the Teutonic Knights, and fought against Duke Konrad.

"Later, I shot my brother's future wife with an arrow in another jealous pique."

"You shot your brother's wife?"

"Well, she was not his wife at the time, and I thought she was a boy—she was a soldier."

"Ah, yes. I have heard the story of the warrior maiden who fought with Duke Konrad's soldiers. So you shot her in battle?"

"Not exactly. She was sent to scout out our whereabouts. But I shot her because I was jealous of my brother's attention and concern for him—her. I was angry my brother had not followed me and joined with the Teutonic Knights. When we were boys, he followed my lead, and I led him into many disobedient acts, I'm afraid. But when we were grown, he listened to Father and not to me. He became the 'good' son, while I was always the 'bad' son. I decided I might as well be bad, since everyone else saw me that way."

"Did anyone tell you that you were the bad son?"

"I heard the servants whispering about it more than once. They said I was the one who would be a disappointment to my father and mother. It made me very angry, because the rest of my brothers and sisters were so good, while I was so . . . angry."

"Did you ever speak to your father about this?"

"No. I was ashamed."

"Is there more?"

"Yes. I have killed many men."

"In battle?"

"Yes, all in battle or in self-defense. But I was on the wrong side of the battle. I only fought for my own selfish ends—I wanted to be a knight, and the best way I could think to be knighted was to distinguish myself with the Teutonic Knights."

"Some would say you were fighting on the side of God and righteousness if you were fighting with the Teutonic Knights."

"But I knew their intentions were oppressive in this particular fight. They were trying to take over land that was not rightfully theirs. I knew it was wrong. In my heart . . . I was grieved over what I was doing, but I was angry, defiant, crazed." Steffan's voice was barely a whisper as he put a hand over his eyes. If only the things he was saying weren't true. But they were.

"I also killed several men in the last few days who had taken and were holding children captive and working them in the mine."

The priest nodded.

"And I had many thoughts of kissing a maiden."

When Steffan did not go on, the priest said, "Is the maiden married?"

"No."

"Are you married?"

"No."

"Then thinking about kissing her is not a sin."

"But . . . I also kissed her."

"Against her will?"

"No."

"I do not believe that is a sin either, if you only kissed."

"But I am not worthy of her. She is much too pure and good for me." When he said it out loud, it sounded rather silly.

"Many a maiden has loved a man unworthy of her. But it is not a sin to love."

Steffan sat thinking about that. If Katerina did love him . . .

"My son, have you finished your confession?"

"Yes."

"As penance, you must confess your childhood sins to your father and mother and your sisters and brothers in accordance to how you wronged them and ask their forgiveness."

"I have already done that."

"Then you must pray for an hour at the altar. And you must accept God's forgiveness even as the thief on the cross accepted our Lord's forgiveness as he hung there, and stop carrying your weight of guilt. Your guilt feelings are not serving any good purpose."

The priest's eyelids fluttered open and closed as he held his hand toward Steffan and said the words of absolution. "God, the Father of mercies, through the death and resurrection of His Son, has reconciled the world to Himself and sent the Holy Spirit among us for the forgiveness of sins; through the ministry of the Church may God give you pardon and peace, and I absolve you from your sins in the name of the Father, and of the Son, and of the Holy Spirit. Go in peace."

"Thank you."

"And do not worry about being worthy. If you love the maiden, and if you submit to God and ask Him to make you worthy, then you will be worthy. Only God can make a man worthy, after all." He put a hand on Steffan's shoulder and looked intently into his face. After a few moments, he gave a tiny nod. "You have a good heart. You just need to trust."

Trust? Trust wasn't Steffan's struggle; it was Katerina's.

Steffan thought he'd feel worthy if he saved the children and captured Hennek, but he'd done that, and his father had even praised him for it, and he still didn't feel worthy. Perhaps he needed to . . . trust . . . that God and his father had forgiven him, that his heart—and his actions—had changed.

Steffan went back inside the church and knelt before the altar to pray. He gazed up at the crucifix. Jesus sacrificed Himself, not so Steffan could feel guilty but so he did not have to.

By the time he left, his shoulders felt lighter, as if a weight had been lifted off. Even his face, his eyes and mouth, felt relaxed and less tense. Could people see it? Could he now allow himself to forget about all those bad things that had happened in the past, the things he had done that he was now ashamed of?

His siblings, who were all so good . . . had they ever felt this way? This joy and lightness of spirit? Had Katerina? They were good already, but he . . . he had been forgiven much, and he would never forget it, never forget this feeling. "Thank You, God."

Twenty-Seven

When Steffan came to the house, his father and Katerina were speaking with the men of the town council, discussing who would be in charge of the town treasury and tax revenue.

"It should be someone other than the new mayor," Katerina said.

Father nodded. "The town needs a treasurer who will work with the Bürgermeister. And the ledgers and bookkeeping should be open to the town council to verify that the information there is correct and that no one is being corrupt."

Steffan listened while they continued the discussion. Always Katerina was there, adding her opinion occasionally, the other men listening and treating her with respect. Steffan suspected that was because his father was there and had set the example, giving her deference and valuing her opinions. But it was also due to Katerina's own spirit, to the fact that she had been the one to discover what had happened to the children, and she had fought for them, fought against Hennek, and won.

With Steffan's help, of course. Steffan was good at fighting, but discussing business and running a town? He would rather get injured in battle.

"One of the first things we need to do is build up a strong guard," Father said.

It was on the tip of Steffan's tongue to say something. He even opened his mouth. But then he closed it as Katerina turned to look at him.

"I agree," she said.

Steffan could help with that. He was a soldier by training as well as experience. Father had once told him, when he was frustrated with him for some disobedient act, *You could be a leader. You have it in you.*

Would Father think of him now? Would he suggest they appoint Steffan as the captain of the guard of Hamlin? Or did he still plan to make Steffan the mayor?

Steffan opened his mouth again, ready to say that he would be pleased to help build up the guard. But again, something stopped him.

"Steffan and I will be traveling back to Hagenheim."

So Father did not intend to make him the mayor after all.

"But I believe you are capable and fully able to get things back in order here. Hans and Katerina have helped us discover who among the guard were loyal to Hennek, and they have been dismissed. I will leave many of my men here until you can train more guards. We shall depart today."

Steffan's stomach sank into his toes. He blew out a pent-up breath.

"Therefore, I wish to appoint a new Bürgermeister whom I believe will serve quite well and will continue to serve for years to come. And I wish to make the announcement in one hour, in the town square."

Father looked up at Hans, who was standing guard at the back of the room. "Have the guards spread the news through town that there will be an announcement in the square."

Hans nodded and strode from the room.

Father looked Steffan in the eye. "You will be ready to leave this afternoon?"

He hesitated, but then said, "Yes, Father."

He turned around to go talk to Katerina—and came face-to-face with her.

"I hope you and your father have a good trip back to Hagenheim. I know your mother and the rest of your family will be very glad to see you after so long an absence."

"Thank you. I . . . I would like to come back to Hamlin, after I visit my mother. Perhaps I could help the new mayor with the guard. I've had a lot of training."

"Oh yes. I think—"

"We should make our way to the town square," Father said loudly for the whole room to hear. "I want all of you there."

They all started moving toward the door. Steffan was careful to stay near Katerina. She was dressed more femininely today than usual. Her hair was flowing down her back with a few tiny braids plaited with purple ribbons. Her dress was a pale lavender, of the kind of fine fabric that a Bürgermeister's daughter might wear.

No wonder she'd never dressed as a wealthy young maiden. Not only did she despise the source of the wealth—her stepfather, Hennek—but after all Hennek and his men had done to make her afraid of being harassed and attacked, she probably wore old, rough, patched clothing to make herself less appealing. And the fact that she so often carried a crossbow and arrows probably attracted less attention when wearing the clothing of a peasant.

She was walking slightly in front of him. Thinking of leaving her made his heart clench in his chest. He wanted to take her on picnics, to hold her hand and kiss her and touch her soft cheek. He wanted . . . to marry her.

Did she even want him to come back?

They reached the town square. Father was waiting for the rest of the townspeople to arrive. This could be his last chance. He touched Katerina's arm and she turned to look at him. At least she didn't flinch anymore when he touched her.

He bent his head toward a small tree growing in front of the Rathous on the otherwise bare cobblestone town square. She followed him until they were on the other side of the tree, away from his father and the men of the town council. She drew close and even leaned in, as if eager to hear what he had to say.

"You look beautiful today."

"Thank you." She squinted slightly and crossed her arms over her chest.

Had he said the wrong thing?

"You always look beautiful."

She unfolded her arms and gave him an amused half smile. "Always?"

"Yes. To me you do."

"I think you're somewhat well-looking too."

"You do? Only somewhat?"

She laughed. Such a beautiful sound, even if she was laughing at him. He smiled back.

"I'm sure you've heard it before from other maidens."

"I *am* known as one of Duke Wilhelm's most handsome sons."

She took a deep breath and sighed. "I think you are very handsome."

Air rushed into Steffan's lungs. Perhaps she *would* want him to return to Hamlin. He had to tell her that he wanted her to wait for him, not to let anyone, like that Hans, get too close to her until he returned. But how would he tell her?

―――――◦‖◦―――――

Katerina had always been honest. Part of her panicked at telling Steffan he was handsome, but she did think he was handsome. To say otherwise would be to tell a lie. And she had never been manipulative in the way other girls she knew would pout and tell a man one thing when the truth was something else.

"I must go visit my mother, but will you be glad to see me return?"

"How long will you be gone?"

"Three weeks? Maybe less."

Three weeks was not a long visit when it would take him at least two days to get there and two days to get back. But it seemed like a long time for him to be away.

She gazed up at him, letting herself be captured by his blue eyes. It wasn't often she even let herself look directly into them, for it was like looking directly into the sun—dangerous. And it was frightening how much she had grown attached to him. She had an urge to touch his cheek and feel the short stubble on his jawline, as the memory of their kiss swept over her.

He held out his hand, and she lifted her own and placed it in his. He held it gently. "Katerina, do you like flowers?"

"Yes."

"I want to know everything you like, to talk with you, dance with you."

"But there's no music. And I don't like dancing." Had he gone daft?

"What I mean to say is, I want to be where you are, and if you don't like dancing at festivals, we can just listen to the music, go hunting, have picnics. I want to know . . . if you want me to return to Hamlin."

A bit of fear gripped her. If she said yes, what would that mean? But she would be honest with him. "I think I would like listening to music with you, going hunting, and having picnics, if you stay as you are now, kind and respectful, noble and good. As I know you are." She leaned a bit closer to his broad chest as she said this. She wanted to kiss him, but she'd promised herself she would not, that the next time she would let him kiss her, if indeed he wanted to kiss her. But there were so many people around them, even in their out-of-the-way spot, more people were walking past them as the crowd grew in the town square.

He moved closer to her, and soon her forehead was resting against his shoulder as he wrapped one arm around her, loosely, casually. "Katerina." He whispered her name. Her heart tripped.

He was still holding her hand. She felt him lifting it and then kissing it. She was so aware of his lips on the back of her hand, his breathing, his head bent beside hers, his chin now just brushing against her hair.

Someone was calling the crowd to attention. Duke Wilhelm's name broke into her consciousness.

"Katerina Ludken?"

Kat stepped away from Steffan, who seemed reluctant to let go of her hand. A guard was standing behind her.

"Yes?"

"Duke Wilhelm would like you to hear the announcement."

"Of course."

She gave Steffan a quizzical glance, and they both walked

toward the fountain, where his father was standing. The guard walked them through the hushed crowd right up to Duke Wilhelm's side, who smiled at her just before he began speaking in a loud voice.

"I am here due to the bravery of two people. The town of Hamlin has had its children returned to their rightful parents, thanks to the good hearts, clever thinking, and determination in the face of danger of my son, Steffan Gerstenberg, and Hamlin's own courageous Katerina Ludken."

Many cheers went up from the crowd, both whoops and shouted words of gratitude and praise. Kat felt her cheeks growing hot. Even through blurred vision, she saw people she knew, women she'd bought things from in the marketplace, friends she'd played games with when she was a child, and men who had been friends with her father. And there was her mother, tears running down her face.

Steffan was standing so close, she let her shoulder lean into his side. His hand bumped hers, hidden between them. She took his hand in hers, and he squeezed it.

The Duke of Hagenheim went on. "I have been discussing with the men of the town council and a few others whom I should appoint as the next Bürgermeister. We all agreed the new mayor should be full of integrity, should love his townspeople above even his own life, and should fear God and not man. And the person I have chosen to be the next Bürgermeister, if she will accept it, is Katerina Ludken."

Katerina went numb all over. Did Duke Wilhelm just appoint her as the new mayor?

She glanced around. Were people angry to have a young woman as their mayor? The first faces she saw were women with joyful smiles, so she quickly looked back at Duke Wilhelm so she wouldn't see anyone else. She did hear some whoops and cheers and even some hands clapping.

Katerina, the new Bürgermeister. Was this a dream? It was so strange, and yet, so wonderful!

―――――•―――――

Steffan's heart jumped into his throat as Father called out Katerina's name. He'd never heard of a woman being given such a position, but he was so proud, of her and of his father for appointing her.

Father stared intently into her face as the crowd quieted. "Will you accept this office?"

"I will."

Father handed her a sheet of parchment paper and hung a ribbon with a medal attached around her neck. "Henceforth you shall be known as Bürgermeister Katerina Ludken."

She was the mayor. Would she think of him differently now? She looked truly happy, though a bit frightened, to be made the Bürgermeister in her stepfather's place.

People began to crowd around her and congratulate her. He should have been the first one to tell her how glad he was that the town was getting the best possible mayor, but he was too late. People crowded him out until he had to step back. And she was smiling and receiving the well wishes. As she should. He was happy for her.

And now he had to leave her.

He looked around at the people and saw more than one man scowling. Another was shaking his head. They obviously disagreed with Father's decision. Steffan did his best to catch their eye and stare them down. One saw him and immediately changed his expression to one of sheepishness, but two others started muttering to each other.

Perhaps Steffan should not leave.

He kept an eye on Katerina, glancing all around. Of course, Father's guards were also watching over her.

Father approached him. "Will you be ready to leave in an hour?"

"Father, are you sure Katerina is safe? Some people are probably not very pleased with you making a young maiden the mayor of their town."

"I'm leaving most of my men here. They will watch over her."

"I know, but . . ."

"I understand." Father put his hand on Steffan's shoulder. "It is your decision if you wish to stay or go back with me to have a longer visit with your mother. It has been more than a year since she spent more than a few hours with you."

"I am aware, Father. And I want to spend time with Mother."

"Good. Then come home and you can return to Hamlin in a few weeks to make sure Katerina is well and everything is working smoothly here."

He knew that was what he needed to do, but it was frustrating.

Katerina was looking around now as the crowd was thinning out. Steffan hurried over to her.

"You will be an excellent Bürgermeister, Katerina. I am very happy for you."

"Thank you, Steffan. But I thought your father would appoint you. In fact, I heard him say it. I was standing outside your door in Keiterhafen and I heard him tell you he wished to make you the mayor of Hamlin."

"He did say that, but I told him I thought you were a better choice. You know the town and love its people, and I assured him you would be very capable."

"You said that?"

"No one is better for this job than you, Katerina."

She leaned toward him until her face was pressed against his chest. He put his arms around her.

"How does it feel?" he asked, his breath blowing a few strands of her loose hair.

"It feels strange. I can hardly believe it."

"I think he may have talked with some of the members of the town council, but he must have been very confident you were the best person for the job. I know no one will work as hard as you will, or love the people as much as you do."

"It's all so overwhelming. I hope I will not disgrace your father by failing miserably."

"That could never be." But how strange for him, remembering he had been wishing, hoping the new Bürgermeister would appoint him as the captain of the guard, and now if he wished for such a position, he would have to ask . . . Katerina.

Twenty-Eight

By nightfall Katerina was exhausted. And now she kept thinking how Steffan had left and they had not been able to say fare well in private. Everyone had been standing there, watching them.

She had been so busy, with so many people wanting to talk to her. The next thing she knew, Duke Wilhelm and his men were mounting their horses to leave, and Steffan was standing there, his expression stoic, and yet she could see sadness in his eyes.

Katerina had wanted to embrace him, but knowing he would not want to show vulnerability to the men surrounding him, and feeling strange herself, as if her new position demanded that she be dignified, she had simply said, "Thank you for everything."

Everyone else was already mounted on their horses. Steffan had no choice but to mount up and leave with them.

Her heart twisted as she watched his back slowly disappear from her view and wondered . . . When would she see him again?

But she was quickly distracted by more people demanding her attention, not least of which was Herr Schuman, who had been appointed the town treasurer. Thankfully that was one task Katerina would not be responsible for, though she was to oversee his work.

Herr Schuman was a fastidious man, was married to a woman who had always been kind and friendly with Katerina and her mother, and was known for never cheating anyone in his brick-making business. But he was always scowling, and many times when he spoke, Katerina had to ask him to repeat himself because his voice was so low and growly.

One good thing about her new position was that she had been able to make Hans her new interim guard captain.

Katerina read over the financial report Herr Schuman had given her. There was one, and only one, thing that she could be thankful to Hennek for doing, and that was hiring a tutor to teach her when she was young. So many people barely knew how to read, and most could not read at all.

"Katerina?"

She looked up to see Hans standing in the doorway of the office that used to belong to Hennek. "Yes?"

"I thought I would let you know that Klaus and Reynart will be guarding Hennek—Klaus tonight and Reynart taking over in the morning."

"They are Duke Wilhelm's men?"

"Yes. And I've sent Wendel to gate duty. He will not be guarding Hennek anymore."

"Did Wendel not wish to guard Hennek? Or did you need him at the gate?"

Hans shifted his weight from one foot to the other and stared at the wall behind her. "Wendel said Hennek was trying to bribe him to let him out, and I didn't want to risk the possibility that Wendel wouldn't be able to resist the temptation."

Katerina took in this information and nodded. "That sounds wise. Who will take Wendel's place?"

"I have not decided yet."

"It might also be wise to try and find out what Hennek was trying to bribe him with."

"Silver coins, I believe."

"You can tell the other guards that Hennek has nothing anymore. He had a hiding place in the mine, but the silver has been removed and is in safekeeping."

"Yes, I will tell them." Hans was staring first at the floor, then the wall.

"Is something wrong, Hans?"

"No." His eyes went wide, then he smiled. "No, all is well. I'm very pleased you are the new Bürgermeister. I cannot imagine a better one."

"That is kind of you to say."

"You are educated and clever. You will do well. And I'm very pleased you trust me enough to be your interim captain. I will always do my best for you."

"Thank you, Hans. I am grateful to have someone I can trust in such a position."

Hans bowed his head. "I shall go, if you do not need me. I was at the gate all day, and I interviewed boys for several hours who want to train as soldiers."

"Very good. Yes, go home and get some rest. Thank you."

As he left, she couldn't help thinking of Steffan. He would be wonderful at training Hamlin's new guards. But would he want to remain in the little town of Hamlin training soldiers? Steffan had been to places she'd never heard of, seen things she'd never imagined. And no doubt he had seen beautiful women who were good at dancing and wore beautiful gowns and whose fathers knew the king—or were even related to the king!

She groaned inwardly as she remembered kissing him. She might never see him again, but she would never forget him, never stop thinking about him—the look in his eyes the first time she flinched when he touched her, as if she'd kicked him in the stomach; the way he'd stepped in front of a wolf to protect her; the way his rock-hard arms felt around her. And she hoped she never forgot how it felt to kiss him, or the way he brushed her cheek with his knuckles, or the way he whispered her name that day in the town square, her forehead resting on his shoulder.

She let out a long sigh. She might be the Bürgermeister, but she was still a woman with a heart that couldn't help falling in love.

———————

Katerina sat at her desk signing off on the receipt for the treasurer to pay all the town's soldiers.

It had been three weeks and one day since Steffan had left. He'd told her he'd be gone no more than three weeks. Was he well? She hoped no harm had befallen him. Or had he forgotten about her?

When she wondered whether he would keep his word, a sharp little pang stabbed her chest.

But she was so busy, she hardly had time to fret over that, even though things were going well most days. Other days ended with her collapsing on her bed and wondering if she'd ever learn all she needed to know about taking care of a town.

It was early. Katerina hadn't been able to sleep and had risen to work on the receipts when it was peaceful and quiet. But now the sun was coming up. Why weren't the servants making breakfast? They were noisy every other morning, but the house was eerily quiet today.

And where was Hans? He usually came around at this time to let her know of any problems that happened during the night.

Katerina's fingertips were tingling as she stood up and went to the office doorway, listening. She stepped toward the kitchen and opened the door. No one was there, and it didn't look as if anyone had been there. Everything was tidy and in its place.

She turned toward the stairs. As she put her foot on the bottom step, a loud thud came from the upper floor.

Katerina loosened the knife she always kept in a sheath hanging from her belt, then ran to grab her sword, the first thing she bought after her appointment as mayor. She'd laughed at herself, but she'd always wanted one, and now she had the money Duke Wilhelm had given her as her first year's payment to buy one.

Katerina picked up the sword and hurried to the steps. She climbed them two at a time, but stopped abruptly when a man appeared at the top. No, two people, but it was too dark to see who it was.

"Who is there?" Kat demanded.

"It is only your stepfather and mother."

Katerina's heart stopped and a cold sensation went through her.

Hennek. She made out his aggressive, smirky smile. He was holding Mother around her neck, a knife point at her ear.

How could he have escaped? Where were the servants? How could this be happening? She had been so sure she and Mother were finally safe.

Katerina stared hard at the man holding Mother at knifepoint.

She had to think. She could not let anger and fear muddy her thoughts. She gripped her sword tightly, the point resting on the step she was standing on.

"Come on down, Hennek," she said, "and tell me what it is you want."

"It is simple." He started down the first step, forcing Mother to come with him. "I want my silver."

"Your silver?" Katerina matched him step for step as she went back down, holding tightly to her sword handle.

"The silver from my mine." Hennek's hair seemed whiter than she remembered and was all askew and sticking straight up in places. "It belongs to me and you've taken it."

"Silver that you enslaved children to mine? A mine that did not belong to you?"

"I discovered it. I mined it. And you've stolen it from me."

Mother looked pale and frightened, but she did not make a sound as Hennek dragged her along with him slowly down the stairs one step at a time, his hand wrapped around her throat.

"I suppose it must still be in the mine. Where did you last see it? Perhaps you mislaid it."

"You mock me. You always were a rebellious girl. You have a demonic, rebellious spirit! You never would submit to those in authority over you. God shall smite you for being rebellious and controlling. You always did want to be in control, and now you've bewitched Duke Wilhelm into believing all your lies about me."

"Was it a lie that you enslaved children after stealing them off the streets?"

"Could I help it if they heard my music and decided to follow me? They liked the music. They came willingly."

"Your mind is sick."

"No, you are the one who is sick!" Hennek's jaw was clenched, his eyes wild as he pointed his dagger at Katerina now.

Kat was nearly to the bottom of the stairs.

"You're not entitled to whatever you want, Hennek. You don't deserve the silver in that mine just because you desire it."

"Silence! You unsubmissive, unrepentant girl! I shall kill both you and your mother. Throw down your sword," Hennek shouted, "or I will kill her this moment."

Katerina threw down her sword and it clattered on the floor.

"Hennek."

Kat glanced over her shoulder to see Hans standing there. *Thank God.* But why did he not have his sword drawn?

"Hans." Her voice squeaked. She swallowed the lump in her throat. "Hennek has escaped."

"Get what you want and get out."

Was Hans speaking to Hennek? He must be trying to make Hennek think he was helping him so that he wouldn't hurt Mother.

"Yes," Kat added, "take whatever you want, but leave my mother alone. She has nothing to do with this."

"Katerina, just tell him where to find the silver and he will let you both go."

Kat turned to look at Hans. "What?"

"Just give him what he wants so he can leave."

Hans must have a plan to recapture Hennek. But would Hennek let her mother go if she told him where the silver was?

"Very well. The silver that was taken from the mine is now in the strong box in the Rathous undercroft."

"Give me the key to the strong box," Hennek said in a raspy voice, his expression dark. "I know you have it."

"Give it to him, Katerina."

Katerina went into the study and toward the desk that used to belong to Hennek but was now where she worked.

"Is it in the desk? Step aside and let Hans get it." Hennek motioned to Hans, who immediately strode over to the desk.

"Where is it, Katerina?"

Something was wrong. She stared hard at Hans.

"Hans, how did Hennek escape?"

"Hans took the key and opened the cell door," Hennek crowed.

Hans's face told her what she feared was true. He stared back at her, his cheek pale. He looked down and started shuffling through the desk.

"Hans, why?" She felt hollow inside. She had trusted him. He'd been the only man she'd trusted. "Did you do it for money? Silver coins?"

"Grete married someone else because she didn't want to marry a poor soldier in the Hamlin town guard. Do you know how humiliating that was?"

"He doesn't have to explain it to you," Hennek said, contempt dripping from his voice. "You are no better than him. You probably only saved the children to get the silver."

The accusation was too ludicrous to acknowledge.

"Hans, please don't do this."

"Shut your mouth and stop talking to him!"

Mother cried out. Hennek must have been squeezing her throat. Katerina whipped around, panic rising when she saw her mother's lips were turning purple.

"Hans, make haste." He curled his lip at Katerina. "I should kill your mother just to make you watch. You always were a thorn in my side. I fed you and clothed you and educated you and you

never appreciated it. You never appreciated what I did for you."
He dragged Mother closer.

If Kat could knock the dagger from his hand, she could kill
Hennek before he could hurt Mother. But if she struck at Hennek
and missed . . . he was ruthless enough to kill Mother, and it
would only take a moment.

"Run," Mother said, looking at Katerina.

"Be quiet." Hennek began choking her. "You know you still
love me." He spoke the words in her ear while looking at Kat.

Mother pulled at his hand, but he did not loosen his hold.

"Stop it. Hans, make him stop!"

"Hennek, you said you wouldn't kill them."

"Shut up. I will only kill them if they force me to. Disobedient
women!" He finally loosened his grip and Mother gasped. "Your
haughty, lying spirit, Katerina, is what is causing your mother so
much pain. You destroyed your mother's and my marriage. You
did this, and it is sad that you were able to bewitch Duke Wilhelm
with your hypocritical ways and turn him against me too."

"You are insane, Hennek. The only hypocrite here is you."

He pressed the knife point into Mother's neck. She barely
flinched. "Kill me, Hennek. I no longer care. Katerina is all that
matters."

Would Hans truly not help them? How could he stand there
and watch this and do nothing?

"God will not be pleased with what you are doing, Hennek."
She spoke in a calm, even voice. "God does not like what you are
doing."

"You dare to speak for God? I am the head of this household.
You answer to me. You have a rebellious spirit, and rebellion is as
the sin of witchcraft. You are the one who is not pleasing God."

"Murder is a grave sin, Hennek."

"Quiet! I will not listen to another word out of your perverse mouth. Hans, what are you doing? Why have you not found the key?"

"I don't know where it is. I've looked everywhere. Tell her to come and find it."

Katerina went over to the desk. She clenched her fists. Hennek was besting her, after all that he had done to harm her. The man was so wicked and yet would accept no blame or responsibility. But for the moment, she had little choice but to give Hennek the key. She could not allow him to kill Mother.

Katerina reached under the desk and took the key from where she had hidden it. She threw it at Hennek and it landed on the floor at his feet.

"Get the key, Hans."

Hans obediently went over and picked up the key.

"Give it to me," Hennek demanded, a satisfied sneer on his face.

Hans handed it over. Finally Hennek let go of Mother, giving her a push, and took the key, closing it into his fist. "Hans, you know what to do. Get rid of our new mayor, and her mother."

Hennek strode out of the house, and Hans turned toward her.

"Wait." Katerina stared hard at Hans.

He stopped and stared back at her while Mother sobbed softly on the stairs.

"I won't kill you," he said quietly, "if you will take your mother and go. Get out of town."

"I thought you were my friend, Hans. I never, ever expected something like this from you." As she talked, she moved closer to Hans.

"You and your mother need to go before I change my mind."
He stared at her, no signs of relenting in his eyes.

"Very well." Katerina moved to walk past him toward her
mother. "Come, Mother."

But as she moved past Hans, she reached out and snatched his
sword from its sheath across his back. Then she stabbed him in
the leg just above his knee.

Hans cried out and she stabbed him again, this time in the arm.

Katerina, still clutching the sword, grabbed Mother's arm with
her other hand, and they ran out of the house and down the street
toward the town gate in the opposite direction from the Rathous.

Twenty-Nine

Katerina dry-heaved, then let out a sob as she ran, still holding on to Mother's arm.

But there was Hennek, and he had spotted her. And one of Hennek's guards was with him.

Worst of all, Hennek and his guard were between her and the town gate and the two guards she had been running to find.

Hennek and his guard advanced slowly toward her and Mother.

Katerina raised her sword—Hans's sword—and prepared to fight. Hennek's guard had a sword, but while he was fighting Kat, Hennek would be able to grab Mother and hold her hostage again. However, the gate guards were not close enough to hear her scream.

"Stay behind me, Mother."

Mother started sobbing and calling for God to help them.

At that moment, a horse and rider became visible as it passed through the gate and galloped in their direction. Were her eyes deceiving her? Was that . . .

Steffan rode up behind Hennek and his guard. He swung his sword and knocked the guard's sword out of his hand, sending it flying through the air to land several feet across the cobblestone street.

Hennek pulled out a long knife and ran toward Katerina, yelling, his eyes wide and crazed.

Kat raised her sword and prepared to stab Hennek, locking her eyes on his chest. If she could stab Hans, she could surely stab Hennek.

Just before he reached the end of her sword, Steffan, now on foot, slammed his sword blade in a wide arc down on Hennek's knife hand. The knife fell to the ground, and Steffan kicked it away.

Hennek yelled, falling to his knees and clutching his hand.

Hennek's guard started running toward Hennek's dagger, which was lying in the street. A man who had stopped to watch the fight and was standing by the knife picked it up, looked at the guard, then threw the knife behind him. It clattered at the feet of two of Hamlin's guards who were running toward them.

Hennek stared at his bloody hand, which was obviously broken, as one of the guards grabbed him from behind and ordered him, "Lie down! On your back, now!" He held his sword to Hennek's throat as the other guard chased after Hennek's guard.

More guards were coming from the other way. Men and women were emerging from the shops and homes and wandering closer.

Steffan was staring at her. He calmly put his sword back in its scabbard. Katerina realized she was still clutching Hans's bloody sword, and she dropped it. Steffan stepped toward her and she threw herself against his chest. He enveloped her in his arms, holding her close.

After a moment he said, "Should I go after Hennek's guard?"

"No!" She pulled away enough to look into his eyes. "Please don't leave me." She never wanted him to leave her, ever again.

Steffan had never seen that look on Katerina's face before. "I promise I won't leave you." Then he noticed the blood spatters on her dress. "Are you hurt?" His heart lurched.

"No, but I need someone to go fetch the healer for Hans. He was stabbed . . . in my house. You there!" She called out to a man gawking at Hennek and the soldier who had him on the ground.

The man looked up. "Yes, Bürgermeister Katerina?"

"Go and fetch the healer and take her to my house. There is an injured man there. Or if he is not there, find him. His name is Hans Schuster."

"Yes, Fräulein." He hurried away.

Steffan's soaring heart sank. "Hans? Your friend?" He swallowed. "He was injured?"

"I stabbed him." Her voice was devoid of emotion and her eyes stared blankly at Steffan's chest.

"You stabbed him?"

"He betrayed me. He helped Hennek escape . . . for money." Her chin trembled.

He pulled her close. His insides twisted at seeing her pain. Then he felt her shoulders shaking. She was sobbing.

He caressed her shoulder. "It is all right. I will not let anyone hurt you or your mother ever again."

"Mother?" She pulled away and turned around. She held out her hand to her mother, who came to her and they embraced.

People were still gathering. He heard a few shouts far down the street, and hoped that meant Hennek's guard had been captured. Hennek was lying on the ground, calling down curses and God's wrath on everyone around him.

Steffan wasn't sure what to do. Katerina was wiping her face with her hands, breathing deeply and no longer crying.

How dare that Hans betray Katerina? He was the only person she trusted. Steffan was glad Katerina had stabbed him.

"Should I go and help them find Hans?"

"No," she said quickly, stepping toward him. She slipped her arms around him. "I need you here. With me."

He held her tight and whispered next to her ear, "I wasn't sure you wanted me."

"Of course I want you." She nestled her head against his shoulder. "You make me feel safe."

"I shall guard you night and day, whether you want me to or not."

She said softly, "I want you to."

His heart beat faster. It was not exactly the reunion he had expected, but it was almost better than the one he'd hoped for.

She lifted her head, and he pulled away enough to look into her eyes. She placed her hand on his chest, over his heart. "If you don't mind living in our little town, would you be the captain of the guard? I need someone I trust, someone who is brave and good."

"I would be honored to be your captain of the guard."

"Thank you." She was staring at his lips. She reached up and touched his cheek, cupping his jaw in her hand.

He leaned down and kissed her lips lightly, then more firmly, and she kissed him back.

Hennek's voice invaded his thoughts. He broke off the kiss to see the guards leading Hennek away as he spit angry words at everyone around him.

Steffan gazed down at Katerina. "You aren't hurt, are you?"

"No. But I am glad you came when you did."

"If you stabbed Hans, you must have been doing well on your own."

He immediately regretted his words, as tears filled her eyes.

"It was—" She stopped and pressed two fingers against her lips. She let out a breath and started again. "It was horrible. I didn't want to hurt him. He was my friend." Her voice suddenly took on a harder tone. "Or so I thought. He let Hennek hurt my mother. But it was still very hard to stab him." She pressed her face against his shirt.

He rubbed her arm. "I wish I'd been here to protect you. I'm so sorry."

"You are a good man."

He leaned down and kissed her temple as she hugged him tight.

The next several weeks were a blur. Katerina was still trying to learn all her duties and do them well. Steffan was the new captain of the guard, and he was busy training new guards and managing all the others. But Steffan made time to take Katerina on picnics, go for a ride in the hills, and take a long walk. And he made certain that everyone knew he was there to protect the town, but his first loyalty was to the mayor.

One day he came to see Katerina at the end of the day, and a man was complaining to her, very loudly, because he'd been arrested for assaulting a vegetable vendor in the marketplace. Steffan heard the man berating her as he walked in the door. Kat was trying to reason with him, but Steffan took him by the collar and escorted him out.

"No one talks to the mayor like that," Steffan told the man. "You will mind your manners or you will not be allowed the privilege of speaking with her at all."

The man picked up his hat, which fell into the street when Steffan ushered him out the door, and hurried away, grumbling as he went, but under his breath.

"You probably only made him angrier." Katerina was waiting for him when he came back inside. She smiled and wrapped her arms around him.

"I had better not hear of his coming in here to you again with his loud complaints." Steffan hugged her in a gentle squeeze. "No one shouts at my mayor."

She stood on her toes and kissed his cheek. He kissed her lips, but only briefly, as there always seemed to be someone nearby bringing her a proclamation to sign, or showing her the records of the treasury, or some other thing.

"Should I give you my report of the day's activities?" Steffan asked, still holding her in his embrace.

"Is that why you came? I thought you were here to give me my daily kiss and chase off grumpy men."

He kissed her again, this time making her lose her breath. When he pulled away, he said, "I came to inform you that I will be getting rid of our town's rat population this evening, just at sunset."

"Oh! How do you plan to do it?"

"First I wish to know how much reward money the mayor is offering for ridding Hamlin of its rats."

She placed a finger to her chin. "Hmm. Ten silver guilders?"

"I'll take it." He released her, then took her hand in his. "Now come and see."

They went out onto the main street of town. Steffan took out his pipe. He took a deep breath, then began to play a lively tune.

The people on the street looked startled and searched for the source of the pipe playing. No doubt everyone in town now knew how Hennek had lured the children away. They all watched as Steffan stood there playing for a few moments, then started walking.

Rats were coming down the street toward him. Kat backed away, pressing herself against the wall of her house and standing on a little stool to get away from them. The rats continued to come down the street from both directions and from the smaller streets and alleys. And Steffan continued to play and walk, moving toward the marketplace.

Katerina followed. People opened their windows and looked out of their homes. Others followed, curious to see what would happen to all the rats following him.

Once he was in the marketplace, which was the center of town, he led them down the street until he came to one of the town gates. He led the rats through it, still playing his lively tune, onto the road and up the hill just outside town, the same hill where the entrance to the silver mine was hidden. A few people, including Katerina, continued to follow the massive herd of rats that accompanied Steffan out of town, but the rest stood at the gate and watched until they were out of sight.

They went the rest of the way up the hill, and Steffan kept playing until he reached the opening in the mine. He went down into the hole, holding the pipe. Would the rats follow him into the hole? The rodents crowded around the opening, then began to fall into it until they had all disappeared into the mine.

The people standing around the entrance to the mine looked

at each other. Finally, Katerina stepped forward and went down to see what was happening.

She could hear the hollow sound of Steffan playing his pipe. She followed the music, keeping her hand on the wall. She found a lighted torch and took it with her. Every so often she found another lighted torch. Had Steffan come down here and lit them ahead of time?

She followed the sound of the pipe into the tunnel that led to the deep hole where the children had entombed the guards. She finally saw Steffan on the other side, still playing, as the rats were streaming forward and falling to their doom.

When the last rat had fallen in, Steffan stopped playing and met her eye in the torchlight.

"You did it!" Katerina grinned across the chasm at him.

"All for you, Lady Mayor."

"Just be careful getting back around that hole." She watched, holding her breath, as Steffan carefully plastered himself against the wall of the passageway and moved toward her. She breathed a sigh of relief when he was safely next to her and put her arm around him.

"Do you think the rats will be able to get out?"

"It couldn't hurt to send some men to throw some large rocks in and cover them up. But for now, let's get out of here."

"Yes. If I never see this place again, I will not be sad."

Soon Katerina and Steffan came back down the hill, but without the rats.

Men and women cheered as they entered the gate and walked down the street. They crowded around Steffan and patted him on the back. When they were finally back at her home, Kat said, "You know we have to have a celebration now that the rats are gone."

Steffan leaned against the wall. "And we should have a festival to celebrate the children being brought back."

"We could also celebrate that the Beasts of Hamlin are dead."

"Good idea."

"So why do you think the rats were here? Why so many of them?"

Steffan sat down in one of the cushioned chairs. "My guess is that the mining drove them out of their homes in the ground and into town."

"That makes sense, I suppose. But are you sure we should leave all those rats in that hole? The mine will smell like rotting rodent, and then no one will want to work in the mine."

"At least they aren't running around town."

Katerina shook her head. "But how did you know they would follow you?"

"A few of the children said the rats followed Hennek when he played his pipe."

"I think you need a reward for ridding our town of the rats."

"Oh yes, I definitely am entitled to a reward."

But before Kat could say anything else, people were knocking on the door wanting to thank the Rat Slayer of Hamlin.

———◈———

A few days later, a guard knocked at the door and handed Kat a missive.

"What is it?" Steffan, who happened to be there making his report to the mayor as the captain of the guard, came to look over her shoulder.

"The town council wants to present you with a reward in the

square for getting rid of the rats, for killing the Beasts of Hamlin, and for saving the children."

Steffan pointed at the writing, "It also mentions you. You're getting a proclamation read over you too."

"The town council agreed that we should have a festival to celebrate the return of our children and the end of the rat plague."

Another week passed and the marketplace was teeming with musicians, food, and wares. People sang and danced and ate bread rolls made in the shape of rats.

Katerina walked arm in arm with her piper, who was dressed almost as colorfully as a jongleur.

"Herr Pied Piper!" one man called to him. "Did you get your reward for ridding the town of its rats?"

"Not yet!" Steffan called back.

All the people standing around suddenly stilled, the musicians stopped playing, and a hush fell on the entire marketplace.

"What is going on?" Katerina asked. But when she turned to Steffan, he leaped onto the stone fountain in the center of the town square.

"May I please have your attention!" Steffan called. "The reward that I request for the favor of ridding the town of the rat pestilence is to marry your beautiful Bürgermeister, Katerina Ludken. And if she will accept me, I promise to love her until I die." He stretched out his hand to Katerina. "Do you?"

Kat could feel her face blushing. "I do!"

Steffan jumped back down and kissed her, and neither one of them seemed to notice that the whole town was watching.

*E*pilogue

*A*fter Steffan led the rats into the mine, and the men of the town used some big rocks to fill up the deep hole, a rat could occasionally be seen in town, but Hamlin was never plagued with large numbers of them again.

Hennek was tried and sentenced to a year imprisonment in Hagenheim's dungeon to be followed by a lifetime of banishment in the frozen North Country. Duke Wilhelm arranged to have the Church give Katerina's mother a writ of divorce, freeing her from Hennek's tyranny. It was as if a weight had been lifted off Katerina's shoulders to know she never had to see him again.

Two weeks later, Steffan and Katerina and the town councilman who was now in charge of the orphanage, as well as Verena and her mother, traveled to Keiterhafen to visit the orphans who had been left with Herr and Frau Gruber. They seemed to be settling in well and were happy to see Verena. Albrecht and Verena talked quietly together and exchanged letters, and Katerina offered to provide a courier to take letters back and forth between Hamlin and Keiterhafen.

The banns were cried for Katerina and Steffan, and after four weeks they stood on the steps of the Hamlin Cathedral and vowed to remain true to each other until death, for better or for worse, in sickness and in health.

The sun was shining as they walked back home from the church with Katerina's hand tucked in Steffan's arm. Katerina wore her hair loose down her back, a few ribbons and flowers interwoven.

After they waved to all the people who walked with them, Katerina and Steffan went inside their home.

"Thank you for not giving up on me," she said just before he kissed her.

"Giving up on you?"

"Yes, when I was so rude to you and called you arrogant and told you I didn't need you and that you should go back to Hagenheim."

"Maybe you should confess to the priest. I've forgotten all about that." He kissed her again.

"Maybe I should." She laughed.

"And thank you for not running away from me when I told you I was a bad man."

She realized they could thank each other for hours, but instead she said, "I'm just glad you came to Hamlin when you did."

"Yes. It's been very rewarding."

*A*uthor's Note

*T*he idea for *The Piper's Pursuit*, you might say, started way back in 1992 when I visited the German town of Hameln, Hamelin, or Hamlin, depending on how you wish to spell it. I was fortunate enough to see the modern-day results of the "Pied Piper of Hamlin" fairy tale—all kinds of rat-shaped souvenirs being sold all over town, as well as a church glockenspiel that plays the story of the Pied Piper of Hamlin, an annual play, and various displays of a man wearing colorful clothing and playing a pipe. I myself came home with a picture of me standing next to a colorful statue of the Pied Piper, and a bread roll in the shape of a rat, very intricately done, and shellacked with something that has preserved it to this day. (I can see the cringes on some of your faces, but it's still in perfect condition, complete with straws of hay for whiskers!)

I was familiar with the fairy tale story of the Pied Piper when I started to plan my own version of the tale and how it could work into my Hagenheim series, but I discovered in my research something that surprised me. Unlike most of Grimm's fairy tales, the tale of the Pied Piper was actually a true story.

The first known depiction of the story of the Pied Piper of Hamlin was on a stained glass window in the Market Church in Hamlin, which was built in 1300 and survived until 1633. And the town's written record begins with this ominous statement: "It is 100 years since our children left." That was written in 1384.

According to the Lüneburg Manuscript, written in the 1400s, "In the year of 1284, on the day of Saints John and Paul on June 26, by a piper, clothed in many kinds of colours, 130 children born in Hamelin were seduced, and lost at the place of execution near the koppen." The word koppen means "hills."

And these are the best, most reliable, and most contemporary accounts to the event. The stained glass window that depicted a pied piper luring children up to a hill just outside of town has been recreated using written descriptions and can be found online. There are many theories as to what actually happened to the children of Hamlin that were lost, but it was the stained glass window, more than anything, I suppose, that inspired my own story.

Another inspiration for me was the story of the Beast of Gévaudan, which I happened to stumble across one day. Between the years 1764 and 1767, an animal in south-central France attacked between 90 and 210 people, depending on the source. At least 60 people, and as many as 113, were killed by this large animal. No one was ever sure if the beast was a wolf or possibly the offspring of a wolf and a very large dog, but by all accounts, it was larger than a normal wolf. There were accounts of at least a couple of women who successfully fought off the attacking beast. And these women inspired my heroine, Katerina.

I hope you enjoyed *The Piper's Pursuit*, which was born of both history and imagination. And love and romance too, of course.

Acknowledgments

$\mathcal{I}$ want to thank my editors, Kimberly Carlton and Julie Breihan, for all their hard work on this story, for helping me catch weaknesses and errors, and for all their insights. I also want to thank my agent, Natasha Kern, for all she does for me, my books, and my career. And many thanks to my publisher and everyone at Thomas Nelson and HarperCollins Christian Publishing for all they do to make my books beautiful and successful.

I have to thank my two wonderful girls, Grace and Faith, for helping me brainstorm this story and being willing to let me talk it out with them. They are just the best, if I do say so myself.

Thanks to any and all friends who helped me brainstorm, offered their homes for me to write in, and asked me, "How's the writing going?" over the course of almost a year that I spent, off and on, writing and editing this story. Moral support means a lot.

I should probably also thank Atlanta Bread Company for all the times they let me sit for a couple of hours so many mornings for the price of a hot tea and a pastry.

As always, thanks to my wonderful readers whom I love and appreciate so much. Thanks for buying my books, and especially for telling your friends about my books, posting reviews, posting my books on Instagram, and all the other things you do to get the word out. If it weren't for you, I'd have to get a real job, and that would stink! God bless you.

Discussion Questions

1. Why was it so shocking for Katerina to find Bridda? What did the townspeople think had happened to all the children who had gone missing?

2. What were Katerina's first impressions of Steffan? How were her opinions of him influenced by her own past experiences? Have you ever had a wrong first impression of someone?

3. Why did Steffan come to Hamlin? Did his purpose or motives change through the course of the story? If so, how?

4. Steffan admits to growing up with a lot of anger and rebelling against his father. What caused these feelings? What things had he done that he felt shame and guilt about? What is the difference between guilt and shame?

5. Katerina does not allow herself to trust men. How does she overcome her mistrust of Steffan?

6. Can mistrust be a good thing? How can it be a bad thing? Do you consider yourself a trusting person? Why or why not?

7. What were some of the things Hennek did to fool people into thinking he was a good person?

DISCUSSION QUESTIONS

8. How did Steffan's past affect the way he viewed children? Did his feelings toward children change?

9. What was Katerina's greatest fear?

10. What was Steffan's fear that kept him from going home?

11. What did Katerina hope to accomplish by killing the Beast of Hamlin?

12. What made Katerina's friend Hans betray her?

13. What did you think of Duke Wilhelm's choice of mayor for Hamlin? What did Steffan think?

14. What were Steffan's and Katerina's goals? Did they achieve them?

THE PEASANT'S DREAM

COMING JULY 2020!

In this reverse Cinderella story, a poor farmer's son, who dreams of using his talent as a wood-carver to make a better life for himself, falls in love with a duke's daughter and must fight for a chance to win her heart.

THOMAS NELSON
Since 1798

A fresh reimagining of the classic Mulan tale, set in fifteenth century Lithuania, where love and war challenge the strongest hearts.

From *New York Times* bestselling author
Melanie Dickerson comes an inspired
retelling of the beloved folk tale Aladdin.

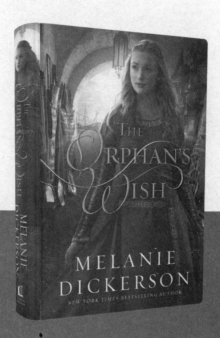

She lost everything to the scheme of an evil servant. But she might just gain what she's always wanted . . . if she makes it in time.

The Silent Songbird

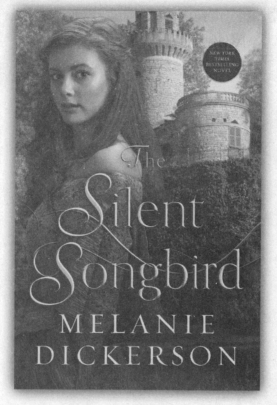

The
GOLDEN BRAID

The one who needs rescuing isn't always the one in the tower.

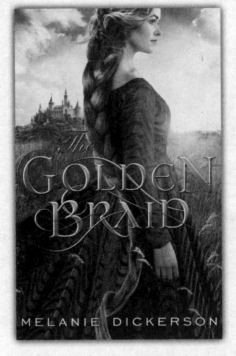

Rapunzel can throw a knife better than any man around. And her skills as an artist rival those of any artist she's met. But for a woman in medieval times, the one skill she most desires is the hardest one to obtain: the ability to read.

Available in print, e-book, and audio!

THOMAS NELSON
Since 1798

About the Author

Melanie Dickerson is a *New York Times* bestselling author and a Christy Award winner. Her book *The Healer's Apprentice* won the National Readers' Choice Award for Best First Book in 2010, and *The Merchant's Daughter* won the 2012 Carol Award. Melanie spends her time daydreaming, researching the most fascinating historical time periods, and writing stories at her home near Huntsville, Alabama, where she gathers dandelion greens for her two adorable guinea pigs between writing and editing her happily-ever-afters.

Visit her online at MelanieDickerson.com
Instagram: MelanieDickerson123
Facebook: MelanieDickersonBooks
Twitter: @MelanieAuthor